M
HAR

Hart, Carolyn G.

Dead man's island.

$19.95

DATE		

BAKER & TAYLOR BOOKS

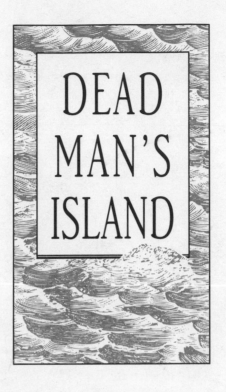

DEAD
MAN'S
ISLAND

Also by Carolyn G. Hart

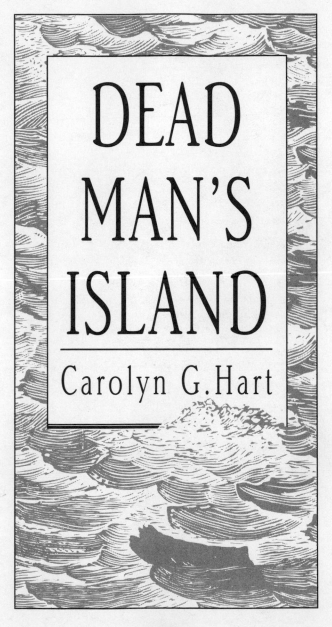

DEAD MAN'S ISLAND

Carolyn G. Hart

BANTAM BOOKS

NEW YORK · TORONTO · LONDON · SYDNEY · AUCKLAND

DEAD MAN'S ISLAND
A Bantam Book / September 1993

BOOK DESIGN BY DONNA SINISGALLI

Library of Congress Cataloging-in-Publication Data
Hart, Carolyn G.
   Dead man's island / Carolyn G. Hart.
     p. cm.
   ISBN 0-553-09173-5 : $19.95
   I. Title.
  PS3558.A676D43   1993
  813'.54—dc20   93-3107
                                    CIP

PRINTED IN THE UNITED STATES OF AMERICA

BVG   0 9 8 7 6 5 4 3 2 1

With love to Sarah and Bruce

I would like to thank the following for sharing with me their knowledge and expertise:

Tom Siebe, Chief Deputy Coroner of Sonoma County, California.

Lt. Robert S. Young, U.S. Coast Guard, Air Station Savannah, Georgia.

Prologue

I don't consider myself an angel, avenging or otherwise, but I can't always accept fate as the answer. Timing makes all the difference.

There exists a rather charming school of thought that the motorist who looms out of the fog at precisely the right moment or the fatherly old man who takes a lost child's hand and leads her to safety are heaven-sent messengers.

Unknown to themselves, of course.

It was the episode in the hotel lobby that made me, Henrietta O'Dwyer Collins, ponder the imponderable and my role in it.

Had I come downstairs one minute later, Willa Benson would have been sitting pretty.

But I was strolling past the reception area a few minutes after eight with nothing more in mind than a leisurely jog. Midway down the polished pink-and-white-marbled hallway, my right shoelace flopped loose. I propped my Reebok on the edge of the heavy blue porcelain planter. As I tied the lace, I glanced at the mirror that reflected me in navy sweats and, behind me, the hallway and the ornate mahogany front desk.

That's why I saw the sleek, satisfied, sly look on Willa Benson's plump face as she turned away from the front desk and looked down at the envelope in her pudgy hands. What made it doubly interesting was the contrast between that unguarded expression, one of malice laced with amusement and contemptuous pleasure, and her usual demeanor of chirpy congeniality as she dealt with the needs of Mamie Duvall, the frail, elderly woman whom she served as a companion.

So I yanked on the shoelace, reworked it, and continued to watch the mirror and the pink-cheeked, motherly-looking woman with the envelope in her hand.

What made it triply interesting was that she didn't open the envelope. Instead, she moved out of sight of the clerk, ripped the envelope—the unopened envelope—in half, then stuffed the pieces in her purse, still looking pleased and satisfied in a thoroughly nasty way.

I suppose most people might have seen all of the above and shrugged, thinking it none of their business, no matter how intriguing. Not I. As soon as the elevator door closed behind Willa, I walked to the lobby desk.

There are clerks and clerks. This young lady had a big smile and she always tried to please.

"Any messages for me, Anita?"

"No, Mrs. Collins. I just sorted the mail."

I half-turned, then paused. "Oh, Mrs. Duvall's expecting an important letter. I told her I'd ask."

"It's on its way to her right now. The lady who's with her, Mrs. Benson, just picked it up."

So I was right. This was mail for Mamie Duvall—not for her canary-faced companion.

I breathed an audible sigh of relief. "Oh, I do hope it was the letter from Sheila, the one she's hoping for."

"Well," Anita said brightly, "it was postmarked from Phoenix—and it looked like a woman's handwriting."

"That's the one." I beamed. "I believe I'll go right up and talk to her."

As I waited for the elevator, I saw my own reflection: dark hair silvered at the temples, dark eyes that have seen much and remembered much, a Roman-coin profile, a lean and angular body with an appearance of forward motion even when at rest —and the angry light in my eyes. I can't abide meanness. And I didn't need a minute's consideration to decide that Willa Benson was up to something very mean indeed.

I didn't go to Mrs. Duvall's room, of course, but to my own and my telephone. Sometimes you pick up as much by what people don't say as what they do, and I figured I had a line on Mamie Duvall.

I'd played bridge several evenings with a trio of elderly women, one of whom was Mrs. Duvall. Mamie Duvall was a soft-voiced widow with a pale, aristocratic face, mournful blue eyes, and a sad droop to her mouth. She had the least to say, but she listened hungrily to the other players' tales of family and friends. Bonhomie was encouraged at Monahan House, an amiable, quietly friendly compound in the Shenandoahs offering golf and horseback riding, tennis and croquet, gently spectacular views of wooded ridges and valleys, sedate activities—bird walks, bridge, guest lectures—for guests, even spa waters for wan health-seekers. Not, actually, my usual kind of vacation spot, but an old friend owned it, and I'd come for a week's visit. I was leaving tomorrow. So, I understood, was Mrs. Duvall.

I had a laptop and modem with me. It was child's play to tap into the hotel system. I pulled up the Duvall registration: Mrs. Marguerite Duvall, 2903 Egret Marsh Road, Pensacola, FL 32505. Ten minutes later, courtesy of the Pensacola library system, I had the telephone numbers of her neighbors on either side and across the street. I did a little more exploratory work — newspaper morgues are so helpful — and came up with the date of death for Marguerite's husband and, more important, the obituary list of survivors: his daughter, Pamela Duvall Wilson of Phoenix, Arizona, and one grandson, Thomas Charles Wilson, also of Phoenix.

Dolly Garrison, who lived across the street from Mrs. Duvall, never suspected I wasn't a long-lost cousin of Mrs. Duvall's trying to get in touch. "Why, it's the funniest thing. First Mamie's daughter called, oh, a couple of days ago, and now you! Pam says her mother's number is unlisted! Why on earth! Nobody I know has an unlisted number. . . ."

I worked fast. Needless to say, I missed my jog, but by the end of the day I knew all about Marguerite Duvall, her daughter, Pam, and her grandson, Tommy. I knew about Mamie Duvall's broken hip and the woman, Willa Benson, who'd answered her ad for live-in help. But the real low-down came when I talked to Pam. "I've written and written. . . ."

The last-minute airline ticket and the change to my own reservations and the purchase of two more last-minute tickets was pricey, but I happen, thanks to some recently published novels, to be rather well-heeled at the moment. (Is that perhaps a qualification for avenging angels?)

I made a great show of delight and surprise when I reached row 10 on the flight to Pensacola and found I had the window seat next to Mrs. Duvall and Willa. I insisted that Mrs. Duvall take the window seat. I was happy to sit in the center.

I took particular pleasure in noting Willa's not-quite-concealed relief at being relieved of duty.

I haven't asked tough questions for more than half a century without learning how to get people to talk.

Mamie Duvall was a heartbreak waiting to be unloaded.

". . . can't find any trace of my daughter. Willa's helped me. She's called everyone who knew Pam, but she and Tommy left her apartment without leaving an address and I haven't heard from her—not a phone call, not a letter—for almost a year now. Willa even talked to the police in Phoenix—that's where Pam lived—but they told her all they could do was file a missing-persons report." Mamie's face crumpled. "Something awful's happened to Pam and Tommy. No word, nothing . . ."

I dredged it all out, how Willa had handled everything, had made all the inquiries.

Mamie pressed a sodden handkerchief to her reddened eyes. "I don't know what I would do without Willa. She's the only person I have in the whole world now."

I reached out, gently held a frail arm in my hand. "No, you aren't alone. In fact, I have wonderful news for you. Pam is all right. She's been trying to get in touch with you for more than a year. She loves you very much, and she and Tommy will be at the airport when we land."

My voice is clear. It carries.

Willa's head jerked toward me. Shock loosened the muscles in her face. There was no smugness there now.

1

I flew to St. Louis the next day, then drove to Derry Hills, my present fairly permanent residence. I kept thinking of mother and daughter reunited, the saccharine interloper vanquished. In contrast, how fortunate I was in my life, even though I was now a widow. My relationship with my own daughter, Emily, is strong and loving, and I take great delight in Emily's family. For myself, I'd spent more than fifty years as a reporter, enjoying every minute. Those days are behind me now, but I face new challenges every day. I welcome them.

My life is full. And happy.

I was glad to be back, suddenly eager to get to work on my new book. I hurried inside the house. I was just unzipping my suitcase when the phone rang. I reached for it with no hesitation.

"My dear, it's good to hear your voice."

That was all Chase said. He didn't identify himself. He didn't need to. Even after all these years I recognized that confident, assertive voice. Truth to tell, I would know it anywhere this side of the grave. Still, it was characteristic of Chase to assume he would instantly be known, characteristic of that fine, careless arrogance that had vaulted him to immense wealth and power.

I didn't answer.

"Henrie, please hear me out." There was a faint sound that might have been the ghost of laughter. "Or should I call you Henrie O?"

That caught my attention as nothing else could have. It argued knowledge of me, Henrietta O'Dwyer Collins, long past the time we'd shared.

"Hello, Chase." I said it pleasantly and evenly, as though we had parted the day before, not four decades before. I heard my own voice, controlled and noncommittal, with a sudden sense of inevitability. Subconsciously I had, for more than half a lifetime, expected this call. "What do you want?"

That drew a familiar bark of laughter. "God, you never change, do you?"

I didn't contradict him. But, of course, I had. The young woman he recalled was almost lost in the mists of memory, and those particular memories I had no intention of resurrecting. The reckless young reporter whom Chase had known so well was now a woman who had spent five decades covering fires, disasters, wars, revolutions, murders, and public scandals.

"What do you want?" It wasn't quite a challenge, but it came near.

He was silent. That was unexpected. Chase with nothing to say? Had the glaciers melted? The sun turned back in its orbit?

Finally, grudgingly, he spoke in a troubled tone I'd never imagined hearing from Chase. "Henrie O"—and there was no hint of laughter now, there was only a naked, helpless honesty —"Henrie O, I need your help."

I wanted to put down that telephone as if the call had never come. I wanted to return to my life as I had lived it for so long. But I continued to hold the receiver in a tight grip. Finally, as reluctantly as he had spoken, I answered. It was the answer that had been foreordained more than forty years before.

I took time to glance at my mail and substitute fresh clothes for soiled ones. Before I closed the suitcase, I took out the two framed photographs I always carry with me. I glanced at the picture of my late husband, Richard, and wished that he was here now, with his grave thoughtfulness and quick, steadying humor. It was Richard who had first called me Henrie O. He claimed I packed more twists and surprises into a single day than O. Henry ever did in a short story. The studio portrait of my daughter was recent, and it captured Emily's beauty, glossy ebony hair, vivid aquamarine eyes, a finely boned face. Emily— the delight of my life. I looked from one familiar, beloved face to the other, then placed the photographs on my bed and closed the suitcase. I called Emily's home in the Rio Grande valley and left the message that I would be gone for another week, visiting a friend in South Carolina. Then I was ready to leave. It was easy enough, physically, simply to turn around, pick up the bags, and head back toward St. Louis and the airport. Chase had already made a reservation for me at the Marriott there, where the ticket for tomorrow's flight awaited me.

The rental car smelled like stale cigars. I had all the windows down despite the late-afternoon August heat and humidity-sodden air. I hadn't been to the South Carolina Low Country in some years. Not, in fact, since 1979 when I'd covered the aftermath of Hurricane David, which had left 78 dead and caused nearly half a billion dollars in damages. Hurricane Hugo had killed 21 when it struck a decade later. Worse was to come. The most devastating natural disaster in United States history was Hurricane Andrew. Striking in the early morning hours of late August 1992, this ferocious storm killed 38 while cutting a swath of destruction across the southern tip of Florida, obliterating 25,000 homes and causing $20 billion in damages and another $10 billion in clean-up costs. Experts had long feared that a hurricane on this scale would wreak havoc along the heavily populated corridor running from the tip of Florida all the way to Washington, D.C., but forecasting has become so expert that evacuation measures worked well in saving lives.

I glanced down at the sheet containing directions. I'd received the sheet in a Federal Express packet that morning at the hotel. My flights had been uneventful, St. Louis to Atlanta, Atlanta to Charleston. I'd had plenty of time to refuse to undertake excursions down memory lane and to speculate about what lay ahead. The directions I'd been sent showed the route to follow, but they shed no light on what to expect at journey's end. Simply a two-sentence note in Chase's unmistakable, backward-slanted handwriting:

You've always had an uncanny ability to sniff out the truth, Henrie O. I'm counting on you. Chase.

I fiddled with the static-ridden radio, caught the latest news—cesspool politics dominated the election with heated charges and countercharges over crime and welfare issues; more Americans out of work as Labor Day approached; Tropical Storm Derek churned toward the Caribbean, picking up speed, and was predicted to reach hurricane status by tomorrow—and enjoyed the occasional glimpse of herons and snowy egrets in patches of lush marsh. Once off the interstate I was grateful for the map as I followed first one, then another and another and another pine-shrouded blacktop, each more distant from habitation, more remote. I almost missed the final turnoff, but at the last minute braked and wheeled to my right into Coffin Point Lane. Gray dust swirled up from beneath my wheels. I blinked and coughed. This track could scarcely count as a road. It was just two deep ruts in the gray dirt. Longleaf pines towered overhead, blocking out the hazy sunlight. Resurrection ferns poked into the dusky lane, slapping against the car. Several miles farther on the track plunged out from beneath the pines to run beside a lagoon. A tawny red doe and her two half-grown fawns, feasting on the leaves of a sweet myrtle bush, turned startled eyes toward me. I slammed on my brakes, and they bolted into the pinewoods.

I came to the end of the lane, literally, about two hundred yards farther on. And this curious odyssey turned curiouser indeed. The weathered Low Country shack on pilings was to be expected, as was the narrow planked pier extending into the salt marsh and out to the lime-green water of the sound. But the row of cars parked at the end of the lane looked as out of place in this remote marshland as tinsel stars tacked to an evergreen. A blue BMW, a Ford van, a rust-spotted Plymouth, a cream Mercedes sedan, a black Porsche, a yellow classic MG, a red Maserati, and a jade Jaguar. So much for "Buy American" among these drivers.

There was not a soul to be seen. No one near the cars. No

one on the pier. No one on the sagging porch of the house. Not a living person other than me moved in that heavy hot air. But my instructions had been precise. This was as far as I would go by automobile. Passage across the water would come next.

I rolled up the windows and locked the car, retrieved my bags from the trunk, and walked toward the pier. Swirling clouds of no-see-ums attacked my bare face and arms, and I knew there would soon be prickly red welts.

I dug into my carry-on bag for some skin lotion to discourage the frenzied insects, slapped it on my arms, then paced up and down the narrow pier. Sweat trickled down my face. A stiff breeze stirred my hair, but the air was so oppressive that it only made me more uncomfortable. Fifteen minutes passed. Then I heard, faintly, the *pop-pop-pop* of an outboard motor. I waited at the end of the pier, shielding my eyes from the late-afternoon sun and looked out across the whitecapped sound.

The motorboat rode low in the water and its paint job had seen better days, but the stocky black man at the stern handled it with casual competence. As the boat knocked up against the pier, he tied up, then stepped out of the boat and climbed the ladder. The rickety pier quivered as he scrambled up to stand beside me.

"Miz Collins?" He was a muscular man who looked like he worked outdoors, his T-shirt tight against a muscular chest, his dungarees faded and stained.

I nodded.

Without another word, his heavy face somber and unfriendly, he picked up my bags. He tucked both under one arm and descended the ladder.

I looked after him thoughtfully as he stowed the luggage. He knew my name. That meant he had to be the person instructed to convey me to the island. But I didn't like his scarcely veiled hostility, and I didn't much like the entire appearance of this venture, the expensive cars haphazardly parked in this isolated, godforsaken wilderness, the slapdash provision for the transference of guests. It created an aura that didn't reek of welcome.

What kind of gathering was in progress? What the hell was Chase up to?

The boatman looked up at me. I could see the sweat beading his face, the wetness of his shirt against his skin. "Miz Collins?" His deep voice was impatient.

"Who are you?" I asked abruptly.

I thought at first that he wasn't going to answer. Finally, sullenly, he said, "Frank Hudson. I work for Mr. Prescott— when he comes 'round. I'm supposed to take you over to the island."

Hudson. That was the name in my packet of information. I started down the ladder.

He made no move to offer a helping hand. I didn't need help, and, in fact, I resent the automatic assumption that everyone past fifty requires assistance in physical efforts, but I was a little surprised nonetheless. I reached the bottom rung and stepped onto the boat.

As I settled into the backseat, he cast off.

"Whom do the cars belong to?" I looked back at the array of expensive vehicles.

"The others."

"What others?" He might not want to talk, but that didn't discourage me in the slightest. I've been asking questions for most of my lifetime.

"The people going over to the island. You're the last."

I felt a flicker of irritation. I'd asked Chase, of course, why he needed help, and he'd said only that I would find out. He said he wanted me because I had an instinct for truth. What kind of truth was he seeking? And why here, so far from the sophisticated world where he moved with so much power? I knew something about his life, of course. It would have been hard not to: twice chosen *Time* Man of the Year, the subject of countless admiring articles in *Fortune* and the *Wall Street Journal.* I knew he owned a number of homes: an old one—a monument to rapacious aggrandizement—in Newport, a cottage in Carmel, an estate in Atlanta, a brownstone in New York, a flat in London. I'd never read about an island home. But, for all I knew, this was some kind of exclusive resort. That would be very much like Chase.

I looked across the sound. I thought perhaps I saw a green smudge of land against the horizon, low and lumpy.

I shaded my eyes. "How far is it?"

" 'Bout six miles."

"You can only get there by boat?"

"Yeah."

I looked at Frank Hudson's back. His shoulders were hunched. There was no sense of holiday pleasure here. I wished I could see his face. Why was he angry?

The boat picked up speed, spanked across the whitecaps. I raised my voice to be heard over the engine. "So there are no cars on the island?"

Hudson eased up on the throttle and looked briefly, contemptuously, back at me. "No cars. No phones. No TV. Nothing."

"Is everything brought in by boat? People, supplies, newspapers?"

"Or it don't come." He pulled down on the bill of his cap, shading his hostile eyes.

"Who lives there?" I shifted a little in my seat. The Naugahyde upholstery was patched and a little lumpy. But the boat was well cared for, clean and tidy.

"Nobody. Not now." The deep voice sounded angrier. "I don't call comin' a few weeks at a time livin' there. 'Course he can do what he wants, can't he? He owns the island, every inch of it. That's what he said when he bought it and started to build. Said he could do what he wanted, where he wanted."

I knew there were many small, privately owned islands off the coast, most of them serving as hunting preserves. I looked across the water with growing interest. A private island. With only Chase and his chosen guests.

Hudson shoved the throttle forward; the engine rose to a roar.

The sun slid behind a heavy bank of clouds. It was still hot, August, Low Country hot, but now the day had turned gray and ominous, the clouds edged by crimson. In the heavy, moisture-laden air the throb of the motorboat sounded like the buzz of an angry wasp.

Then I saw the island, dark and vividly green, low against the murky horizon. An isolated patch of land with no link to the mainland and therefore no connection with the sprawling, powerful empire of Chase Prescott, media magnate.

This was a Chase Prescott I didn't know. What had happened to make the information mogul of America leave behind all the trappings of power? Chase seeking respite? That was at odds with everything I remembered. No matter how much he enjoyed drama, Chase surely wasn't recalling the reclusive, nerve-ridden decline of Joseph Pulitzer, who had spent his final years in a tower with foot-thick walls where he still suffered acute pain from the smallest of noises.

As we grew nearer, the boat bouncing on the short, choppy waves, I could see the ripple of spartina grass. The tide was coming in. Dense and impenetrable undergrowth choked the towering pines. There was no sight of a house or a dock. The island must have appeared just the same—fecund, wild, forbidding—to a party of seventeenth-century Spanish adventurers or to a brigantine filled with pirates.

Abruptly, as if reading my mind, Frank Hudson slowed his

boat. "The house is at the other end of the island. You can't see it from here."

The motorboat turned south. Across the glistening, thick spartina grass of the marsh, I saw the low-lying land, the snarled tendrils of vines and ferns and bushes, a toppled pine, its trunk gashed by lightning.

It wasn't hospitable. In no way did it evoke the image of a South Sea island, where life is easy and languorous. "Did Mr. Prescott have the house built or was it there when he bought the island?"

"Built it."

"I would imagine that brought in quite a bit of money to the local economy." I tried to envision the many, many barges it would take to haul in everything needed for the kind of house Chase would want. Barges and workmen.

"Yeah." But the answer was a harsh sound in his throat.

"Do you live on the island?"

Hudson's hands, large, work-worn hands, tightened on the wheel. "Not anymore. Not since Mr. Prescott took it."

"Did he make you move?" Now I understood that anger. "Didn't he have to pay for your property?"

Explosive rage burned in the dark eyes that looked back at me. "White men always have papers. The papers said the island belonged to some people up north. They came down to hunt a couple of times a year. It didn't matter how long we'd lived there. They tore our houses down and made us move to the mainland. Us and the Willetts and the Browns and the Jorys. Oh, he gave us some money—for relocation"—the word was savage—"but it ain't the same. It'll never be the same."

It was abruptly cooler beneath the darkened sky. The skin on my bare arms prickled.

"Does the island have a name?" I asked.

The waves slapped against the hull. Blackbirds cawed. Hudson's heavy shoulders shook. I realized he was laughing.

"Oh, yes'm. It has a name. Mr. Prescott don't like it. He calls it Prescott Island. But that's not the real name."

"What is it?" I grabbed a railing as the boat picked up speed.

"Dead Man's Island." His deep voice resounded with satisfaction.

I stared at the dense, forbidding tangle of growth.

Dead Man's Island. There had to be a reason.

"Why?"

Hudson, too, was watching the island slide by. "Everybody still talks about it—and it was almost a hundred years ago. The big storm. The biggest one ever. After it was over, they come to the island to see how it went here. You know what they found"—eyes darker than coal searched mine—"when they come over? Not a living soul. Everybody drowned. Every last one of them. The bodies—swollen and smelly—they was snagged in the trees and caught in the brush. Up there on the high ground, the ground where Mr. Prescott built his house. Before that storm this was Fortune Island. But from that day to this ain't nobody called it nothing but Dead Man's Island."

I shivered. From the sudden breeze, of course.

But in my heart I knew better. My Irish mother would have said a goose had walked across my grave.

2

Opulence.

That was my immediate judgment.

The massive pale yellow house dominated the ridge. It was in the Georgian colonial style, the two-story central segment balanced by two-story wings on either side. Colonnaded porches extended from every portion. Scarlet bougainvillea cascaded over walls and balconies. But the eye was caught and held by bed after curving bed of roses, roses so vivid, so gorgeous the eye was dazzled: crimson and rose, pink and vermilion, butter yellow and white, primrose and palest ivory, mauve and deep coral. A central fountain, bordered by pink marble, flung a shining column of water skyward. Dark green cypress bordered the flower beds.

This house and its gardens were a spectacular achievement, a paean to human ingenuity and determination.

But it was also an aberration.

Elegance had no place on this wild and untamed island. The Georgian house and its fairy-tale gardens were at war with the luxuriant vines and unchecked shrubbery and encroaching weeds, the unstoppable, uncontrollable fecundity of subtropical land.

The house was light and bright and airy.

Behind it loomed the darkness of the vine-choked maritime forest.

As the motorboat entered the small harbor, a slender, small-boned man in crisp khakis and a short-sleeved sport shirt bustled out onto the pier. This, of course, was a substantial pier, so new the wood was hardly weathered. Midway jutted a covered boathouse.

Hudson held the boat steady as I climbed up the ladder to the dock.

The young man on the pier beamed a welcoming smile, but it was as automatic and meaningless as a showgirl's curved lips. "Mrs. Collins, how lovely to see you. Mr. Prescott asked me to welcome you to Prescott Island. I'm his personal secretary, Burton Andrews."

Burton Andrews had a boyish build and a youthful manner, but face-to-face I could see the faint pouches under his eyes and the fine lines on his forehead. His discontented air betrayed that nothing ever quite lived up to his expectations.

He took my bags, ordered Hudson with, I thought, unnecessary condescension, to be sure to return the following week — "Mr. Prescott said the guests will all be staying for a week.

Now, that's Thursday next, do you understand?"—then chattered as he led the way ashore past the boathouse and the cabin cruiser docked inside. "That's the *Miranda B,* just back from her yearly overhaul in Miami. A gorgeous boat. Mahogany trim throughout. I'm sure Mr. Prescott will take everyone for a spin sometime this week. It has a crew of three, but Mr. Prescott's given them a holiday. He usually does that when he's in residence on the island. He likes to have as few people here as possible. To be *intime,* you know. That's why Hudson's bringing over the guests. Of course, arriving in Hudson's old outboard isn't nearly as pleasant as traveling on the *Miranda B.*"

Behind us the *pop-pop* of Hudson's boat faded. We reached the end of the pier.

"Mind your step now, Mrs. Collins. It's six steps down—"

Did the fool think I couldn't count?

"—and the oyster shells can be a little tricky, humpy, *vous savez.*"

I didn't bother to answer. I lengthened my stride. How did Chase put up with this nattering idiot?

As we walked, Burton Andrews kept up a swift stream of comment in his flat midwestern—Iowa, perhaps—accent, peppered with bad French. "The main house is eight thousand square feet. Every comfort imaginable, *bien sûr.* Behind it there are separate quarters for the servants and a huge storage building that houses our own gas-powered generator, extra foodstuffs, garden machinery, and supplies. It even has a restaurant-size freezer room. We never lack for anything here on the island. Mr. Prescott expects excellence, and he wants all who stay on Prescott Island—"

That afforded me a flicker of grim amusement. Prescott Island: Dead Man's Island. I looked forward to discussing nomenclature with Chase.

"—to be healed by its special peace. Peace and quiet, that's what you will find here, Mrs. Collins. The ring of the telephone, the bleat of the fax machine—none of that intrudes here. Peace and quiet and, of course, the ultimate in service. We have a staff that can attend to every need, but the main work—trimming, gardening, thorough cleaning, restocking of supplies—occurs only once each week." His arm swept out, encompassing the dazzling gardens. "Every Wednesday a crew arrives from Charleston. That makes it possible for six days out of seven to be devoid of irritants. No lawn mowers, no leaf blowers, no hedge trimmers. Instead we have sailing and swimming, books, films, hammocks for siestas. It's quite heaven on earth, Mrs. Collins. Even for those of us who have to work while we're here."

I wondered how that description would strike Frank Hudson. And I didn't miss the little sting in the tail of Burton's panegyric.

The secretary prattled on. "It's a brilliant arrangement. But, of course, Mr. Prescott specializes in brilliance, as I'm sure you are aware, being such an old *amie*." His oyster-gray eyes slid toward me, curious and expectant.

I didn't ante. "It's been a number of years since Mr. Prescott and I have seen each other."

Every word Burton uttered made me further regret my decision to come here. I despise ostentation.

Now I should be clear. I do enjoy *luxury*, but I prefer it to be luxury within decent bounds. Thorstein Veblen understood conspicuous consumption; the 1890s in the United States was the heyday of the vulgar display of riches. Until now. One hundred years later greed still runs rampant. Today's CEOs receive obscenely bloated paychecks even as businesses and industries scramble to "downsize," a comfortable euphemism for the wholesale firing of middle management.

Prescott Island was not my kind of place. I would have preferred Dead Man's Island, with its four families.

We had reached the gardens. The scent of roses swirled

around me, a thick, sweet, heady perfume. And hot—only Houston or Calcutta could be more oppressive. I was awash with sweat.

"I'm sure you'd like to have a chance to rest from your journey." The secretary's voice had the jolly assurance of a ward nurse. I itched to tell him so. "I'll take you to your room. Mr. Prescott would like for you to join him in his study in an hour." He glanced at his watch and said precisely, "That will be at seven minutes after five."

I paused—we had just reached the central fountain—and looked at the open-air porches. There were three: one a living area, another obviously a breakfast nook, and a third, the clos- est to the swimming pool, a leisure lanai with hammocks and deck furniture. All were unoccupied.

The air was so hot it shimmered. I recognized another scent threaded through that of the roses, the faint, acrid stink of insecticide. That figured. Otherwise, this idyllic retreat would be uninhabitable. I doubted that even heavy spraying would prevent swarms of mosquitoes at dusk.

No insects.

And no people.

"Where is everyone?"

Burton Andrews blinked, then looked about and gave a twittery laugh. *"Eh bien,* it does seem deserted, doesn't it? But that's the charm of Prescott Island, Mrs. Collins. So different from life on the mainland, where it's people, people everywhere. Here we are far from the vale of tears that is the world. And"— his voice became more matter-of-fact—"it's terribly hot this time of day. Guests are encouraged to do what they wish, when they wish. Mrs. Prescott presides over tea every afternoon in the living room. Inside, of course. With the air-conditioning. I'm sure some of the guests are with her now. Others may be rest- ing, walking—" He looked around. "Well, of course, the heat!" He shifted my larger case from his left hand to his right. I had my carry-on piece. "But Mr. Prescott told me to take you straight to your room, to give you a chance to relax and—"

So Chase wanted me whisked to my room. Why? So I wouldn't meet any of my fellow sojourners until after I'd talked with him? What difference could it make? I had no idea. I would make every effort to figure it out, but first things first.

"Thanks," I said briskly, "but I'd like to meet my hostess—and tea sounds wonderful." I handed him my carry-on. "Just drop the bags by my room. I'll find my way there later."

"But Mr. Prescott—"

"Oh, I'll see Chase in his study. At seven minutes after five. Now"—I shaded my eyes—"that looks like a main door. *Merci beaucoup* for your help, Mr. Andrews." And I started up the path.

Burton scrambled after me. "Mrs. Collins, your room—I'll show you—I can have refreshment brought to you. You needn't take tea today—"

"I prefer to join the others." I favored him with a steely glance and marched ahead of him up the steps and into the main hall.

Burton wasn't happy about it, but he pointed me in the right direction for the living room and started up the stairs with my luggage, pausing every step or so in the vain hope, I suppose, that I might change my mind. Worthier men than he have tried to deflect me from a chosen course. Without, I might add, the slightest bit of success.

In the cool, shadowy entrance hall I paused to look in the magnificent ormolu mirror that reflected a Ming vase, a Rodin sculpture, a William Merritt Chase seascape, and the staircase. I smoothed back a strand of hair, straightened my travel-crumpled aquamarine smooth-weave cotton dress, and watched until Burton's pants cuffs and shiny brown cordovans finally disappeared from the mirror. Then I set out in search of my hostess.

I favor comfortable shoes. These were crepe-soled and silent. I reached the open double doorway and had an uninterrupted moment to survey the scene and those who had arrived on this island before me.

That's when I got my first surprise. Burton had indicated that Chase's wife presided over tea. I dredged a name from my memory. Miranda Prescott. But this must be a granddaughter, a slim girl in a watercolor-pastel dress as delicate and shimmering as sunlight on water. The round shawl collar with an organdy bow recalled the elegance of long-ago fêtes or canoes gliding on moonlit canals. Raven-black hair curled softly to frame a heart-shaped face. She sat behind the magnificent George III tea service, pouring with the care and precision of a little girl playing house, her face absorbed, her gestures—

Light from the chandeliers caught the fire and brilliance of the rings on her slender left hand.

Wedding rings.

I felt a surge of dismay. She was so young. Too young. Dismay and disappointment. In Chase. I would not have expected this of him.

I scanned the others in the opulent room: a hard-faced woman with too much makeup but an aristocratic air; an extraordinarily handsome young man with sullen, downturned lips; a chunky mid-fortyish fellow with cherubic cheeks and a genial smile; a tightly coiled, bold-featured redhead who had A-type stamped all over him; and an exquisitely groomed blond man my mother would have tartly deemed too smooth by half.

I stepped inside, calling out a cheery hello. Everyone looked my way, and the men hurriedly got to their feet.

Reporters are accustomed to evoking odd responses. It comes with the territory. Even so, Miranda Prescott's reaction was outside the norm.

My young hostess became absolutely immobile, her face rigid, her slender body taut. She looked steeled to confront enormous challenge. But when she saw me, her eyes widened and her mouth curved into a soundless O of surprise.

That she had expected someone entirely different was abundantly clear.

"Mrs. Collins?" Her girlish voice rose in disbelief.

"Yes. But, please, call me Henrie O. Everyone does. And do sit down, gentlemen."

But the men, even the sulky, bored youth, waited politely until I'd taken a seat next to my hostess. An interesting social custom, and one that can provide endless diversion upon discussion. Should women be treated with deference? Or, in fact, is this actually a show of respect or is it more truly a subtle indicator that men are all-powerful, choosing to honor the "weaker" sex?

Miranda struggled for words. "Mrs. Collins . . . Mrs. Collins, you are . . . How nice you've arrived in time for tea."

"I'm glad, too." I accepted a cup and glanced around. This was an enormously comfortable room, the kind of comfort easily secured when cost is no question. As a young reporter, I spent some time doing "house" features. I would have described this living room as "perfect for entertaining in a casual, relaxed manner."

But there was nothing relaxed about our hostess this afternoon. As everyone resettled, Miranda offered me delectable sandwiches: watercress, smoked salmon, egg salad. She managed a social smile, but it did nothing to hide the misery in her vulnerable dark blue eyes. There was definitely something very wrong here. It showed in the slight tremble of those beautifully manicured, girlish hands, such soft unworn hands, and in the unhappy droop of her gentle mouth.

Nervy. That's an old-fashioned word, but it says it all, a mixture of fear and uncertainty and anxiety.

I couldn't for the life of me trace her uneasiness to a source. It was more than my unanticipated arrival. Certainly it couldn't be the surroundings. The living room itself was delightful, comfortable chairs and sofas upholstered in a chintz pattern of a vase with rosebuds that was repeated in the drapes. Cheerful rose-and-white-striped silk covered another sofa and the comfortable easy chairs. Red velvet straight chairs echoed the crimson lacquer of a coffee table. The needlepoint carpet featured squares of lush roses mixed with peonies. A vivid Matisse garden scene hung on one wall, a Dufy beach view on another. The red Bohemian glass of the twin chandeliers sparkled like Chianti in sunlight.

But nervy the young wife was. I paid close attention as she made the introductions.

Valerie St. Vincent—"No doubt you've seen her onstage, Mrs. Collins. One of Broadway's great stars."

Platinum hair framed smooth, controlled features, but it was the coldness of Ms. St. Vincent's blue eyes that I noticed. They briefly touched me. She made no effort to disguise the look of total, chilling disinterest, despite her reputed theatrical abilities.

I gave Valerie St. Vincent a gimlet look. I don't like to be dismissed. So, without a smile, I said briskly, "I don't believe I've had that pleasure." I had, of course. Her Lady Macbeth had been an unforgettable tour de force. "But I have a tendency to remember the leads, not character actors. Hello, Miss St. . . ." I paused. ". . . Velman, is it?"

If looks could kill—

I flashed the actress my most charming smile.

Haskell Lee—"Chase's stepson."

The sulky, gorgeous youngster. Haskell must be the son of Chase's second wife, Carrie Lee, who had died several years ago in an accident.

"Haskell gave up a tennis tournament to be with us." Miranda's lips curved into a meaningless smile that her stepson—

so young, yet older than she—didn't bother to return. "He works in Chase's Atlanta office."

I doubted that Haskell was integral to the success of Prescott Communications. This handsome youth (he must have been a very young child when his mother married Chase) looked much too indolent to excel in anything, except perhaps social tennis. Obviously wishing he was elsewhere, he sprawled back against the chintz cushions, tanned and well-muscled. He popped a tea sandwich in his mouth and managed a barely civil nod. Then he shifted petulantly in his seat and reached for his drink in its cut-glass tumbler. No tea for him.

Miranda hurried ahead with her introductions.

Roger Prescott—"Chase's son. I know you and Roger will enjoy each other. Roger is a writer, too."

Roger was as unlike his father as possible. He was blond, stocky, red-faced, and overweight. But he gave me a spontaneous, cheerful smile. "I write polemics. Critics sometimes describe them as diatribes. How about you?"

I grinned back at him. "Used to be a reporter. Now I write thrillers."

"What's the difference?" It was a sardonic drawl, but not offensive.

"In my fiction I have to tone everything down. I could give you facts that no one would ever believe." I spoke lightly enough, but I wasn't kidding.

"I would believe them." Roger Prescott leaned forward, his pale blue eyes ablaze with sudden emotion. "Did you know, Mrs. Collins, that if we continue our present environmental policies one-fourth of all plant and animal species existent in the mid-eighties will be extinct in twenty-five years? Did you know that air pollution from cars costs the United States forty billion dollars a *year* in health care? Did you know that cigarette smoking kills more people every year than all other diseases, including AIDS, yet our government continues to support tobacco farming? Did you know that—"

"Now, Roger, let me introduce everyone." It was said so charmingly that it had no sting, and Roger gave Miranda an indulgent smile. "Mrs. Collins, this is Lyle Stedman."

Lyle Stedman—"Lyle's also from the Atlanta office."

Stedman radiated power. There was a sense of strength barely contained despite his relaxed posture, a superbly muscled arm along the back of the couch, feet crossed. I was confident Lyle Stedman would react quickly to challenge, physical or mental. He was instantly noticeable, red hair so dark and bright it glittered like a sun-splashed ruby, a hard-bitten face with a bold nose and a blunt chin, a big chest and muscular legs, large strong hands.

"Your reputation precedes you, Mrs. Collins." Stedman's voice was deep and assertive. "How many National Press Club awards *do* you have?"

I was surprised he knew of me. I judged him to be on the young side of thirty. "One of the fruits of longevity is establishing a reputation you may not deserve, Mr. Stedman."

He chuckled deep in his throat and his eyes assessed me shrewdly. "Well, you've established a hell of one."

"I'll do my best to live it down."

"Mrs. Collins, this is Trevor Dunnaway." Miranda was regaining some composure. I was glad. There is nothing so painful as the open distress of the very young. "Trevor is the general counsel for Chase." She looked at him with a touch of awe.

Out of the corner of my eye I saw Lyle Stedman's self-assured mouth crook in disdain.

Everything about Trevor Dunnaway spelled success. From the confident tilt of his head to his carefully manicured nails and expensive and perfectly fitted sports clothes, Dunnaway was definitely a Monday's child. The attorney's features were regular and strong, his hair thick and blond. His blue eyes were good-humored and his mouth curved easily into a generous smile. "Mrs. Collins, this is a real treat. I read your last book, *Casablanca Course*. It's what we called a ripping good read when I was a boy." A faint remnant of a British accent was overlaid by many years in America. "You've certainly seen a lot of the world, haven't you?"

I am not immune to charm, and Dunnaway didn't lay it on too thick, but I wondered, behind my modest smile, whether this young man automatically flattered everyone he met, or whether this was a special effort for me. And, if so, why?

"Enough to question most verities, Mr. Dunnaway." I turned away and smiled at my hostess. "These scones are delicious." Which, of course, resulted in the offer of more. I do have a weakness for scones and tea sandwiches. My plate replenished, I smiled a great deal, sipped the hot Darjeeling from the Capo di Monte cup, made an occasional comment, and studied my fellow sojourners.

Valerie St. Vincent exhibited a regal charm for the benefit of Lyle Stedman, and he politely discussed New York theater with her. But his eyes probed every face in turn, seeking an answer for a question I didn't know. Miranda listened, with an occasional horrified exclamation, to Roger Prescott's impassioned indictment of medical experimentation on animals and the cruelties involved. "So you think cats and dogs run away from home? Let me tell you what *really* happens, Miranda." Trevor Dunnaway lightly regaled me with his recent tribulations during a polo match. "So that was the end of it for my second horse. I mounted the third and was just out on the field when the cinch slipped and . . ." It was done with a rueful smile and a great deal of modesty. Of course.

Nothing especially riveting about any of it. It was pleasant, undistinguished social intercourse, notable only because of where we were. Guests at a multimillionaire's secluded retreat. We were an intriguing assortment: an actress, a stepson, a son, an employee, a lawyer. A journalist turned novelist.

But it couldn't be as aimless as it appeared. In some fashion these particular people met a certain criterion.

I wondered if Chase was going to tell me what that was.

Or whether I should have to find out for myself.

On that thought, known only to me, of course, I excused myself, professing much pleasure with both the tea and the company. I had business to take care of before I met Chase.

I had no difficulty following Miranda's directions. The travertine marble staircase in the foyer led to the second floor. A marble-topped Louis XVI–style side table sat on the landing. Firecracker plants flamed in jade pots. The hallway was wide and spacious, the walls a cool lemon with crisp white moldings.

My room was in the south wing, the last bedroom on the right. It would have been a perfect room for a visiting teenager. Pink walls, pale pink shutters (open to provide a slatted but glorious view of the sound), pink bedding (roses again, climbing a trellis). White wicker furniture afforded a bit of contrast. But surprisingly the pink didn't cloy; it was light and delicate, as faint as the first wash of sunrise.

My emptied suitcase was in the closet, my clothes were hung, my lingerie was neatly folded in the lavender-scented drawers of a wicker dresser.

But, I was pleased to note, my carry-on bag sat on the desk, unopened.

A superbly trained maid had attended to my belongings.

I closed the door and went directly to my carry-on bag. I never travel without the tools of my trade: a laptop computer, a tiny state-of-the-art recorder, and, of course, my latest addition.

Opening the bag, I lifted out the carrying case of the cellular telephone and unzipped it. Taking the phone, I stepped out on a now shadowy balcony to make the call.

That was my first intimation of just how tenuous was our connection to the mainland. It rang, but faintly. Still, I felt a surge of triumph when Lavinia answered on the first ring.

Lavinia is an old and dear friend. She looks like a Betty Crocker ad from the fifties. Many too-slick money dealers, to their chagrin, have been fooled by the gingham dresses and sweet rosebud mouth. Lavinia was once a top financial columnist for a New York newspaper, and she has a mind like a Sony microchip.

"I got right to work yesterday afternoon as soon as I got your message. And let me tell you, Henrie O, you . . ."

Her voice faded.

That set the pattern. We were barely within a transmission area. Snatches of information. Fadeaway. Information. Fadeaway.

But when I hung up I knew a good deal more than when I started. What I'd learned was damned interesting. Now I wondered just what my function was to be. Perhaps the other guests didn't matter. Perhaps Chase wanted me here to study documents. Though if that was the case, he would have been smarter to invite someone with Lavinia's skills. In any event, Lavinia's information put a whole new face on my mission. But Lavinia's parting, half-heard advice gave me even more food for thought: *"Keep a close . . . hurricane nearing Cuba . . . listen to wea . . . keep out . . . trouble . . ."*

Then the connection died.

At six minutes after five I knocked on the door to Chase's study, turned the brass handle, and opened the door.

He was crossing the room to meet me. He still moved with that commanding grace, the easy, confident, predatory swagger

of a panther—beautiful, dark, fascinating, and infinitely dangerous. The kind of man to whom women lose their hearts.

On one level, it was a disturbing encounter.

On another, it was the most natural event in the world.

Chase Prescott. Forty years later. So much had not
changed. The aura of power, of greedy desire, of iron-hard determination. It was there in his eyes, in his still darkly handsome
face. Oh, time had touched him. The handsome face was lined,
almost gaunt. He was much thinner than I remembered. His
glossy black hair was threaded with white, his once smooth,
youthful skin lined, the eager fire in his eyes transmuted to icy
resolve.

"Henrie O." And it was the familiar deep, compelling
voice.

He took my hands in his, a strong, warm, vibrant grip. We
looked at each other.

I knew what he saw. A slender, intense woman whose fire
for life has not been quenched, a woman who still loves to laugh
but who knows the world is bathed in tears.

"You came," he said simply.

"Yes." I kept my voice easy. I didn't want to admit how
difficult this journey had been.

"Because—"

I cut him off. "Let's not look back, Chase."

A quick frown drew his brows down, then it was gone, like
a cloud slipping by a summer sun. He dropped my hands. "All
right. If that's the way you want it."

"It's the way it has to be."

I was prepared to turn on my heel and leave.

He knew it. "But you came. Goddammit, you came." He
pounded a fist into his open palm. A grin of triumph curved his
mobile mouth, and it was oh, so familiar, the old, reckless, dare-
devil Chase, on top of the world. "I feel like there's no way I can

lose, Henrie. Not now. Not with you here." He took my elbow and propelled me to a chair near the fireplace. He remained standing. Yanking a pack of cigarettes from his pocket, he pulled one free, stuck it in his mouth, lit it.

So he still smoked. All of us smoked when we were young. Those were the years when Lucky Green went to war, and smoking was common and quite acceptable. I managed to quit thirty-some years ago. It was the most difficult thing I'd ever done. I was sorry to see that he hadn't. I heard almost immediately that rattly smoker's cough.

Dark shadows marked the hollows beneath his eyes. But most worrisome of all was the feverish quickness of his movements. That frantic edge contrasted sharply with the somnolent richness of his study: cypress paneling, floor-to-ceiling bookshelves on three walls, antique French parquet flooring, a Georgian mantel over the fireplace, Georgian tables and armchairs, Impressionist drawings, and a jewellike collection of nineteenth-century music boxes.

He paced in front of the fireplace, then impatiently tossed the cigarette onto unlit logs piled on the hearth and turned toward me.

"Henrie—"

"Chase, you have eighty-three million in interest on loans due in thirty-five days. If you can't meet that payment, it will throw your entire empire—holding companies, conglomerates, and all—into bankruptcy. The word in New York and London is there's no way you can come up with the money." Lavinia had found out a lot in less than a day.

His face froze in shock. Then anger crackled in his eyes with the same violence as fire licking at the edge of a forest. "So that's the word that's out. Listen, Henrie O, I'm going to beat the bastards. You can count on that. God, it makes me mad, the way they'll suck up to your face and sharpen their knives behind your back. But they're going to eat their words. Prescott Communications isn't going down. I'll die first. I've never failed —and I won't fail now."

There was no mistaking the total conviction in his words. This was a Chase I knew well, single-minded, ruthless, absolutely certain of success.

"No, Henrie O, I'd give anything if that was the problem. Money, hell, I can always get money. I've got new financing in the wings. That's going to be all right." With a wave of his hand he indicated that eighty-three million dollars of debt wasn't worth talking about. "That's no problem—if I live long enough to swing it."

"Live long enough? Chase, are you ill?" That could explain the thinness, the haunted look in his eyes, the quick mood swings.

He managed a tight grin, but there was hurt in his eyes, hurt and an unwillingness to believe, and a wildness. "No. I'm fine. Everything would be perfect—I'd be on top of the world, the financial crunch behind me or soon to be, rich beyond most men's dreams, blessed with a beautiful wife, ready to expand my empire"—he leaned toward me—"the next frontier will be the ultimate utilization of home computers for news delivery, information retrieval, books, purchasing, banking, you name it. It can be done, and I'm going to be there, Henrie O, I promise you . . ." He paused. The excitement seeped out of his face. ". . . unless someone, someone here on my island, kills me first."

3

Chase paced and talked, smoking one cigarette after another. It was as if a dam burst; a torrent of words and fears and passionate conjectures buffeted me.

Finally, he slumped exhausted in a club chair and stared at me with desperate eyes. "You know a lot about murder."

Yes, I know a lot about murder.

Murderers will often urinate involuntarily after committing the crime.

Murder makes a killer hungry. Check the fast-food outlets close to the scene of a crime.

Two to six hours after death rigor mortis begins, starting with the head and spreading down the whole body.

If the position of a body is changed after death, it will affect postmortem lividity.

Toothlike projections from a bloodstain will indicate the blood fell from a moving body and will show the direction of movement.

I could continue. But this knowledge was useless in trying to prevent a crime.

I suppose it was a combination of fear and inadequacy that made me snap at him. "For Christ's sake, Chase, why didn't you call the police?"

But I knew the answer to that. What good would it have done? Calling the police in the instance he'd described would have been about as effective as a battered wife getting a court order forbidding harassment. There are a lot of death statistics tied to the latter.

"All right, all right." I opened my purse, grabbed my notepad. "Let me see if I'm clear on the timing. And the people."

He bounded up from his chair. "You're going to help."

"If I can, if I can. I'm not a sorcerer."

"You're the smartest goddamn reporter I ever knew." He was once again Chase-in-charge, Chase-on-top-of-the-heap.

I won't say the tribute didn't please me. But what Chase wanted was a far cry from what I did best, ferreting out facts — gouging them out, if need be — and purveying information as clearly, cleanly, and justly as I could.

I said as much.

And the old Chase exhorted me. "But that is *exactly* what I want." He was pacing and gesturing again, lighting one cigarette from the remnant of another, just as he had when I was a young reporter and he was an intense, hard-driving bureau chief. Those days—I wrenched my mind back to the present; I don't like the melancholy ache of remembrance.

Chase gripped my arm, his hand warm against my skin. "Think of it as a story, Henrie O, the way you always have. Dig out the truth. That's what I want: the truth." His hand slipped away. His face was suddenly tight and grim. "Then I will deal with it."

"Deal with it? How?" I was still sorting out the implications of what he'd told me and what he wanted; I hadn't given a second's thought to what might be done if I figured out who the culprit was.

He dropped onto the sofa and now he was relaxed, one arm flung casually along the back. He gave me an impish grin. "It will be fun." But the grin abruptly tilted sideways and disappeared.

I understood. Just how much fun would it be to discover who it was, among people whom you knew intimately, who actively, malevolently, stealthily wanted you dead?

"Sort of fun," he amended wryly. He reached for another cigarette but didn't light it. "Also simple and foolproof. If you come up with the name, all I have to do is give a sealed envelope containing that information to my lawyer and to the executor of my estate—an envelope to be opened in the event of my death by any other than natural means. Then I inform the person named in that letter."

"Hard cheese for them if someone else should do you in," I pointed out.

He pulled out his gold cigarette lighter and touched the flame to the tip of the cigarette. "Tough." His voice was cool.

I could see his point. Why be overly solicitous of a person who wants you dead?

"Still, that is a drawback," I pointed out crisply. "But one we can deal with later. All right, Chase, let's see if I have it straight."

I read aloud:

"Date of Attempted Murder of Chase Prescott: July 25, a Saturday.

"Location: the Prescott brownstone apartment, Central Park West, New York City.

"Modus operandi: poison."

Chase took a deep drag on the cigarette, smothered a cough. "If I hadn't seen it happen, I still wouldn't believe it. I went into my study to work on some of the financial stuff, you know, getting ready for the refinancing. I was right in the middle of that. Anyway, I went into my study and found a box of chocolates sitting on my desk. From my favorite store. I was pleased. I thought probably Miranda"—he broke off, took a deep breath, coughed—"probably Miranda had got them for me. I opened it up, and it was a box of turtles—"

Chocolate turtles. That brought back a few memories of my own. Chase's taste hadn't changed.

Chase flashed that well-remembered boyish grin with just the smallest tinge of embarrassment. "I've always been crazy about them. Hadn't had any for a while. The damn cholesterol business."

I restrained myself from suggesting that cigarettes were a good deal more deadly—usually—than chocolate turtles.

Smoke wreathed his face. "So I grabbed the box and pulled out the nearest one and I lost my grip on it. The damn thing tumbled right off the desk." Chase's lips pressed together for a moment, then he spoke so quietly I could scarcely hear him. "God, it was awful. Chesterfield—my retriever—came across the room in two bounds. He bit a candy and, I swear to

God, Henrie O, he was dead in five seconds." Chase managed a grim smile. "Turns out there really is a smell of bitter almonds. A stink. Anyway, there was only the one poisoned candy in the box. I had the rest of them tested. I had the box dusted for fingerprints. Not a single damn print on it or in it but mine. Just mine."

Pain was replaced by a dogged matter-of-factness. "I worked it out. The poisoner had to know I was the only person in that house who would eat a chocolate turtle. My staff is superbly trained. Anyone seeing the box on my desk would assume it was for me and leave it be. The poisoner had to know I was in New York that weekend. He must have been in the house on Friday or Saturday—a guest, an employee, or . . . or someone who lived there."

Miranda, of course, would not be a guest.

"I checked my daybook. Dropping in on either Friday or Saturday were Valerie St. Vincent; my stepson, Haskell; my son, Roger; and my lawyer, Trevor Dunnaway. Lyle Stedman was up from Atlanta for the weekend."

I made a note. "How about the people living or working in the house?"

"Miranda, of course. My secretary, Burton Andrews. You've met him. And the staff that's here this week: Enrique, my manservant; his wife, Rosalia, the housekeeper; and Betty, the maid."

"No one else was in the apartment on either Friday or Saturday? A repairman? A friend of Miranda's? A guest of a member of the staff? A delivery person?"

"I checked. Believe me, I checked." He brushed back a lock of ebony hair that had fallen across his forehead, making him look—for an instant—younger, vulnerable. "No one else. It's one of them. It *has* to be one of them." He ground out his cigarette in an overflowing ashtray.

I wondered if Chase's insistence had to do with conviction

or fear. It would be even more horrifying to think you had a deadly enemy abroad and no hint as to his or her identity. It was better, if terrible, to be able to draw a circle around a particular group.

But he should be able to do better than that.

"Chase, how about leveling with me? You know these people. You know them damn well. Who hates you? Who would benefit?"

His feverish eyes slid away from mine. "Henrie O, I promise you, I've looked at it from every angle, and I don't have any idea. Not a single damn idea."

I knew it as clearly as if it were splashed on a billboard. He was lying. He had an idea, all right. That made me mad.

"Chase, dammit, I can't work in the dark. Whom do you suspect?"

He stared stubbornly down at the floor and shook his head, once, with finality.

It was an impasse, and it was I who finally surrendered. He wouldn't say. Perhaps if he put his suspicion into words it would destroy for him forever that gossamer trust that binds friends and lovers.

I looked down at my notebook, recalled the faces I'd met at tea, and wondered how I was going to undertake what might be the hardest assignment I'd ever had.

I don't suppose Chase has ever borne silence well. "Well, what do you think?" His deep voice crackled with impatience.

I looked up in surprise and some irritation.

He was regarding me with the demanding air of a small boy awaiting the production of a rabbit from a magician's hat.

"Chase, I have yet to talk with anyone. I scarcely have any ideas." And the few I had, I didn't intend to share for now.

"But you're so good with instinct." He sounded almost

querulous. Once again he pushed back that stray lock of hair. "That's why I wanted to talk to you before you met any of them, so you could be prepared, be on the lookout . . ."

His voice trailed off.

I suddenly felt terribly sorry for him. Did he think I was the human equivalent of a divining rod, able to sniff out the presence of evil like a dowser locating water? Was that why he had instructed his secretary to sweep me to my room upon arrival? To keep my faculties untainted by exposure to his intimate circle of suspects?

"I thought I'd tell you everything. Then maybe at dinner tonight, maybe you'd just *know*." His eyes flickered around the room, touched my face, moved on, returned. "But maybe—what do you think, Henrie O? Do you know which one did it?" He lit a cigarette, drew on it, stubbed it out.

How interesting. Obviously, Chase knew I'd crashed Miranda's tea party and he believed his would-be killer had been there, too. Apparently he had included the members of his staff on his list of suspects simply because they had opportunity. I wondered how wise it was to dismiss them from his suspicions. It's always astonished me that more of those who live out their lives cosseting the very rich do not harbor enormous resentment. Personally, every time I see a Mercedes arrogantly encamped in a no-parking zone or hogging two slots, I've wished I was in the turret of a tank.

I tapped my notebook with my pen. "Chase, I'm not into instant Rorschach—"

"Henrie O, I want your gut response."

"My gut response? My gut response is that you're acting like a fool."

His head jerked up. A muscle twitched in his jaw. "What the hell do you mean?"

"Hasn't it occurred to you, Chase, how dangerous this

could be? Let's say one of these people intends to kill you. And you've conveniently gathered here—with no means of escape other than a single boat, which you control—a handful of people who were on the premises when your candy was poisoned. I should think the temptation—for the guilty one—would be overwhelming."

He pushed up from the couch. Jamming his hands in his pockets, he stared down at me with burning eyes. "So it's a gamble, Henrie O. The ultimate gamble. Black or red, which will it be? Will I win? Or lose? Well, I don't intend to lose, my dear." His voice was harsh. "I've never been a loser. Never. The house always wins. Ultimately, the house always wins. Well, I'm the house and I damn sure intend to win. Look at it"—he pulled his hands free, smacked a fist into a palm—"I've got the advantage. I know one of them's a killer. I'm on guard. I've got my defenses up. Even more than you know about. But you're my secret weapon, Henrie O. No one knows who you are. No one knows what a devil you are for the truth."

I rose. "Chase, you're talking years ago. I haven't gone after a story in almost a decade. And how can I do it here? No telephones, no files, no contacts, no way to find out about each of these people." I certainly didn't consider the intermittent working of my cellular phone an adequate resource and did not believe this was the time to mention it. "You know how I did a story. I looked and searched and scraped back the surface and peeled off the facade. I knew whom I was dealing with. I knew more about them than their doctors or their lovers, never mind their mothers. How the hell can I do that here? Look, this is an ill-conceived idea from start—"

He turned away, striding to a bank of filing cabinets tucked in an alcove. Pulling a key from his pocket, he unlocked the top drawer and lifted out files, one after another, then swung around, his arms full, his face triumphant. "Henrie O, I haven't forgotten how you work. I've got it all here for you.

Everything that can be found out about each and every one of them."

I stared at the green folders.

That they were full of information I didn't doubt.

But it was information I hadn't gathered.

I am always suspicious of facts gathered by anyone other than myself.

I learned that distrust in the real world. Words are, quite simply, weapons. How a person or an act or a thought looks depends entirely upon how—and by whom—it is described.

As an example, think for a moment about a presidential press conference. Do you describe the president as thoughtful or worried, as voluble or chatty, as combative or defensive, as vigorous or hyper? Think about it.

So I took the folders in my arms with considerable concern. Besides, I well knew that Chase had no scruples. He had proved that to me many years ago. So I had no way of knowing what slant he'd taken or, as it's put today, what kind of spin he'd applied. Still, some information was better than none. . . .

And I wouldn't forget the source.

But I was still unhappy.

"That's not the only problem, Chase. So I have records and people to talk to—but what makes you think they'll talk to me? Why should they?"

He leaned against the mantel, once again the lord of the manor. His armor was in place. There was no hint of the troubled, fearful man who had looked at me moments earlier with pain-filled eyes. "You're with me. I knew I could count on you. And it's going to be easy, Henrie O. Here's what we're going to do. . . ."

As I closed the study door behind me, I still had plenty of misgivings, but I knew Chase was determined. I knew, too, what that meant. No matter how dangerous and ill-considered I might see this venture, my choices were simple: I was either with him or against him.

Once, years ago, I was on a runaway horse. Even now I can hear the thud of hooves, smell the horse's panicked sweat, feel the tremble of his muscles between my legs. I had no control and yet I was a part of a blurring, headlong race through time and space.

I was feeling the same way when I regained my room. I put the folders in the top dresser drawer, pushing aside my lingerie. There was a folder for every person on the island, including Chase and me. Our inclusion interested me. I well knew how wily his mind was. What did he want me to learn from his folder, and what indeed from my own? But I wasn't going to read them now. Instead, I placed my purse on the desk and left. We were to gather for drinks at seven. It was a few minutes short of six. I wanted to take a preliminary survey of my surroundings. I felt an imperative need to flesh out my picture of this unique island.

I have a friend who is always sharing moments from her past lives. My standard response is always "So what?" I mean, so she was a discarded mistress of Louis XIV or a pioneer wife who died of a rattlesnake bite on the way to Idaho, what does that have to do with the price of computer disks today? Especially since she presently faces neither a rival for a king's love nor snake-infested environs.

So I can reasonably attribute my customary restlessness until I have checked out my surroundings to an early enchantment with *The Last of the Mohicans*. But could I have once been a scout for a wagon train? Or long ago a shepherd tending an unruly flock? If so, no doubt next time I'm almost certain to return as a bloodhound. I believe in consistency.

In any event, I indulged my itch to look around.

I stepped out on my balcony, which overlooked the front of the house and the sweep of the rosebeds and the sound.

It was like stepping into a sauna.

Instantly I felt the press of the hot moist air against me. The sky had a copper-yellow glaze, and the air was sticky and still. The breeze I'd enjoyed as I crossed to the island in Frank Hudson's boat had died away. Not a breath stirred the leaves of the magnolias and the live oaks or the fronds of the palmetto palms.

The tall slender cypress were like black cutouts against the glassy sky, making them even more ominous than usual. I've always found cypress to be cheerless trees. They remind me of the tombs along the Appian Way and the dust-choked heat of Rome.

As I surveyed the gardens, the luminaria-style lanterns around the pool came on and, faintly, I heard the strains of Hawaiian music, the splashing of water, and laughter. I was tempted to go for a quick swim before dinner. There was still time, and it would be enormously refreshing.

But that itch had to be satisfied.

Once out in the hallway I saw closed doors on either side. I wanted to know who was staying where. In fact, I wanted a plan of the house. So I set out to make one.

There were eight guest bedrooms on the second floor, four in each wing. The central portion of the second floor contained Chase's study, a library, a music room, and a billiard room. On the ground floor the central portion held the dining room—with an elegant three-pedestal mahogany table accompanied by a set of fourteen Sheraton chairs—and the living room, where we'd had tea. The back portion of the ground floor was given over to the kitchen and a laundry. The kitchen was humming with activity. Rosalia, Chase's housekeeper, was tall and slender. Too slender. She nodded shyly and didn't look in the least surprised when I unexpectedly invaded her territory. Her face had a grave, deep sadness. I wondered what her story was. Most people have stories, especially those with unsmiling mouths. I found the maid setting the table for dinner. Betty's black and white uniform was too tight, and she looked haggard. Briskly she asked if she could help me, but I felt almost certain I caught a flash of fear in her weary eyes and I filed that away for future investigation. Enrique was selecting the wines for dinner. Chase's valet was carefully polite when I spoke to him. I began to think the servants might have a much clearer idea of why I was a guest than anyone I'd met at tea. But why should they care? I persisted with my questions to Enrique until I had a good idea of the layout of the house. I learned that Chase and Miranda occupied all of the north wing's ground floor. Their quarters overlooked—but at a nice distance—the swimming pool, he said. The south wing on the ground floor contained a movie theater and a small art gallery.

I took time to visit the gallery and was impressed by the collection of American pastoral art.

But the house was only a part of my quest. I stepped out onto the front porch. Struck once again by the furnace-hot heat, I walked slowly through the fragrant gardens to the pier. Just past the boathouse I came upon a lone figure, leaning on the railing, staring out at the sound. He didn't turn at the sound of my footsteps.

I came up beside him. He was certainly a spectacularly handsome young man despite the perpetual scowl on his face.

"Where would you rather be, Haskell? Out on the water?"

That caught his attention. Chase's stepson turned toward me. No mid-century matinee idol had ever looked better. With his thick chestnut hair, deep-set eyes with long dark lashes, smooth olive skin, firm chin, and sensual lips, he surely cut a wide swath among the ladies.

His look was half-surprised, half-skeptical. "How did you know?"

"There's something about a man who loves water." I looked beyond him, out to the sound, remembering languid seas I'd shared with Richard. It's easy to tell when a man loves the sea. There's something about the lift of their heads when they look out on the water, something about the way they stand. "And," I added more prosaically, "you have a tan that you've acquired over a period of years and you're wearing boaters."

He glanced down at his shoes. A faint smile tugged at those sensual lips.

"You spend a lot of time on the water."

That brought back his scowl. "Except when I'm at the fucking office." His dark eyes slid toward me. "Sorry," he said stiffly.

I felt a wrench of my heart at his youth. It has been a good many years since anyone apologized to me about language.

"If you don't like the office, why do you go?" I leaned against the railing, listening to the water sucking at the pilings beneath us.

"Because he makes me." His anger toward Chase crackled through his voice. "What business is it of his? It's my money. It *should* be my money. Why did my mom put him in charge? Everything I do, he has to approve. He wouldn't let me have a penny if I didn't do things his way. And I'm running out of time."

Time. Haskell couldn't be a day over twenty-five. If that. Old? Ah, the perspective of youth. I kept my amusement out of my reply. "Too old? Too old for what?"

His dark eyes flashed. "To race."

I understood. "Powerboat?"

The transformation of his face told it all. The sullenness and resentment were gone. His eyes glowed, like those of a big cat. He was fully alive, eager, excited.

I looked at him intently now, with no amusement and with sharp interest. Speed is an addiction. Racing takes exquisite timing and a certain kind of madness—and blindness to the consequences.

"Chase won't let you race?" Why should Chase care?

Haskell turned back to stare out at the sound, his face once again heavy with anger. "He says weekend racing's good enough. He won't let me have the money to buy a superboat. If I had that kind of boat, I could go on the circuit." Eyes brilliant with anger turned on me. "I could win the Gold Cup. I know I could."

I said nothing.

"I could." It was almost a shout. Then he turned and walked swiftly away.

I looked after him. Watched him stride, handsome head down, hands jammed in his pockets, through the lush gardens and into the big house.

I pushed away from the railing and began to walk back toward shore. I would have to talk to Chase about Haskell. There is nothing so dangerous as thwarting dreams.

Faintly I heard the cheery *plink* of music wafting from the pool. It was nice to return to lightheartedness. And I had, from this vantage point on the pier, the spectacular view I'd sought of the house and its gardens. Lights glowed in almost every window. I reached the steps, hurried down to the oyster-shell path, and headed for the pool. The luminarias still shone brightly and the saccharine music played on, but the pool was deserted now. Probably the swimmers had gone to bathe and change for dinner. The pale green water reflected the spill of lights. There were a dozen or so white-webbed deck chairs and lounges. Thick white towels were crumpled on several. Stepping-stones led to the cabana. A nearby wooden hot tub was convenient both to the pool and to Chase and Miranda's lanai.

I followed another oyster-shell path, this one heading due

south, passed the front of the house, and reached a wide shell path that marked the perimeter of the cultivated property. I turned east. The shells crunched underfoot, and I smelled the winy scent of the motionless cypress sentinels always on my right.

Two big buildings sat about a hundred yards behind the main house, both thickly screened by pittosporum bushes. I guessed that the two-story stucco provided quarters for the servants. The square, single-story, cement-block building with two overhead garage-style doors had to be the storage facility. I tried a side door. It wasn't locked. But, on an island with controlled access, why would it be? I stepped inside and heard the hum of a generator. The air was scented with gasoline. Of course, here was the supply of electricity for the island. I flipped a switch. Bright overhead lights beamed down on a collection of lawn and garden machinery: a tractor, a riding lawn mower, edgers, blowers. There were several rooms: one a walk-in freezer, another stocked with lawn and garden supplies, another a mini-warehouse for foodstuffs. All were superbly supplied and meticulously clean.

I came back out into the twilight. Behind the storage building I found a neat landfill and an incinerator. A wisp of smoke curled out of the incinerator chimney. A luxuriant herb garden flourished between the storage building and the servants' quarters. The pittosporum and banana shrubs provided a lovely and aromatic screen between the service buildings and the main house. A wedge of pines separated the service buildings from two clay tennis courts. These, too, remained private, with a grove of weeping willows between the courts and a small cinder jogging track. Everything had been carefully designed so that it was possible to enjoy any aspect of the island in almost total seclusion.

Chase's vacation retreat had all the appurtenances of the most elegant spa. But the springy grass and sandy soil couldn't be disguised and, once I passed the cypress border, I faced the harsh reality of Dead Man's Island: waxy-leaved live oaks, crackling-frond palmettos, prickly slash pines; sea myrtle, yucca and bayberry, yaupon, winged sumac, and Hercules'-club; cinnamon ferns, ebony spleenwort, and resurrection ferns; cordgrass, sea oxeye daisy, and cattails.

There was only one break in that exuberant fecundity, another oyster-shell track plunging into the untamed maritime forest. I took only a few steps, then knew this exploration would have to wait for daylight. Beneath the canopy of trees, it was already dark, a darkness that had never known electric lights. Leaves rustled, something seemed to slip beneath the bushes. I smelled rotting plants, pine resin, dank water, insecticides. Despite the latter, the whine of insects rose above the crackling of twigs.

I swatted a mosquito and turned to go, then stopped short and looked into the wary, intelligent eyes of a crouching raccoon. The masked face appeared amused, but I knew that was only an anthropomorphic reaction on my part.

But I carried with me a memory of that sleek, sardonic, uncaring face as I retraced my steps. I used the entrance, also unlocked, at the end of the south wing and ran lightly up the stairs to the second floor. I had satisfied the itch but only supplanted it with a different, less easily assuaged discomfort.

As I stepped into my pink room, I was trying to dispel the sense of alienation and menace my walk had given me. I was so preoccupied that I almost passed by the desk without noticing.

I suppose if I hadn't been in so many hundreds of strange rooms in past years, sometimes in countries where the press is often perceived as an enemy, I might not have noticed. But I have been in those rooms . . . and I did notice.

My purse, which I had through habit aligned so exactly, was not where I had left it. Oh, it was only a matter of less than an inch. But purses do not move themselves, no matter how infinitesimal the distance.

Someone—either careless or hurried—had picked it up and, no doubt, rifled through it.

I did so myself. Nothing was gone.

I checked the dresser. The files were there. They were not in the same order.

Ah, that was careless.

Or, assuming a clever adversary, it might have been quite deliberate.

The overall effect was the same. I wasn't afraid. But I was damned alert. The equation had changed. Someone was much too interested in me. But there was nothing in this room or among my things to reveal the truth about me. Thank God.

Dinner was exquisite: beef tournedos, asparagus and carrots, fresh raspberries for dessert, California Chardonnay. The service was flawless. Enrique moved on cat feet, always at the right place at the right time. The surroundings couldn't have been more charming. Not even the Waterford crystal could match the glisten of the parquet de Versailles floors. But the conversations were tense and unilluminating. Roger Prescott provided the only flash of vigor toward the meal's end when he passionately, despite Chase's grim disapproval, persisted in debating his father about the tragedy of the homeless.

"You know why they're out there, thousands of them—it's because government stopped funding mental hospitals. We the people magnanimously gave the mentally ill their freedom. Jesus, how great to be free to walk the streets, frightened and helpless with no place to go and nobody to give a damn. Jesus, that was generous, wasn't it?" Roger downed his second glass of wine, all in one gulp. "We're not talking about bums, Dad.

We're talking about people who are too sick to work. And the ones who are on the streets because of alcohol and drug problems, they're sick, too, but society doesn't want to treat them. And now we have the New Poor, the people who used to have jobs, good solid members of the middle class who have been discarded by a business system trying to recover from the ravages of Reaganomics. Everywhere you turn government's cutting services, less money for drug treatment, less money for the mentally ill. Is it any wonder crime increases? Why don't you cover *that* story?"

Chase glared at his son. "If you want a soapbox, Roger, earn it. Prescott Communications covers what I want covered because it belongs to *me*. It's as simple as that. I earned my way in this world. That's the American way. Take the proceeds from your latest book and buy yourself a newspaper."

Roger's plump cheeks flamed.

I wondered if his book had been self-published. Or was the dig merely that it hadn't made money?

Lyle Stedman broke in. "We do cover the homeless issue, Roger. From all sides. Including the truth that people can't expect jobs if they have no skills and if they aren't willing to learn any. And if you've studied any history, you know Johnson's Great Society didn't work. So don't come at us with a lot of retreaded ideas." The newspaperman's eyes were cold and bored.

"That's half an answer," Roger retorted angrily. "Of course it didn't work. Because all the money went into that stupid war. As for your coverage, it sucks. You carry wire news. That's only the tip of the iceberg. You're great on murders and society rape and business, oh, God, yes, let's cover business. But business isn't so much fun anymore, is it? IBM's laying off. GM's laying off. You pick up the paper, and it's a new giant scrapping people and lives every day."

A frown furrowed Valerie St. Vincent's perfect face. The

actress had chosen a rich floral silk chemise. "Even in times of economic woe, people must have art. All it will take to revive Broadway is one good show, one really good show. Chase, darling, after dinner, we must have a moment, just the two of us, to talk about the future. You've always been willing to gamble. I knew when you asked me to come here this weekend that something wonderful was going to happen." She lifted her head. Her upswept platinum hair glistened.

"I only gamble on a sure thing, Valerie." Chase's cold voice was dismissive. "You haven't been in a hit in six years."

The actress's hand tightened on the stem of her crystal wineglass. Now her beautiful face had the empty look of a car-crash dummy.

I surveyed my fellow guests with interest during these exchanges. I had no illusions that I could "dowse" guilt for Chase, but I was beginning to have a feel for these people and I wanted to match these judgments against my take of the would-be murderer.

Burton Andrews was a toady, quick to offer an admiring laugh at Chase's smallest quip, eager to trumpet agreement with the boss's opinions. But dislike flickered in his eyes when Chase wasn't looking in his direction.

Valerie St. Vincent was self-absorbed to the point of narcissism. The actress desperately hungered for love and admiration and praise. Why had Chase turned on her so brutally? She still had a look of shock, her lips so compressed that tiny white patches marked the corners of her mouth.

Lyle Stedman sipped his wine and smiled grimly. "You'd better be damned glad somebody's covering business, Roger. It may not be the best system, but you show me one that works better."

Miranda Prescott sat at the end of the table opposite her husband. She was lovely tonight in a turquoise silk sarong. An orchid was tucked in her softly curling black hair. But the eyes above her social smile looked anxious, and they constantly sought her husband.

Chase seemed unaware of her scrutiny.

He seemed, in fact, even more feverish than when we'd met earlier in his study. His conversation erupted in staccato bursts and he jumped restlessly from topic to topic: the new church-state relations in Mexico, the concern over stability in the Russian nations, the continuing unrest in the Balkans. He ate little. But the mound of stubs in the ashtray grew fast.

Trevor Dunnaway sat between Miranda and Haskell Lee, who was on my left. I couldn't see the lawyer very well, but I heard him. It would be difficult not to hear Trevor Dunnaway. His smooth, golden voice rolled on and on, cheerfully describing the latest addition to his collection of trompe l'oeil, an eighteenth-century French oil that absolutely, he exclaimed, looked like a bas-relief sculpture.

I certainly gave Dunnaway good marks for his efforts to be an entertaining guest at a less than rollicking social occasion. But, more than that, I found myself more interested in the handsome lawyer than I had been before. Those who enjoy the art that attempts to look something other than what it is must have, at the very least, a wry sense of humor. I looked forward to talking to him in more depth.

Haskell concentrated on his food and made no effort to talk to me or to Trevor. His was the obdurate, scarcely veiled rudeness of a spoiled child, still so caught up in his own wants that he fails to see other human beings as real. They were, at best, purveyors of satisfaction. They were, at worst, obstacles.

As for Roger, his round face still had a high flush and his voice was querulous. Chase's son had drunk too much, which made me wonder how much he'd consumed before coming to dinner. Roger was an emotional man consumed by causes. The world thinks highly of cause bearers who succeed, calling them visionaries; those who fail it dismisses as crazies. But there is one certain truth about zealots: They are never bound by the rules the rest of us follow.

Much as he hated to accept it, Chase believed that someone now seated at his dining table was a poisoner.

What did I know about our potential murderer?

Poisoning is a stealthy crime. The killer is seldom present at the fatal moment. In my view, poisoning argues either cowardice or enormous caution.

Valerie St. Vincent would be cautious, as would Chase's secretary and his lawyer. All three were manipulative, always alert to improve their situation, always hiding their desires beneath carefully preserved facades of beauty or amiability.

Lyle Stedman, on the other hand, would be careful but not cautious. I had trouble picturing that combative man sliding the tip of a syringe filled with cyanide into a piece of candy.

I looked down the table.

My glance locked for an instant with Miranda's. Her worried eyes probed mine, demanding . . . demanding what?

I saw Miranda Prescott as neither cautious nor cowardly. Emotions flitted across her face so openly, many of them emotions that should have been alien to her youth and to her position.

For very different reasons, neither Haskell nor Roger would be cautious. Both were impulsive, emotional, passionate. Neither, I felt certain, was a coward.

But poisoning requires more forethought and meticulous preparation than I would expect of Haskell.

As for Roger—Roger would kill for a better good, but it would be an agony for him to do so.

Tomorrow, tomorrow I would . . .

"My friends." Chase's rich voice held no trace of irony. He pushed back his chair and stood.

The dessert had been served and removed and fresh coffee brought. Enrique moved so quietly that he seemed all but invisible.

"I have an announcement to make." Chase looked at each of us in turn. "I've asked you to the island for a special reason."

Roger reached for his coffee cup. The sound of china ringing against china seemed strident in the waiting quiet.

Every eye focused on Chase.

It was a very clear indication of the power he wielded in each and every life in this room.

Too much power.

"I am very lucky to have persuaded one of the finest writers of our time to agree to work with me in preparing a biography." He flashed me the ingenuous smile I'd found so charming forty years before. "Henrietta O'Dwyer Collins." He paused; everyone looked at me.

I managed a frosty smile.

Chase rocked back on his heels, his face genial, his tone expansive. "We all know that each person is perceived differently by those around them. That's why you're here. Each of you knows me in a different way. Your part in this is simple. Tell Henrie O what you know, how you feel. Be honest. I want you to tell her exactly what you think of me—what your dealings with me have been. Because this is to be a frank biography. She won't have any trouble finding people who will tell her nice things. I want the truth. Because, you know, I'm not ashamed of a goddamned thing I've ever done."

It was fitting that Valerie St. Vincent enjoyed the last word. She flung down her napkin, shot Chase a contemptuous glance, and said with her lovely actress's diction: "If you aren't, my dear Chase, you certainly should be," then swung about to exit, her golden head high and her shoulders flung back.

A beautifully flung barb, a gorgeous departure.

That's how I might have judged it, except for the effect on Miranda.

Her eyes huge and questioning, Chase's young wife stared after the actress. Then slowly, painfully, her bewildered gaze turned toward her husband.

But Chase was unaware of Miranda. Instead, his face oddly smug, he watched Valerie stride away.

4

Chase was in high good humor as he offered liqueurs to his guests. He seemed totally unaware of Miranda's pale face and silence. Valerie did not join the rest of us in the living room. I had no chance to talk to him with any freedom. But tomorrow would do well enough. I declined a game of bridge and, at about a quarter to ten, bid everyone good night.

But I wasn't going to bed.

I was going to think.

I glanced at the fresh carafe of water on my nightstand.
It could so easily be poisoned.

So could the golden box of expensive chocolates that rested
near the carafe.

But I assumed Chase could think of that, too.

The maid—I must try to talk with Betty tomorrow—had
turned down the silken covers. A mauve card propped on the
pillow contained information in elegant calligraphy about other
amenities available in the room: an alcove contained a coffee or
tea maker and a small refrigerator plus a cupboard with snacks.
I checked the pink refrigerator. A fluted crystal dish contained
chocolate mousse laced with raspberry. The enticing dessert
was at once both pleasing and disconcerting. It indicated how
thoroughly had Chase investigated my likes and dislikes. I
shrugged, resisted the temptation, and settled at the desk.

I thumbed through the stack of folders until I found my
own.

I didn't want to read it first because of ego. I've long since
slaked that hunger. But I had to find out what Chase knew
about me and my life.

Nothing in the first few lines conveyed the color and sub-
stance and feel of my youth. It merely reported that my father
was Douglas O'Dwyer, a foreign correspondent, and my
mother, Eileen Cameron, was a poet.

That was enough to trigger memory, of course. Early memories swirled and blended: the rumble of railroad wheels, the
thick smell of coal, the lusty whistle of a steam engine. Movement, always movement. I suppose it was a slapdash, uncertain,
unstructured growing up, but I knew how to haggle in Arabic
and sing roundelays in French and read a railway timetable
before I was ten.

I also learned about loss early when Mother went to a
sanitarium for tuberculosis and never came home.

I learned to go to a different school every few months and

keep a clean apartment for my father and me. The file didn't mention the day I met a very young foreign correspondent, Richard Corley Collins.

I learned to run and hide when the Germans goose-stepped into Paris. My father was in the south of France, caught up by the invasion. I never saw him again.

I wasn't yet seventeen when I managed to get out of France and into Spain. The file made it sound easy. It wasn't. The Pyrenees in winter claimed the lives of many refugees. I found my way to Portugal and a freighter home to America.

The dossier gave my next address as Lawrence, Kansas. And it began the long list of newspapers I worked for.

Because what else in life would I want to do?

The clatter of a typewriter; the scent of melted lead; the desperately difficult task of mastering words, making them sing; the unending challenge of seeking truth, balancing viewpoints.

Conventional wisdom is right: There are two sides to almost every story. That poses the task for the honest reporter.

Almost every story.

I've never been impressed that Hitler loved little blond children.

That isn't enough.

But generally it's hard to find white or black hats. Villains are seldom easy to spot. They know how to smile, too. Truth is harder to grasp than an eel and always as quick to slip away.

By the time the war was over, I was well launched on the only career I'd ever wanted. The dossier summed it up in a dry, unrevealing list of newspapers and place names.

It charted me to Washington, D.C.

I met Richard Collins again. For the first time I met Chase Prescott.

I read the next few lines carefully, but, once again, it was simply bare bones: place names, the newspaper, the date Richard and I married, Emily's birth.

I scanned the rest of it and found it all accurate and absolutely uninformative. If the rest of the folders were this spare
with information—real information, like the loves and hates of
lives, the traumas and mistakes and triumphs—they would be of
little help.

I put my own aside and picked up Chase's. I was grinning
by the time I finished it. I wondered what young hopeful on
Chase's staff had prepared it. Although it still didn't give me
meat, real meat, it was a great deal more forthcoming than my
own.

All served up, of course, in the most laudatory of terms. I
was interested to see that it addressed Chase's current financial
crunch. That meant Lavinia's information was accurate. It even
contained a recent quote of his—from a speech to a men's dinner club—that Prescott Communications was in no danger of
dissolution and the announcement that new money would be
infused by fall.

I did learn facts about Chase that I hadn't known:

He was raised by an aunt in Chicago (both parents dead in
a train crash). Chase and his aunt Sylvia were achingly poor.

He married his first wife, Elizabeth Warren, the same year
Richard and I married. Their son, Roger, was born a year after
Emily. Elizabeth inherited six newspapers and two radio stations from her father. These became the core of Chase's vast
media chain. Cancer killed Elizabeth when Roger was eighteen.

I understood what that meant to Roger.

Chase married Carrie Lee the following fall. Valerie St.
Vincent was Carrie Lee's sister. Chase's second wife died four
years ago in a small plane crash en route to their summer home
in Aspen. Chase was in Paris on business; Haskell was in Spain.
Roger's whereabouts weren't mentioned.

Two years later Chase and Miranda Temple married on
Valentine Day. She was an evening-news co-anchor for his Chicago television station.

The list of Chase's awards, achievements, honorary de-
grees, and publications ran six single-spaced pages. Chase was
the subject of a recent unauthorized biography, *The Man Who
Picks Presidents,* by Jeremy Hubbard. Immediately before the
book's publication Chase filed a libel suit. Litigation was pend-
ing.

It was hard not to be aware of the book at the time, for it
dominated bestseller lists and trashy headlines for months. I had
not read it, however. And not simply because Chase was a
closed chapter in my life. I refuse to increase the profits of
garbage journalists by purchasing their frothy cocktails of gossip, innuendo, and half-truths. I have a similar policy for the
kind of fiction that excites critics because of its viciousness and
commercially crafted violence. But now I made a check mark in
the margin. I wanted a copy of *The Man Who Picks Presidents.*
Chase unquestionably had one here on the island.

I took a chocolate break after I finished Chase's folder. My
hand hesitated for only a moment above the selection of as-
sorted truffles in the candy box. After all, nobody wanted to
poison me.

The ineffable essence of chocolate laced my bloodstream,
and I returned to the folder stack with renewed energy.

It was slow going. But I was determined to read them all
tonight. I intended to get an early start tomorrow talking to my
fellow guests, and I wanted all the ammunition I could carry. I
made notes, jotted down lines of questioning, even came up with
a few theories.

The lights went out.

"Damn." I said it softly, without too much rancor. After all,
it was late now—quite late. The luminous dial of my watch read
ten minutes after two. And a power outage on a remote island
certainly was no cause for surprise. I'd recently done a series of
stories in the Virgin Islands. It was rather more a matter of

celebrating when the lights were on than remarking when they were off. I knew from my earlier nosing about that this island had its own generator. I didn't know what would cause it to fail, but I was confident it would come back on. Eventually.

I never travel without a flashlight, of course. Hotel fires do happen. I always put my flashlight and my room key—when in a hotel—on the television set, so I would know immediately where to find them in an emergency. Here I'd placed the flashlight on the delicate writing desk. I picked it up and turned it on. I had enough light to finish the folder on Lyle Stedman, but I was suddenly tired. Enough was enough.

But I was restless. Tired, yes, but not ready for sleep.

I enjoy moving about in the night, walking quietly in the darkness while others sleep. Now I slipped down the stairs and stepped outside through the unlocked door. I was getting accustomed to the lack of locks on Dead Man's Island.

It was dark beyond belief. I almost went back upstairs for the flashlight but didn't. My eyes would soon adjust to the darkness. The lights in the gardens and near the house were extinguished, and not a gleam of starlight pierced the thick overcast.

I walked cautiously down the shell path to the pier. An erratic wind skittered leaves one way, then another. The air felt sodden. Waves slapped unseen against the pier, flinging up spray to sting my face.

With no warning the lights on the pier came on. I turned away from the brooding water. The massive house was dark, except for my room in the south wing of the second floor.

I was at the steps leading down to the gardens when I heard footsteps crunching on a shell path.

Of course. Someone—probably the manservant—had been to the generator and restored the power.

I hurried down the steps and headed that way. I wanted to

intercept Enrique. Chase's valet had been in Chase's New York brownstone the day the poisoned chocolate piece had killed the dog.

I always like to catch people at an unexpected time or place. Knowledge they might otherwise hide is more likely to slip out. My fatigue from studying the dossiers evaporated. I walked swiftly, eager to plunge into the quest Chase had assigned me. What better time than now?

I suppose I made a good deal of noise on the path. I had no reason to be quiet. Just as I came around the side of the house, I realized the other footsteps had ceased.

I'm fairly good about sounds.

I was almost certain the other footsteps—when I'd last heard them—were still some distance from the house.

Lights only spottily illuminated the long swath of lawn behind the house. The tennis courts were dark. The wind rustled the shrubs.

It was silent except for the sounds of night.

"Hello," I called out.

The rattle of the palmettos, the rustle of magnolias, the scratch of leaves . . . but not another telltale footstep.

Someone was out there, hidden in the shadows. Watching me?

An old homicide cop once told me, "If something don't seem kosher, run like hell."

I'm a fairly steady jogger, but my wind-sprint days are gone. Instead, I ducked away from the path into the sanctuary of shadows. Two can play that game. I ran lightly and quickly toward the house.

I regained my room and was pleased to see that it did have a button lock.

But I slept poorly. If not an old friend, danger is a longtime acquaintance. I had definitely sensed danger in the inimical quiet that had followed my call. Who had moved unseen through the night, then waited and watched me? And why?

"Vacation from hell." Valerie St. Vincent glared at the swimming pool where Chase was working out, swimming with a slow, steady freestyle.

The breakfast patio was twenty yards from the pool. In good weather the setting would be idyllic. There was a gorgeous view of the sound, comfortable wicker furniture, and elegantly prepared food: fresh fruit including papaya and kiwi, Danish pastries hot and buttery, cereals, meats, cheeses, eggs, and exquisite coffee. On a sultry August morning with a sullen sky and a wind just high enough to be irritating, however, the patio somehow lacked charm.

As did the actress. In the unflattering light, with the wind disarranging her hair, she looked every one of her forty-two years (that was the official age in her dossier; add at least another five). Her plastic surgery had been skillful, but it wasn't hard to spot the scars. And no operation would add generosity or thoughtfulness to that smooth, self-absorbed face.

Trevor Dunnaway heaped scrambled eggs on his plate, then added three pieces of French toast and several slices of rare roast beef. "Could be worse, Val, could be worse."

I sipped my coffee and enjoyed her prompt attack on him.

"Worse? God, yes. I suppose *Haiti* would be worse!" She looked around venomously. "It doesn't matter how you dress it up, this is nothing more than a sandbar and a swamp. Carrie would have loathed it. And if I have to listen to that damned music much longer I may *drown* someone." The Hawaiian music drifted to us. She had a point.

The lawyer put down his plate and slid eagerly into his chair. "Miranda loves the music." His tone was neutral.

Valerie's head jerked toward him. "Is that a little word to the wise, Trevor dear?"

He shrugged and reached for the coffee carafe. "My mother always told me not to bite the hand, et cetera," he said pleasantly.

"The greedy, greedy hand," the actress hissed, and she looked again toward the pool.

Chase finished his workout—I had to wonder if he wasn't showing off just a bit—with the butterfly, that most spectacular and most difficult stroke. At the wall he pulled himself easily out of the pool and stood for a moment, panting, full of life, proud of both his physique and his conditioning. Then, with a casual wave toward his audience, and, yes, I'm sure he knew we were all watching, he loped across to the hot tub, took the steps two at a time, and jumped into the steamy water.

"All he needs is a bevy of serving girls standing over him with fans and sprinkling pearls and rose petals on the water." The hand gripping Valerie's coffee cup looked clawlike.

Trevor peppered his roast beef. "Why not?" he said lightly. "I'll suggest it. He can afford anything he damn well wants."

I made my first contribution to the breakfast chatter. "Despite the notes coming due?" I spooned brown sugar over my oatmeal.

Trevor poured syrup over his last piece of French toast. "Sure." His tone was unconcerned. "As far as a public announcement goes, we have to hold off a few more weeks. But you'll still be working on the book. Just let me know, midmonth, and I'll get that information to you." An admiring smile lit his handsome features. "You really have to hand it to the old bastard. He can charm money out of the goddamnedest sources."

"Especially women," Valerie snapped.

The lawyer's smile slipped away. "Val, if you've got any sense—"

She jumped to her feet, throwing her napkin down on the table. "I've got sense enough to know when I'm not wanted. So why did he invite me?" Her sandals slapped against the tiles of the porch as she flounced toward the French doors.

I took another sip of coffee and looked inquiringly at the lawyer.

Trevor refilled his coffee cup and added three lumps of sugar. "You mustn't mind Valerie, Mrs. Collins. She's never adjusted to being an ex-sister-in-law." For an instant the lawyer looked bemused. "Actually, the sharp-tongued little vixen has a point. Why *did* Chase invite her here?"

I left his query in the limbo of all good rhetorical questions.

I finished my oatmeal, looked regretfully at the succulent French toast, and downed the rest of my superb coffee. "Believe I'll say good morning to my host."

Trevor nodded but did not respond.

As I wandered casually across the springy lawn toward the hot tub, Trevor popped up and returned to the buffet table and Haskell Lee stepped out on the patio.

Chase raised a hand from the bubbling waters to give me a cheerful salute.

I could feel the heat from the roiling, foaming water when I reached the top of the steps. The hot tub—actually large enough for a small party—was wooden with wooden steps leading up to the lip of the tub. A fenced wooden walkway circled the lip.

Chase was sprawled comfortably, his back to the wall. His face looked dangerously pink to me. "Henrie O—jump in."

I merely smiled.

But he was in high good humor, and he always loved to tease. "You used to be a creature of impulse, Henrie O. Come on in." He was talking too fast, with an unnatural excitement.

I shook my head and started to speak, then a movement caught my eye. I looked beyond the tub, toward the house.

Miranda stood on the patio outside their wing of the house.

She wore a brief nightgown of delicate lace-edged cotton. Her childlike face looked pinched and wan.

I smiled and lifted a hand in greeting.

Abruptly, she whirled and darted back into the house.

I suppose my smile turned to a frown.

"What is it?" Chase was irritated, both, I suppose, because my attention had left him and because I wasn't responding to his playful invitation.

"Miranda."

The playfulness seeped out of his face. Momentarily he looked somber, then he tossed his head and slapped the water with a resounding smack.

Hot, sudsy water spewed up, spattering my walking shorts.

"Henrie O, *this* is *the* way to start the day." He was smiling again.

As always, Chase at play was an infectious spirit, but I knew I needed to concentrate on my task.

"Chase, two items."

That got his attention. "You've made progress?" He pulled himself out of the tub and stood beside me.

I could feel the warmth of his body.

I stepped back a fraction.

"I'm not sure. I have stirred someone up." I told him about the search of my room yesterday before dinner.

He was quiet for a long moment, reaching out absently for a thick towel from a nearby stack. Briskly he buffed his head and chest dry, then wrapped the towel around his waist. "I don't know what the hell that means. It could be anybody. Maybe just Betty straightening up."

"It wasn't Betty." Perhaps I was a little sharp.

He gave me a rueful smile. "Sorry, Henrie O. Of course you're sure. You wouldn't have told me otherwise. Hell of a thing, isn't it! I can believe someone here is trying to kill me, but

I can't believe a guest or employee of mine would invade another guest's privacy. But if someone searched your room—"

"There must be a reason."

"All right. What do you want me to do—call everyone together and—"

"Lord, no." I couldn't believe what I was hearing. "The last thing we want to do is alert the searcher. No, I just wanted to tell you because it may indicate suspicion of me, which wouldn't be helpful. But there's more . . ."

I told him about that cold, inimical sense of being observed late last night and the hair-prickling feeling of danger.

He crossed his arms over his chest; now his face was grim.

Good. I had caught his attention. I was afraid he would dismiss the nonencounter as the figment of a too-active imagination.

"Maybe we better call the whole thing off. I thought it would be all right, that you could find out the truth for me. But I won't put you in danger. I won't."

There was utter finality in his voice.

"Chase, you damned chivalrous fool, use your head. If I'd seen whoever it was, I might have been in a jam. But I didn't. So drop that theme. What I want is for you to think—and to be very careful. Why would anyone turn off the power? Do you have anything to do with the generator? Is there any way you could be put in danger there?"

He didn't brush it off.

I waited patiently. And, truth be told, with a quiver of excitement because this did indeed bring back old times—the good times—to me, working with Chase, watching his quick intelligence sift facts and theories and suppositions. More often than not he'd come up with a new angle, something no one else had figured.

A chair scraped back from the breakfast table, and Trevor

ambled down into the rose garden, pausing occasionally to bend low and sniff the blooms. Roger came through the French doors and called a good morning to Haskell, who acknowledged it with a nod. Roger stretched and yawned. Today he looked like an amiable sleepy bear. His blue-and-white-striped polo shirt was too small and already damp with sweat and his khaki shorts were crumpled. He saw me and his mouth spread into an agreeable smile, then he clapped Haskell on the shoulder and took a chair.

Still Chase stood, straight as an arrow, his eyes speculative.

The water in the tub bubbled and gurgled, churning and reflecting the sunlight in an almost blinding glare.

Finally Chase spoke. "I can't see how I could be in any danger there, Henrie O. I've been in the generator room only once since this place was built. The architect took me through everything. It's not a spot I visit. Ever. And I certainly won't go near it now. So the objective can't be the generator room itself. As for why the lights went out, that's easy enough. Someone wanted to be certain they weren't seen. How long, Henrie O, were we in darkness?"

"Fifteen minutes. Maybe twenty."

Chase threw back his head and laughed heartily. He reached for another towel. "I guess I don't have to worry about any fancy booby traps. There wasn't enough time. But I won't step on anything that looks like fresh digging. Besides, maybe the person you heard didn't have anything to do with our lights going out."

"So why not answer when I called out?"

He gave a sardonic shrug. "There are always secrets, my dear. Perhaps Haskell was nosing around the maid. He wouldn't exactly want to draw attention to it."

"Is that a possibility?"

"It's occurred to me." His eyes held a mixture of salacious amusement and irritation. "He would know I wouldn't like it."

I always have another question. "Why would you care?"

At that, he gave a whoop of laughter. "Then you don't picture me in the role of a stern and moral father figure to my stepson?"

"No. A buccaneer, perhaps. A stern and moral figure, no."

"Suffice it to say, my dear, that that kind of dalliance plays hell with domestic arrangements. Anyway, the point is that your not-quite-close encounter may merely have been an embarrassment to someone."

"I don't think so." I started down the tub steps.

"I know. You're as determined as the witches in *Macbeth* that trouble is brewing. So I'm warned. Believe me, I won't touch any electrical connections of any sort. Now, what do you have planned for today?" He couldn't quite keep his voice casual as he followed me down the steps.

"I'll get to that. But, first, how many of the people now on the island have been here before?"

Chase crossed his arms on his chest. It wasn't the body language of resistance. I could see the ripple of goose bumps on his arms.

"Everyone, my dear, except you."

"So any one of them could know where the generator is." I had expected little else.

"It's hardly a state secret."

"And no one would have any reason to expect you to go to the generator." I was thinking out loud. "Okay, let's drop that for now. Do you, in fact, follow a regular schedule when you are here?"

He gave me a swift look of respect. "I understand. And, yes, I do. I start every morning with a workout in the pool. Then I indulge myself in the hot tub. The only good idea that ever came out of California."

I lifted my chin. Had the circumstances been different, I would have gone to battle immediately. What all of us owe to

California can scarcely be measured and God knows I'm not talking about Hollywood, though it does have its moments. Still, the classic films can almost be recited by memory: *Gone With the Wind, Casablanca, The African Queen, The Bridge on the River Kwai,* and maybe a dozen more. But California started the struggle for a clean environment, including smoke-free lungs. And it's perhaps the last place on earth, certainly this side of heaven, where decent people believe affirmations can affect the small-souled and cold-hearted leaders who happily engage in war although they, of course, are safe in distant capitals.

My glance locked with Chase's. We both knew that this quarrel was merely deferred to another time and place.

"And then?" I prodded. If Chase always followed a particular regimen, we could carefully check out the surroundings, be sure he was safe.

"A shower. Breakfast on the patio. Then I walk down to the point." He gestured to the southeast. "Beyond the pier there's a path that winds through the woods to a huge expanse of beach. Storms dredge the sand from north of here, then, the way the current flows, the sand drops on the south end of the island. The beach has added about four feet in the two years I've had this place. I had a stone platform built there with an attached shed for my painting supplies. I paint like hell all morning every morning. I'm damn good." His grin was pure Chase, egoistical, full of himself.

Obviously, he took this hobby—though I made a mental note not to call it that—seriously.

So I said mildly, "You and Churchill, hmm?"

He gave a tiny shrug, but he made no disclaimer.

It was another reminder of how long ago our paths had parted. For many years now Chase had been treated by those around him with great deference. Wealth can have many drawbacks, but perhaps the greatest is the separation of its possessors from ordinary human give-and-take. It was clear that Chase sincerely believed he was quite special indeed.

"I paint all morning, then I come back to the house about twelve-thirty for lunch. After lunch I get in some work. There's always work. About four I round up Miranda and maybe go for a sail, maybe play some pool. That's when we don't have guests. When we do, she always has tea ready about four-thirty. I come or not, depending on whether any of them are important."

That summed up that.

He continued, oblivious to my sardonic amusement. "I finish up in my office. Read, relax. We have dinner about seven-thirty. And so goes another day on Prescott Island." His tone was easy; his eyes were not. "So what do you propose for today?"

5

I told Chase what I wanted to do.

His look was quizzical. "You're taking that twenty-minute blackout seriously."

"So should you." I didn't smile.

I could read his thoughts: a little bit of irritation at my taking charge, then a rueful realization that, after all, he'd invited me aboard.

In any event, he capitulated. "All right. Come along."

At the French doors leading into his and Miranda's suite, he knocked on the door, then opened it. "Miranda? I've got company." He held the door and nodded for me to enter.

Miranda put down her makeup brush and half-turned from her dressing table. Her pretty heart-shaped face was utterly blank, but her eyes were dark with deep unhappiness. She was dressed for tennis.

Obviously, I was about as welcome as the bogeyman in a child's dream.

Chase must have been aware of her displeasure, but he chose to ignore it. "I'm giving Henrie O a look at how I spend time here on the island. For the book."

She gripped a red headband. "But you always spend the morning at the point. By yourself."

"So I'm doing things a little differently today. It isn't every day we have a world-famous author visiting us."

The room was beautifully decorated. The four-poster was huge to fit modern taste but in the graceful Chippendale style. The painted walls looked like green linen. The bedspread and wall hangings were light in contrast, a cream background for twining clusters of ivy.

"Oh." It was almost a pitiful breath of sound. "Yes. Yes." She turned back toward the mirror, blindly picked up a tube of lipstick. I knew tears brimmed in her eyes.

"Here's my bath, Henrie O. This way." Chase was either oblivious to his wife's pain or totally uninterested.

Two bathrooms opened off either side of the bedroom. His and hers. I didn't care what impression it made on Miranda, but I walked into Chase's bath and examined the shower. I turned it on and off.

At the lavatory I opened the medicine cabinet. Chase used a single-edge razor. I picked it up, unscrewed it, took the blade out, and inserted a new one.

Chase stood in the doorway, watching with eyes that were

half-amused. As I stepped toward him, he said, too low for Miranda to hear, "Dear God, do you think the bastard might smear anthrax germs on my shaving blades?"

"The point, Chase, is that we—and most especially you—must not take anything for granted."

I was glad to see when I stepped back into the bedroom that Miranda was applying eye shadow. But she did so with a hand that trembled. A spot stained her cheek. She gave a little cry and reached for a puff to scrub away the errant mark.

She didn't respond as we said good-bye. Her back was rigid. As we stepped onto the patio, I glanced at Chase. If he was worried about the state of his marriage, his face gave no sign of it. Perhaps I had succeeded in making my point, and he was concentrating on what an enemy could have accomplished in that twenty minutes of darkness.

In fact, as we walked toward the pier, he surveyed the gardens with a quick, nervous intensity as if he'd never seen them before.

That was all to the good.

I took the lead on the path that plunged into the thick tangle of semitropical woods.

I walked slowly.

It takes a good deal of care to search in dim light for traces of digging or for a vine conveniently stretched across a path. I also checked the trees.

He started to look, too.

His face was rather white by the time we reached the point. "Wait here," I instructed.

He watched as once again I surveyed the area, this time paying particular attention to the sand and the stepping-stones leading to the stone platform. I wasn't worried about the platform. It's hard to booby-trap stone.

But the door to the storage shed was another matter altogether.

The door appeared perfectly normal. I found no wires, no sprinkling of sawdust, no sign it had been tampered with.

Still, I gestured for Chase to remain where he was. I moved back a good twenty feet, seized a baseball-size clump of oyster shells, and lofted it toward the shed.

The unlocked door jolted open as the shells split apart and clattered noisily but harmlessly on the platform.

I crossed the platform, then checked out the shed. "Okay, Chase. Everything looks fine here. I'll return at noon, and we'll go to the house together."

He stood at the edge of the platform, staring at me. "You've certainly added a sparkle to my day, Henrie O. I can't wait to get started on a new painting. Maybe some nice skulls. Or a graveyard in the rain. How does that strike you?"

I gave him a little salute as I headed toward the trail. "Just relax on the platform, Chase. It's perfectly safe. More than you can say about a commuter flight or elective surgery. Think how brave Valerie is. It will buck you up."

His laughter wasn't altogether forced. "Go to hell," he called after me.

I walked fast. Actually, I felt pretty good about the morning so far. Chase was safely situated, fully alert to danger, and now I could get started on my real job—the hunt for a killer.

It didn't take long to find everyone.

Trevor and Miranda were playing tennis. I admired their stamina. It was so humid the air felt thick enough to reach out and grab a handful. Lyle jogged around the small track, his running shoes scuffing the smooth surface, sweat staining his blue nylon shorts, his bold-featured face crimson with exertion. He was running too fast for the weather, but maybe he was used to it. Enrique knelt by a sprinkler head in the rose garden. Valerie wore a sun hat even though she sat in the shade of a honeysuckle arbor. She was painting her fingernails, her arched eyebrows drawn down in a tight frown. Not the best facial exercise for redone skin. Haskell floated on a raft in the middle of the pool, a wet towel hiding his face. In the kitchen Rosalia loaded the dishwasher. Betty was dusting in the main entrance hall. In the library Roger was stretched comfortably on a couch, reading. He gave me a friendly smile.

As I had expected, I found Burton Andrews in Chase's study. The personality of the room—the Impressionist paintings, the weight of books, books, books, the vast collection of elegant music boxes—diminished the dapper little secretary, making him look even paler and less substantial than he was. His slicked-down hair was the color of straw. His inexpensive pastel sports shirt hung on slender shoulders. His hands were untanned and thin. Sitting behind Chase's massive desk, he looked like a boy.

I reviewed what I knew about him. Thirty-two. Unmarried. Graduate of a community college. Finance major. He'd been working as a temp in the main Atlanta offices of Prescott Communications when Chase's longtime secretary divorced and moved to Tahiti with an artist friend. (Now that would be an interesting story.) In the dossier Chase touted Burton's efficiency and willingness to work long hours. There was no hint that Chase took any special pleasure in his company; this was a subordinate, a human machine expected to perform given tasks and rewarded on that basis. Burton's salary was twenty-seven thousand a year. Not a high salary for the secretary to such a rich man. Perhaps the least attractive defect of some of the superrich is stinginess. I didn't remember that of Chase. Had he changed? Had he permitted greed to mold him utterly?

"Good morning, Burton."

He rose immediately. "Good morning, Mrs. Collins. What can I do for you?"

I waved him back to his seat. I am accustomed to sizing

people up. Burton's voice and demeanor were that of the perfect secretary, accommodating, respectful, attentive.

"I want a copy of *The Man Who Picks Presidents.*"

Surprise—and a trace of uneasiness?—flickered in Burton's pale eyes, but he made no comment and pulled open the bottom right desk drawer.

He stared into it for a long moment. Frowning, he leaned closer, fumbled with the files. Finally he closed the drawer and looked up. "The copy isn't here." He sounded genuinely puzzled. "I'll check with Mr. Prescott. Perhaps he has it, though . . ."

I waited, but he didn't finish the sentence. So I prompted him. "Though . . . ?"

"Well, I'd be surprised if Mr. Prescott has it. He hasn't asked for it. And it makes him mad every time the book's mentioned." A flash of malicious amusement gave his eyes liveliness for a moment, then they were once again unreadable. "He filed suit immediately, you know, trying to stop publication, but that didn't work. Now there's the libel suit. You know about that?"

I nodded.

"And about the private detective?"

I was beginning to get irritated with Chase. How many things that mattered had he failed to mention to me? But for Burton's benefit I nodded once again, my face bland. "Oh, yes. How's that coming?"

My answer, for some reason, reassured him. "The agency wasn't successful in determining where the information about the family came from. But Mr. Prescott's going to hire another agency. He's determined to find out who leaked the personal information to that author." The secretary looked at me sharply.

Now I got it. Burton was wondering if that was my assignment from Chase. Why should he care? Was he the informer?

My judgment was swift on that. No, he didn't have the

guts, and he wasn't nearly nervous enough for that to be the case.

But, for some other reason, he was extremely wary about any investigation into the background of that book. I tucked that conclusion away for future study and focused on the import of Burton's revelations.

"I certainly don't blame Chase for that. I know that's what upset him the most, the realization that someone he trusted, someone close to him, had betrayed him."

It's an old journalism trick, making a statement that can then be attributed to the unwary person being interviewed if he/ she says yes. *(Chase Prescott's personal secretary confirmed today that unsubstantiated accusations of impropriety in the recent sensational unauthorized biography of the media magnate are believed to have originated either from Prescott's family circle or from close business associates. . . .)*

The secretary nodded. "Mr. Prescott's furious." Was there just a trace of satisfaction in his tone?

"If Mr. Prescott doesn't have the book, who might have taken it?"

"I don't know." He looked thoughtful.

"When did you last see it?" I led him through a series of questions.

In sum, the book was there on Wednesday. Today was Friday.

Anyone on the island could have taken it.

Why?

To keep me from seeing it? That only figured if the person who fed the author confidential information was on the island and feared that I was there for that reason.

A stretch. But the guilty flee . . .

It would be critically important to the informer to remain unknown. Exposure would, at the very least, result in expulsion from the family or the business.

That could be a strong motive for murder.

"If it's important, I can pick up another copy when I go over to the mainland on Monday."

Burton's offer interested me. Obviously, he didn't care whether I saw the notorious biography. So apparently what worried him was the fact that someone would *take* it.

It didn't worry me. It interested me enormously.

"Thanks, Burton. I would appreciate it. Now, let's get to work. This will be only the first of many, many sessions we'll have during the course of my research on Mr. Prescott's biography"—I tried to sound as mellifluous and reassuring as a $200-an-hour shrink—"and today I want to focus on you."

"On me?" His face froze in the startled-deer look made famous by a late-twentieth-century vice president.

"My practice is always to start an interview by finding out about my contact. We'll relax and chat. When I know more about you, I can put your thoughts about Mr. Prescott into a better context."

This is, actually, sound interviewing technique. Stay the hell away from the sensitive questions until you've disarmed your subject. It's also a good way to finger a liar. Feed questions that have no bite—where were you born, where did you grow up, where did you go to school, what was your college major, etc.—then when everything's easy and smooth, slip in a question that matters. It's astonishing what you'll learn. If you watch eyes and hands, you'll never need a lie detector.

Of course, that kind of interviewing also has a secondary effect. It turns contacts into real people for the interviewer. I learned about Burton's older sister, who had raised him after his mother died. (The quick blinking back of tears when he told about her funeral last May.) He collected stamps and raised tropical fish. (*"They have so much personality, just like people."*) The stress of temping. (*"God, you never know what will happen, and they always blame the temp!"*)

I opened my purse, rather ostentatiously dropped my pen and notepad inside, and settled back in a relaxed fashion. *("The better to eat you, my dear.")* "What's it like, working for Chase Prescott?"

He smiled falsely. "Oh, it's fascinating. Always something new and different. Mr. Prescott is brilliant. He's always two steps ahead of everyone."

Poor little guy. It was easy to imagine what kind of hell it could be to try to satisfy the demands of a man who thought himself to be very special indeed.

I waited. Most people can't stand silence.

Burton shifted restlessly in Chase's big chair. "People who don't understand him think he's bad-tempered. It isn't that at all." Cautious pale eyes blinked nervously. "He's impatient. You see, his mind works so quickly, and he expects everyone to be as smart as he is."

Actually, I didn't recall that of Chase. Rather, I felt Chase prided himself on being smarter than anyone around him. Not, really, an attractive quality on his part.

"Are you as smart as Mr. Prescott?" This wasn't, of course, a fair question. But skewering through defenses isn't a pretty exercise.

He flushed. "Are you making fun of me, Mrs. Collins?"

"No."

"If I was as smart as Mr. Prescott, I wouldn't be a secretary. I do the best I can."

"I suspect Chase is more fortunate than he knows to have a secretary like you." I should have been ashamed of myself.

He looked at me warily, unaccustomed to praise.

"In fact, I'll make it a point to tell Chase how outstanding I think you are. He can trust you—which is certainly more than can be said of some of the other people in this house."

I had him eating out of the palm of my hand. His suspicions tumbled over each other.

"Listen, Mrs. Collins, I know it's Roger who spilled that awful stuff about the family to the writer . . . He tries to pretend he likes his father, but it's a lie, a lie. . . . Roger loathes him, I know he does . . . Never made any money on his own. Why, he just barely makes a living . . . Miranda's been acting funny the last few weeks . . . I see her up at night walking around . . . Lyle Stedman thinks he's already as big a deal as Mr. Prescott just because he's been picked to be CEO. I think that's making Mr. Prescott kind of mad. . . . Butter won't melt in that lawyer's mouth. I don't trust him. I tried to tell Mr. Prescott once, but he wouldn't listen. . . . That snotty Haskell Lee treats me like I'm dirt. Asks me to get him things, like I'm some kind of servant . . . I might as well not exist as far as Mrs. St. Vincent's concerned. But she'd better watch how she acts . . ."

There was a lot of venom and resentment stored behind Burton's obsequious facade. When he finally ran down, I inquired mildly, "Who should I talk to next? Who do you think will be the most honest and open about Mr. Prescott?"

The secretary's answer surprised me.

I suppose someday, should I ever make it to Eden, I'll find it much like the sanitized, controlled garden of luxury that Chase had created on Prescott Island, with flowering shrubs and sea-soft air and tiny pockets of privacy at every hand.

As I walked up the shell path, I welcomed the shade from the willows that fenced off the jogging track from both the back gardens and the house. It was only midmorning, but the hot air flowed over me like melted caramel.

As befitted an earthly paradise, there were several comfortable webbed garden chairs beneath the shade of an arbor beside the track. I took a seat and watched Lyle Stedman jog. Lean and muscular, he had the easy grace of an accomplished athlete.

His red hair was plastered limply to his skull. Unsmiling, breathing harshly, Lyle looked tough, absorbed, withdrawn. He slowed to a walk, still moving briskly.

His dossier revealed a young man in a hurry. Lyle Stedman started poor, the only son of a divorced secretary. He learned early that he was good at sports. It became his ticket to college, a track scholarship to the University of Mississippi. He was the house manager in his fraternity. He also played poker. Between the fraternity job, his scholarship, and cards, Stedman put together enough of a nest egg to pay his way to the Middle East. There he badgered every news bureau for a job until he landed one, starting off as a stringer. Three years later Prescott Communications hired him full time. When the Gulf War began, Lyle's stories caught the attention of Chase himself. Chase brought the young journalist back to the Atlanta office. Lyle Stedman outhustled his peers, and six months ago—at the tender age of twenty-seven—he was named Chase's heir apparent.

I imagined he'd made enemies in his scramble to succeed. I doubted that he gave a damn.

Lyle's stride checked. He hesitated, then came toward me, his expression impassive. He picked up a towel from a nearby chair, wiped off his face, then dropped into the chair across from me. Intelligent green eyes challenged me. He waited for me to speak.

I reached up and broke off a spray of honeysuckle. This time I didn't try the dear-old-lady-writer-cozying-up-to-the-subject. Lyle Stedman was a far cry from Burton Andrews. "Having fun?" A South Carolina–size wasp buzzed a little too near.

"You're the hotshot reporter. You tell me."

"Sure. About as much fun as a root canal." I would have guessed his last vacation had been in junior high school.

He did laugh at that. "Okay. Truce. The boss says you're writing his life. Why?"

"Money, of course." This is the kind of answer that usually embarrasses the asker enough to shut down further questions on the subject.

Not Lyle Stedman. He lifted one thick red eyebrow. "I know who you are. You've won every award there is. Covered the world. Then successfully made the switch to big-time fiction. You don't need money."

I tried evasive action. "But Prescott Communications does need money. In a bad way. Want to tell me about it?"

"If the boss heard that, he'd can you on the spot." Lyle leaned back in his chair and regarded me shrewdly. "I don't get this. The party line at the office is: Everything's swell, don't ask stupid questions, the money will come in, Prescott Communications forever with a drum roll and a trumpet tattoo in the background. So what gives?"

I crushed the honeysuckle in my hand, savoring the sweet, thick summertime smell. "Do you think the money's not coming in?"

"Goddamn. You've either got more guts than anybody I've ever met or you play it the way it lies. But in case you're carrying tidbits back to Chase, no, I don't think he's delusional. If the boss says the money's coming in, it will come. So I'm telling everybody to cool it. I'm telling everybody to concentrate on the job. Leave the high finance to the boss. It won't be the first time he's worked a miracle."

Lyle was trying to convince himself, not me. But it gave me a nice opening, and I pounced on it. I learned a lot more that I didn't know about Chase. Lyle got into the spirit of it, and I soon saw that this intelligent, impatient, ambitious young man was one of those rare creatures—a dispassionate observer. He was quick, yes, to say when he thought Chase was at fault—the celebrated unauthorized-biography libel case, for example—but just as quick to extol virtues, painting a vivid picture of a man fanatically devoted to the company he had built from nothing, an impatient, quick-tempered man with an unerring eye for what popular taste craved and a fierce determination to be the first to satisfy that hunger.

"That, in sum, is why he's richer than Croesus." The heir apparent hunched forward in his chair, his voice admiring. I could read the rest of his thought. One of these days, he, too, was going to be just as rich. When it was his turn. "Yeah, the boss was one of the first to get the idea that the simple life was back in style. He started new sections in every paper and a segment in the morning talk shows about back-to-basics, down with conspicuous consumption. People loved it. The letters poured in. Now everybody's on the bandwagon."

"The simple life."

He flashed a surprisingly charming grin. "Just because it's in his newspapers doesn't mean *he's* taken a vow of austerity. Here we are on Prescott Island, in a little grass shack for his buddies. But why the hell not?"

"So why did he ask you here this weekend?" My fingers felt sticky from the honeysuckle.

His smile slid away. "You heard the man at dinner last night. He knows I'll lay it out straight. I do, you know. He's fired me twice, but he always hires me back. I'm the only son of a bitch Chase knows who doesn't stand at attention when he comes into the room."

"But you'd rather be in Atlanta." I waved away a wasp, tossed the crushed honeysuckle onto the grass.

"God, yes." He twirled the towel into a taut line and snapped it twice. "Jesus, this is boring. No offense. But I want to be in the newsroom. I want to know what's going on. And this goddamned island—we're out here like it's a century ago.

What's wrong with him? Maybe he's getting old." He shook his head. "No, that's not it. But, for God's sake, anything could happen in Russia. The damn Libyans could knock down another plane. Hell, we don't know what's happening! For a damn week! And those interest payments come due in October. What's that? Five weeks? And here we sit twiddling our thumbs on this godforsaken island. So he says everything's okay —why doesn't he tell us what's going *on*? The rumors out in the industry are bad." He leaned back, visibly trying to relax. "But I'm not in charge."

"When you are . . ."

"When I am? Lady, I'm going to bite and scratch and gouge and fight and someday Prescott Communications will be the biggest media outfit in the world. In the whole damned *world*."

I knew as I looked at his glittering green eyes that the day he took over couldn't possibly come, as far as he was concerned, soon enough.

Caesar said it best: *"Yond Cassius has a lean and hungry look . . ."*

I was on my way to the tennis courts, hoping to find Miranda, when I took a detour.

The acrid, unmistakable scent of burning drew me to the incinerator. I touched the concrete blocks lightly. They were still warm, though no smoke twined from the vents.

It was the first home incinerator I'd been around in forty years. Believe it or not, home incinerators were a given in Southern California not so long ago. A small shovel hung from a hook on one side, along with gloves. I slipped on the gloves and opened the door. I used the shovel to explore.

Books are hard to burn, as Nazis and others of their ilk have discovered through the years.

This book was blackened and smoldering. Still, it was far from destroyed. I held in my hand the missing copy of *The Man Who Picks Presidents*. I carefully sprinkled it with some sandy dirt, to extinguish even a lingering spark. Then I went to the trouble to empty out all the ashes to see if there was anything else not customarily consigned to incinerators.

All I got for my trouble was an ash in my right eye and a smear of carbon on my walking shorts.

I took the charred book back to my room. There I wrapped it in a quart-size plastic bag (I carry them when traveling for soiled clothing) and tucked it in the middle of the folder stack.

I brushed away most of the cinder smear on my shorts and hurried back outside, my goal again the tennis courts.

Why try to burn Chase's biography?

Obviously, I could easily obtain a copy when back on the mainland. And, in fact, thanks to Burton Andrews, I'd have the book in hand by Monday afternoon.

Panic.

Whatever I'd sensed late last night when I called out and no one answered, it certainly hadn't been panic. No, taking that book to the incinerator was not the point of extinguishing the lights.

I turned up the path to the tennis courts, brushing back some low-lying weeping willow fronds. But when I reached the courts, I was disappointed not to see Chase's young wife. Trevor Dunnaway was zipping up his racket. He looked irritated.

"Where's Miranda?"

"Decided she'd had enough. Quit in the middle of the set." He must have realized he sounded pettish. He managed a smile and gestured toward a lavish wet bar beneath a canopy. "It *is* damned hot. Join me in a drink? Got ice out here and everything. Whiskey, beer, soda."

"Love to." Trevor was on my interview list, of course. Since he was a bird in hand, I'd defer my search for Miranda.

I took plain seltzer. Trevor uncapped a bottle of Dos Equis XXs. "Good and cold," he said approvingly. He pulled two director's chairs deeper into the shade for us. As we settled back, he looked toward the courts. "God, it's fun to play on clay. But they take a lot of work." With elegant timing, the court sprinklers came on at that moment. The aromatic smell of water hitting dry soil drifted to us. "Automatic, see," he explained admiringly. "Kind of an electric eye in reverse. As long as someone's playing, the water stays off. When there isn't any movement for a set period, the sprinklers come on for a while and pretty soon the court's perfect for the next game. Isn't that a hell of a deal?" He tilted the dark brown bottle and drank greedily.

He was certainly at home in this resort setting. As if to the manor born. But he hadn't been. Trevor was that strange hybrid, a middle-class origin but an upper-middle-class background. Both parents were schoolteachers who immigrated to the U.S. from England. Trevor was an only child. They gave him every advantage. Private schools. Music lessons. Good clothes. But the money only stretched so far. He couldn't afford skiing over spring break or jaunts to Europe or the expensive summer camps that cater to the rich. But Trevor brilliantly parlayed good looks and charm and an undeniable British accent, so appreciated by upper-middle-class Americans, into invitations to accompany his classmates' families on vacations: snorkeling in Greece, pyramid climbing in Mexico, salmon fishing in Alaska. And now, as a corporate attorney, he enjoyed a top income and, as always, excelled at eliciting invitations to the mansions and estates of the wealthy.

"Clever," I agreed, watching the drops of water striking the clay. "When a man is rich enough, there's no limit to what he can afford. So you must be complimented that a man who could have any lawyer in America as his corporate counsel should choose you."

His blond brows rose in surprise. "Never thought about it. Damn nice thing for you to say. But I don't know if I can lay it to legal brilliance." His smile was disarming. "Fact of the matter, got to know Chase at the club. Golf, you know. Damn fine player."

"As I'm sure you are." I lifted my glass. The seltzer was tart and refreshing.

"Fair, fair. Good enough, I suppose." He finished off the beer. His open face, still flushed from the tennis, was now relaxed and good-humored, that of an untroubled man on a perfect holiday. He grinned. "More to the point, fellows like Chase want to have a little bet on each hole. I never win *too* often."

I was seeing a superb performance. There was more to this man than amiable bonhomie, but he'd had years of practice at providing what he sensed his audience wanted. One session with me wasn't going to prick that facade, let alone destroy it.

I could try.

"What happens to Chase's estate when he dies?"

The easy look fled. He sat up straighter and looked at me sharply. He was unsmiling. He no longer looked like a lawyer on a holiday. He looked like a lawyer. "Why do you ask that? That has nothing to do with the book you're researching."

"No, perhaps not. Let's say I'm interested because the provisions of a will reveal an enormous amount about the relationship of the testator with the legatees." I met his gaze confidently.

"But this isn't that kind of biography, is it? This is going to be positive, isn't it?"

"Excuse me?" He couldn't have missed the frost in my voice.

It didn't bother him a whit. He compounded the insult. "Look, he's hiring you to write him up. Probably paying a good bit—"

"That's not the way it works, Trevor. I've agreed to write a biography. In fact, I've already had expressions of interest from several publishers. My agent will probably have an auction. But the point is: I write what I find. If it's positive, so be it. If it isn't . . . I'm no hired hand. Which brings me back to my original question: What happens to Chase's estate—"

That's when the shots rang out.

It galls me to admit it, but I was the last to reach the point. Age can be mastered to a great extent, but my seven-minute-mile days are long since past. Sometimes I console myself that not many women my age still jog, even if at the pace of a summer-somnolent armadillo. And sometimes I just swear bitterly and try to ignore the ache in my right knee and the stitch in my side.

I'll never forget the sight that met my eyes.

Everyone known to be on the island was there except for the housekeeper and the maid.

It was easy to see what had happened.

The force of the shots had flung the easel onto the stone floor. Drawing the eye at once and irresistibly were the ragged-edged bullet holes—three of them—almost at the midpoint of the canvas. At the height of the artist's head.

The surface of the stone floor told its story, too. A long, scuffed swath through the drifted pine needles and live oak leaves marked where Chase had thrown himself down. He had scrabbled to safety behind the shed, his back to the sound. That desperate crablike scuttle had cost him. Blood streaked his elbows and knees; dirt stained his white shorts and polo shirt.

Miranda clung to one arm, murmuring his name over and over, tears coursing down her lovely face.

Chase ignored her. His chest heaved like that of a man who had run a long distance. His face was red and stricken. It was also implacably angry.

"Someone shot at me."

Enrique shaded his eyes and looked out at the choppy water. "Hunters, sir. Poachers. The island's posted, of course. But some people—"

"Hunters?" Trevor broke in, his blue eyes skeptical. "We'd have heard a boat. Chase, did you hear a boat? Did you hear anything? Crackling in the underbrush, footsteps? Hunters make noise."

Chase jerked away from Miranda, too angry to be patient with her tears. He looked toward the dark mass of foliage. It appeared even darker and more somber and impenetrable from the brightness of the point with the open Atlantic on one side, the sound on the other.

"Nothing. Not a single sound."

"But that means . . ." Miranda hiccuped and rubbed her reddened eyes, looking bereft and hopelessly childlike.

Chase looked at each face in turn, his eyes probing, challenging. "Yes, it means someone crept up and aimed a gun at me —at my *back*—and shot—and the only reason I'm alive is that most people don't have any idea how hard it is to hit a target. The force of the explosion jerks the gun unless it's held rock-steady. One of you didn't know that."

"This is absolutely the limit."

Valerie's protest was icy, outraged. She tossed her platinum head. "I've been insulted ever since I arrived. But I refuse to be accused of murder. I'm leaving. Right now."

She turned and stalked across the stone floor.

Chase crossed his arms over his chest. "I didn't know you were a channel-ready swimmer, Val."

That stopped her. She whirled to face him. Her beautiful eyes blazed. "The boat will take me to shore. Now."

"No. No one's going anywhere. Not until I say they can go." Chase smiled grimly. "Unless they wish to swim."

"Wait a minute, Dad." Roger's voice was conciliatory. "You're upset. Of course if Val wants to go home, we'll have to—"

"No." A vein pulsed in Chase's temple.

"But, Dad—"

"Shut up, Roger." Chase's breathing was easier now. He squinted at the woods. "Who got here first?"

There was an instant of uneasy silence.

Enrique's face was expressionless. "I think I did, Mr. Prescott."

Chase focused on him. "Who came next?"

Enrique looked toward Valerie.

The actress clenched her hands. Her eyes smoldered. "Wait a minute now, wait just a minute. Is this a put-up job?" Furiously she jabbed a finger. "*You* were here when I came!"

Burton Andrews stepped back as if she'd struck him. "I didn't say I wasn't," he stammered. "I heard the shots — I was over by the track and I came as fast as I could."

Near the track? Why hadn't Trevor and I seen him? Of course, there were all those weeping willows . . .

Chase jerked his head toward me. "Okay, Henrie O, get this down."

I'm not fond of barked instructions, and I serve as no man's scribe. But these were not normal circumstances. I got out my notebook.

The order of arrival sorted out like this:
1. Enrique
2. Burton
3. Valerie
4. Lyle
5. Trevor
6. Haskell
7. Roger
8. Miranda
9. Me

"Enrique, check on Rosalia and Betty." Chase pointed up the path. "Then come back."

Miranda gave a little moan. "Oh, God, do you think something's happened to them? Oh, my God, what's going on here?" Her hands twisted together.

Chase shot an irritated look at his wife. "Nothing's happened to them. If we had a cellar, that's where Rosalia would be. Hiding. She doesn't look for trouble. Enrique will find them. Come here, Burton."

The secretary edged toward Chase, reluctance evident in every line of his body.

"Christ, man," Chase snapped, "what's wrong with you?"

"No-nothing." Burton stared at Chase with those stricken-deer eyes. The secretary had the died-again attitude of the born loser. He'd been blamed so many times for mistakes that weren't his that his automatic response was going to be "I didn't do it."

Chase understood that. He spoke slowly, patiently. "Relax, Burton. Think back. You heard the shots, then what did you do?"

Burton swallowed convulsively. His eyes slewed toward the woods, then jerked back to Chase. "Well, I was up near the track. Sort of. But closer to the woods. I was—" He shot another nervous glance at Chase. "I was taking a quick break, a little walk, before I got back to work. But I was thinking about the appointments for next week, getting the material—"

Chase managed not to bark, but just barely. "Get on with it. You were taking a walk. What happened?"

"Well"—Burton's tongue flicked over his lower lip—"I wasn't paying a lot of attention when *bang!* I heard the shots and then I heard someone running—it must have been Enrique—so I started to run, too. I came up the path and you were just getting up from behind the shed and Enrique was hurrying toward you."

"Did you pass anyone on the path? See anyone?" Chase fumbled for a handkerchief and dabbed at his bloody knees.

Miranda took the square of linen from him and gently touched the deep scratches.

"No." Burton's voice wavered. "I don't think so."

"You did or you didn't." Chase winced and roughly snatched the handkerchief from Miranda.

"No, no, I didn't see anyone until I got here and saw you and Enrique."

I hate to see time wasted. "Chase, obviously Burton didn't see anyone. The gunman would immediately take cover when he heard us coming, then, at the appropriate moment, slip onto the trail, break into a trot, and arrive here at the platform to join in the general hue and cry."

A crunch of footsteps sounded from the tangle of shrubbery and woods. No one said anything until Enrique emerged from the trees.

The valet reported to Chase that Rosalia and Betty had immediately locked themselves in the pantry after Betty ran in from outside and told the housekeeper about the shots.

"Where was Betty? Why was she outside?" I demanded.

Enrique ignored me. He kept looking at Chase, his pockmarked face impassive.

Chase took it up. "Where *was* Betty?"

"The storeroom. Rosalia sent her for some supplies." Enrique's tone was just short of truculent. "I told them to get back to work. Lunch will be served on time."

Lunch. Oh, yes. People are born. They die, naturally or not, and everyday routines continue.

"Good enough." But Chase was not interested in what his employees were doing. His eyes were on me. "Henrie O's right. It doesn't matter when anybody arrived or didn't arrive. Dammit, Henrie O, what *does* matter?"

"A thorough search of the premises and private interviews with everyone on the island to pinpoint the location of each person at the time of the shooting. That's a job for the police. I've got a mobile phone and—"

"No police." Chase's voice slashed through mine.

I looked at Chase an instant too long. By the time I scanned the other watching faces, it was too late. If Chase's announcement afforded relief to anyone, I'd missed it. All I saw on each visage was surprise and puzzlement.

"Hey, Chase, what's the deal? Somebody tries to murder you, of course we've got to call in the cops." Lyle Stedman's gravelly voice betrayed his impatience.

"No cops." Chase's mouth set in a grim, determined line.

"Dad, wait a minute, think a minute." Roger spoke quietly, gently. His face was still white with concern.

"The police?" Miranda's voice was faint.

Chase held up both hands. The voices quieted. "This isn't the way I thought it would turn out, but maybe it's better to put it all on the table. One of you—one of you—" He stopped and stared at his family and staff.

Miranda hugged her arms against her slender body; her eyes were huge and terrified, like a child waking deep in the night.

Haskell's dark good looks might have been carved out of mahogany. He watched Chase with an unwinking gaze.

Roger stepped toward his father, his hand outstretched. If Chase saw the gesture, he didn't respond. Roger's hand fell. His face screwed up in pain.

Valerie's smooth, unlined countenance didn't alter, of course. Perhaps that was an unsung advantage of face-lifts. It would take a hell of a crystal ball to read that lady's thoughts.

Burton looked like a rabbit caught in a trap. I wondered if the secretary was going to faint.

Lyle Stedman's green eyes narrowed.

Trevor Dunnaway was shaking his head slowly. All trace of his usual good humor had fled.

"One of you"—Chase's voice was quiet, but there was steel in his eyes—"tried to kill me today. One of you has tried before."

His upraised hands kept them quiet.

"No. Listen to me. That's why I invited each of you here. All of you—except Henrie O." His face softened. "Henrie O's the best investigator I've ever known. She's smarter than three carloads of cops. That's why when somebody tried to poison me, I thought of her." The look he gave me was as warming as an embrace.

Not so the response from the others. Their combined glances were almost a physical assault. Distrust. Suspicion. Anger. Jealousy. All aimed at me.

"Poison? What the hell are you talking about?" Trevor looked like a bank president whose bank has just been taken over by the FDIC.

"Poison!" Miranda's voice shook. "When? Where? Oh, Chase, I knew something was terribly wrong, I knew it!"

Roger stared at his father and mouthed "Poison," but no sound came.

Chase impassively described the lethal candy and the dog bounding across the room. "His body arched. He tried to breathe. I watched him die."

"That's sickening, absolutely sickening." One hand clutched dramatically at Valerie's throat. She shuddered. Then her eyes narrowed and her perfect cheeks flamed. "How *dare* you suggest I would do such a thing! I'll sue you, Chase, unless you withdraw that accusation."

"There is no accusation, Val. Yet. You are simply one of several who could have placed the candy in my study." Chase looked around the point. "One of you," he said simply. "That's why you're all here. And here you are all going to stay until Henrie O figures out which one of you did it, which hand filled that candy with cyanide, which hand held the gun. She's going to find out the answer."

"That's crazy, Dad." Roger withstood his father's furious glance, and it occurred to me that he was a stronger man than perhaps Chase realized. "You can't keep people hostage here. And there has to be some reasonable explanation—"

"Of that?" Chase asked bitterly, pointing at the fallen canvas and the three darkened holes. "Target practice? Accident? Mistake? Which would you pick, Roger?" His quick movement started blood flowing again from his right elbow. One drop, then another splattered onto the stone. Miranda gave a soft moan. Chase clapped the soiled handkerchief to the wound.

Roger jammed his hands in the pockets of his shorts. He looked hot and unhappy and worried.

Sweat beaded Chase's face, as much, I think, from shock as the heat. "No, this is my island and nobody leaves until I say so. Besides, if any of you give a damn about me you'll want to cooperate." His pugnacious, demanding glare swept from face to face.

Which pretty well put it on the line.

Trevor spoke up, and my respect for him grew.

"Chase, I've stayed with you through a lot of fights, a lot of hard times. I've gone your way even when I didn't agree with you. But this is wrong. Murder isn't a parlor game. You've got to call in the police."

Chase's eyes were steely. "I'm the son of a bitch in charge, Trevor, and you better not forget it."

"One item you've overlooked," I interposed quietly.

I saw the plea in Chase's eyes, the deep, passionate, aching demand.

Our gazes locked.

I wasn't Chase's servant or employee or family. I could tell him to go to hell.

But there was such raw emotion in those eyes that beseeched me.

I could tell him that his proposal was unbalanced, a plan devised by a mind under too much stress. And I certainly didn't share his confidence in my superiority as an investigator. The police are professionals. No amateur can match a professional.

But I couldn't—not for the life of me—turn down the appeal in his eyes.

All right. I wasn't a cop. But I was a damned good reporter. The jobs have more in common than most cops would like to admit.

I could do it.

If I didn't do it, Chase would simply send us all back to the mainland. He couldn't be forced to report the attack to the authorities. And on another day in another way the killer could try again.

It was one of those pivotal moments in life.

Everyone knew it.

Every eye focused on me.

"I will agree"—I saw triumph flare in Chase's eyes—"on one condition."

He stiffened. "That is?"

"You will from this moment on, so long as we stay on this island, be in the company of one or more persons."

Chase's face smoothed out. He even smiled. "Sure. Hell, yes. Look." The smile fled and in an unaffected, open, wondering voice, he said, "I don't want to die." He looked down at the blood-dappled handkerchief. "I don't want to die," he said again, so softly we almost couldn't hear. It was a cry from his heart. Everyone there knew it.

"Dad, oh, God, Dad." Roger stepped forward and wrapped his arms around his father.

For an instant the two held each other in a tight embrace, then Chase broke loose. "Okay. Point well taken, Henrie O. That's easy enough to do. No problem."

That was the most important requirement. I could take on an assignment to search for facts. I wasn't a bodyguard, and I couldn't take the responsibility of Chase's safety.

I wasn't finished. "Further, if I conclude that I cannot successfully complete my task, the police must be contacted."

"I understand what you're saying, Henrie O. But you know and I know what will happen if I go to the police." Chase's mouth twisted. "Hell, it's how I made my first million. Toss the quivering hunk of warm flesh to the wolf pack and ride the story to the end. Maybe it would be poetic justice to see my own family on the receiving end of forty-eight-point heads, but I don't want it to happen."

How could I have forgotten that the police, once in, are news sources? The enterprising press corps would love this one. I could see the headline now:

MEDIA MAGNATE CHEATS DEATH IN POSH LAIR;
MURDER ATTEMPT ON PRESCOTT ISLE FAILS;
POLICE INTERROGATING MEMBERS OF FAMILY

If the newshounds probed deep enough, dug deep enough, my own story could become part of a tabloid frenzy, which would then spill over into the mainstream press through articles sagaciously regretting sleaze journalism but quite thoroughly repeating and relishing each and every charge, every rumor and innuendo, no matter how sensational.

And I had a secret I was determined—no matter what it cost—to conceal. Now I, too, wanted desperately to avoid police involvement.

So I'd damn well better figure this out and figure it out fast.

"Henrie O, give it twenty-four hours. That's all I ask. Twenty-four hours. If you're stymied by this time tomorrow, I'll either get the authorities in or everyone will leave the island."

Twenty-four hours. Chase was agreeing to constant companionship for that period. Certainly we should, with everyone alert, be able to keep him safe for twenty-four hours.

And I had twenty-four hours to meet a deadline that suddenly meant as much to me as it did to him.

"All right. I'll try." I looked swiftly away from the gratitude in his face and said brusquely, "Roger, please lead the way back to the house. Everyone, except for Trevor, is to follow you. Enrique, you go last. Keep your eyes open. Notice if anyone touches anything on the path—or off of it, for that matter. Everyone keep an eye on his neighbor and—"

A scowl twisted Lyle's pugnacious face. "Why is Trevor your buddy?"

"When I heard the shots, he was standing right beside me. I am certain he didn't shoot at Chase. He knows I didn't. So if he's agreeable, we'll do a preliminary examination here. The rest of you are to stay together. Eat lunch, then"—I glanced at my watch—"we'll meet in the living room about one."

As they walked away, Roger in the lead, I checked them out. All wore casual clothes. No one was carrying a gun.

So the gun was either hidden somewhere nearby or the marksman had tossed it as far as possible into the tangle of semitropical foliage.

If the latter were true, the gun would be found only by the greatest good luck.

After a pro forma objection—"As an officer of the court, I feel I must insist that the proper authorities be notified"—Trevor turned out to be an agreeable pupil. We worked in tandem. As I directed him, he made a sketch of the crime scene. We had to estimate distances, but it was close enough. The bullets that had ripped through the canvas were easy to spot on the stone floor. Three of them. I had just suspicious enough a mind to foresee claims of manufactured evidence if I did this on my own. The first imperative was to be sure we had an accurate description of the scene, one we could turn over to investigators at a later time.

The only physical traces of the attack were the knocked-over easel, the trio of bullet holes in the canvas, the bloody path of Chase's frantic scramble to shelter, and the bullets. To the naked eye, they were simply misshapen lumps of lead, but a laboratory could link them to a particular gun. Trevor carefully sketched their position relative to the easel.

That was the easy part.

Then came the painstaking, slow, scratchy business of searching for the marksman's vantage point. I kept an eye out for poison ivy and poison oak.

We worked in silence. I had plenty of questions for Trevor, but this tedious hunt took all our concentration. Mosquitoes whined and bit. Trevor sneezed from the foliage. I was bathed in sweat.

"Look!" Triumphantly, Trevor held aside a plume of fern.

A cartridge case.

He reached for it.

"Wait!" I waved Trevor back. We were about five feet into the woods. From here a marksman, screened by a fir, had an unobstructed view of Chase standing by his easel. Twenty feet of sand intervened before the stone platform. The easel had been in the middle of the platform, adding another ten feet. All three shots had struck the easel. That was good shooting even though it had missed Chase. At the first shot, Chase would have thrown himself down immediately. A moving target is hard to hit. Or had the attacker intended to miss him?

I asked Trevor to sketch the tree, the cartridge, and the easel while I continued to study the ground. I spotted the second cartridge. The third I couldn't find. It could have ricocheted away or fallen into the pine straw. But I felt confident we'd pinpointed the site of the shooting. When Trevor finished his sketch, I eased a hefty fragment of oyster shell under the cartridges and placed them securely on the edge of the platform.

The location told me something about the marksman, too. He/she had played it safe, at no time becoming visible to Chase.

Was it caution or cowardice?

Armed, all anyone had to do was walk up to Chase, walk right up to him, and shoot.

It told me a good deal that the attacker had remained at

arm's length. That was all of a piece with the anonymity of poison.

Three shots fast.

Then what?

Chase, of course, had cried out and dived for the shed. From here it might well have looked to the attacker as if he had succeeded. But there would have been no time to be certain, no time to break out in the open and fire into the fallen figure because the shouts and calls would have begun and the rush of people toward the point.

There was only the single path.

"Okay, Trevor, let's go up this way and see if we can spot where someone could have hidden."

We gave it up midway up the path. Sure, there were places. Behind that twelve-foot stand of Spanish bayonet. Or crouched behind the yaupon or bayberry shrubs. The most likely was a patch of trodden grasses and ferns about a third of the way up the path. But it may have been visited by a different predator. In one piece of moist ground I saw a ragged imprint of an alligator's tail.

We scouted that area well. No gun. We looked again where we'd found the cartridges. No gun.

I gazed at the dense tangle of vines and shrubs and trees. "What would you do if you'd just shot at somebody—maybe you think you succeeded—and you heard people coming?"

Trevor used his arm to wipe the sweat from his face. "Throw the damn thing as far as I could and duck behind the biggest clump of shrub I could find," he said grimly.

Once in my room I slipped the cartridges from the shell into a handy plastic bag, which I nestled in a side pocket of my purse. I managed a shower, soothing lotion on bites, fresh clothes, and a quick lunch in twelve minutes. I went by Chase's study, spent a few minutes getting my supplies, but I still made it to the living room on time. Trevor wasn't with me. I had given him a special task, and I thought he just had time to do it.

Everyone, except Trevor, was in the living room, including Rosalia and Betty.

I placed a legal pad and a handful of pens on the red-lacquered coffee table, then checked with Chase. "You've kept everyone together?"

"Occasional restroom stops, but everyone's been escorted directly to and from the nearest bathroom on this floor. No one's had a chance for a private conversation. And since they were all in here—I told them to stay—I took a shower. If they were all in here, it was safe enough." He shot me a half-defiant, half-embarrassed look. It wasn't, of course, strict compliance with my directive. But I understood. He had to get clean. He had to distance himself from the kind of sweat—sticky and wet and smelly—that fear creates.

I faced a room full of uneasy, bewildered people. "I need everyone's cooperation. I want each of you to write down in some detail precisely where you were when you heard the shots and your subsequent actions until you reached the point. When that statement is finished and signed and given to me, you will be free to come and go as you please with the proviso"—I looked at my weary host—"that you, Chase, stay with Trevor for the rest of the day. And I want everyone in the house after dark. No wandering about alone."

Chase patted the right hand pocket of his blue blazer. It bulged. "Don't worry. And I want everyone to know I'm armed."

"Where did you get it?" How many damn guns were there on this island?

"From the cabin cruiser. I've had it for years. You don't travel in the Caribbean without a gun. I have it, and I know how to use it." His face was pale, but his voice was strong.

Which came as no surprise to me. Chase was the kind of man who would fight death with every tool at his command.

"Is that the only gun you know about?"

"The only one. Whoever shot at me must have brought the gun to the island." His left eyelid flickered. A nervous tic. I'd never seen Chase so shaken.

But those bullets had come close.

"All right. I don't have to warn you to keep the damn thing handy. As I recall, you shoot quite well." My voice was admiring. Actually, I never recalled Chase having anything at all to do with guns, but I wanted to erect every possible psychological barrier between Chase and his stalker.

I picked up the legal pad and ripped out a sheet for each person and handed these out with the pens. I even gave one to Chase. "Think back. Try to remember the minutes just before the shots. Close your eyes. You may remember something—a smell, a sound—something that possibly could help."

I waited patiently, listening to the scratching of the pens and the occasional sigh. One of the writers, I knew, was penning a lie.

Lyle was folding his sheet when the door opened and Trevor slipped in. Good.

I stood by the door to receive the sheets.

Lyle gave me a jaundiced look. "Lady, what if it's a nut? What if Chase was today's target and tomorrow one of the rest of us gets blown away? It's going to be hard to explain to the cops, isn't it?"

"Who else would eat a chocolate turtle from a box on Chase's desk?" I asked.

"Yeah." He glanced back at Chase, almost spoke, then shrugged and walked out.

Miranda, her face sullen, pushed her sheet toward me. "I should be the one to stay with Chase. Why don't I get to stay with him?"

Before I could answer, her girlish face crumpled again in tears. She hurried blindly past me.

Chase didn't notice. He stood stiffly by the Adam mantel, his hand clasped tightly to the gun-bulked pocket of his blazer.

Roger thrust his sheet at me. "Miranda, wait, wait a minute." Over his shoulder he muttered, "Poor little thing's upset. I'll see to her."

Hmm. So Roger was eager to comfort his stepmother. His so-much-younger stepmother. That was worth thinking about.

Haskell ambled over. "I should have had my head examined when I got out of the pool to go see what the noise was all about. Why the hell should I care who tries to blow Chase's head off?"

"Or I?" Valerie demanded, sweeping past me in a cloud of gardenia perfume.

The secretary edged toward me. Burton gave me the sheet, then looked back toward Chase. "Uh, will you want me in the study now?"

Chase waved him away impatiently, and Burton hurried out.

Rosalia was waiting for Betty to complete her sheet. The two women came to the door together. "We will be in the kitchen." She glanced uneasily back at her husband, then stepped through the open door.

Enrique poked his sheet toward me, his dark face sullen, and strode past, coming just a bit too close to be courteous.

As they left, I closed the door. I faced Trevor and Chase. Chase started to speak, but I held up my hand. "Trevor?"

The lawyer had a half-amused, half-embarrassed look on his handsome face. "Damn strange experience. I've never searched anybody's belongings before."

"So?" I prodded.

"I looked for a box of bullets, another gun, any kind of

poison, that sort of thing. No luck." He ran his hand through his thick blond hair and didn't look toward Chase.

"But you did find . . ."

He shot me an agonized glance. "Jesus, prowling in people's private—"

Again Chase started to speak, then subsided. It was no time to be concerned about host-guest niceties.

"What *did* you find?" I hadn't actually expected the search to be productive. We weren't dealing with a fool. Still, our opponent couldn't have predicted an immediate search. If Chase had been killed, it would have taken hours for the authorities to arrive and begin a formal, thorough investigation.

Chase watched, his face expressionless.

Trevor shook his head, as if to clear it. "A few things that matter. Could matter. Nothing to prove they do. Some cocaine in Haskell's room. A letter in Lyle's briefcase, a job offer from Triton TV . . ."

"And?" I prompted.

"Miranda's taking a lot of pills." He kept his eyes away from Chase.

But I didn't.

And I didn't miss the spasm of pain.

The wind was freshening.
Trevor shaded his eyes to look out at the sound. "Choppy."

A gusty wind kicked up frothy whitecaps. High, thin clouds raced across the glazed sky. Not the most pleasant afternoon for an outing on a yacht, but Chase had been adamant. Said he'd be damned if he was going to sit around cooped up with Trevor with nothing to do.

The *Miranda B.*'s motors roared to life.

I lifted my voice. "Trevor, check the weather reports. There was a hurricane heading for Cuba. That's probably why we're getting some higher waves."

"Sure. Listen, Henrie O . . ."

From the deckhouse Chase gestured impatiently for Trevor to come aboard.

Trevor held up a hand. "Coming! Just a second." Then he turned to me and said swiftly, "I've got to talk to you. There's a Lloyd's of London policy that . . ."

His words were drowned by the deep boom of the *Miranda B.*'s horn. It was throaty enough for an ocean liner.

". . . Stedman." The horn boomed again. The lawyer shrugged in a gesture of frustration and scrambled aboard.

As the yacht plowed through the whitecaps heading for the Atlantic side of the island, Chase poked his head out a side window and gave me a vigorous wave, as if this were a holiday outing on an ordinary day, not a temporary respite from suspicion and fear. I looked after him with an upwelling of admiration. I didn't love him. I never could again. But he had been an integral part of my life, and now he was facing a terrifying situation with admirable composure.

I wondered what the lawyer had wanted to tell me. Something about an insurance policy. Something that concerned Lyle Stedman? Stedman was an employee. What would he have to do with insurance for Chase?

I would have to await the yacht's return to find out.

But I had plenty to do, and I was glad I didn't have to worry about Chase while I did it. He was safe from harm, at least for the duration of his outing with Trevor, and I had the island's nervous inhabitants to myself. I hurried back toward the house.

Despite the wind rattling the palmetto fronds, I settled at a table on the breakfast patio. I had to force myself to do it. I itched to set out—immediately—to talk to each and every person on the island. There was so much to do, so much to be discovered, but I learned a long time ago that it's better to think before you approach an adversary.

I studied the sheaf of handwritten reports that pinpointed where each person had been when the shots rang out. No one, unfortunately, had seen anyone else gripping a "smoking gun." Or any gun at all.

Someone, of course, was lying about his or her location.

Only Trevor and I had an alibi.

I was still a little surprised that no one had glimpsed someone else when hurrying toward the point. It did reflect the variety of locations on the island: the pier, the boathouse, the gardens, the pool, the house, the tennis courts, the track, the servants' quarters, the storage building, and the thickets that afforded privacy almost everywhere. Once those running toward the point plunged into the maritime forest, they would be well hidden from view.

I reviewed each person's purported location.

Enrique: checking provisions on the *Miranda B.*

Burton: near the jogging track.

Valerie: sitting beneath an arbor in the rose garden studying a script.

Lyle: doing hand-over-hand on the monkey bars near the track.

Trevor: at the tennis courts with me.

Haskell: floating in the pool.

Roger: in the library reading *Earth in the Balance.*

Miranda: weeding in the herb garden between the storage building and the servants' quarters.

Rosalia: in the kitchen. She apparently didn't hear the shots although Roger, who was also in the house, did.

Betty: on the walk between the storage building and
the kitchen.

I now had a much clearer picture of the location of each
suspect, and no reason to doubt anyone's word. Yet. But the
reports were important from another aspect. All handwritten
missives tell you something of their authors. Enrique's printing
was large, the letters somewhat irregularly formed, but they
marched across the page forcefully, arguing a strong personality. Rosalia had trouble with *B*s and *P*s and might be dyslexic.
Would that indicate she mightn't be all that accurate a marksman? Betty's spelling was atrocious, but she was the only one to
emphasize that the shots came in such quick succession they
could scarcely be counted. Burton wrote in tiny but legible
script. I doubt if he'd ever raised his hand in a classroom. Valerie's flamboyant script reflected, not surprisingly, a penchant for
the dramatic. Her little discourse had style. Haskell couldn't
keep to the line: his writing was poorly formed and erratic.
Even within a single word, an odd letter would be capitalized or
missing or written twice. In his case I didn't fault the school
system but the mood-altering substances so common on school
grounds. Miranda's round, schoolgirlish script had as much personality as a mound of mashed potatoes. Chase wrote so hard
and fast the pen almost punctured the sheet. Lyle scrawled
oversize, thick-inked words that swaggered across the page.

I came back to Betty's ill-spelled, much-crossed-out-and-
over effort: *". . . so hot I wuz mizrabul, hot as a furnuss. I hurd the
shots, fast, fast, fast, fastur than korn pops . . ."*

I closed my eyes for an instant, trying to place myself in the
mind of the gunman.

Bang, bang, bang.

Why such a rush? Why not take another second or two,
adjust the aim, react to the jolt of the gun? Why this pell-mell
haste when a little more time might have spelled success?

I opened my eyes.

I didn't like the feeling seeping through me, the sense that the personality we sought was unstable, impulsive, undisciplined.

No. I must not confuse haste with disorder.

There was nothing disorderly in this attack except for the rapid firing.

Perhaps Chase had started to turn toward the woods, toward his attacker. That might have accounted for the hurry. A determination not to be seen.

That rang true with both episodes. Care and effort were expended to leave not a single trace and to avoid a direct confrontation. The marksman was too cautious or too cowardly to face the victim, yet clever enough to entirely change the method of murder in the second attempt.

I had a tantalizing sense that this was critical, that I was close to understanding something of the mind behind the poisoning and the shooting.

But it was elusive, nothing I could grasp and define.

I gave up on it. I had enough concrete work to do. And I was determined to conduct the interview I'd had in mind when I headed toward the tennis courts that morning.

I wanted to talk to Miranda.

Because, sad to say but true beyond doubt, in the event of murder look first and look hard at the spouse.

Even one as young and lovely as Miranda.

Perhaps especially one as young and lovely and nervy as Miranda.

I didn't find her on any of the porches. She was not in the gardens or near the pool. I paused beside the hot tub. There was something faintly sickening about the smell of chlorine and the shush and gurgle of the foaming, steamy waters. I looked toward the luxurious wing where she and Chase stayed.

"Mrs. Collins, may I help?"

Roger Prescott still had his aura of ineffable good humor. But there was a worried look in his pale blue eyes and a grave cast to his face.

"I'm looking for your stepmother." I raised my voice a little to be heard over the water bubbling in the tub.

He blinked, then gave an odd laugh. "Actually, I never think of Miranda as a stepmother. Absurd, really. I'm almost twice her age."

"But she is your stepmother." I walked toward him. "I need to talk to her."

His face crinkled. "She's pretty upset. Maybe I can help you. I took her to her room."

But it was *their* room, Miranda's and Chase's.

"She's got a pretty rotten headache." His voice was soft.

How interesting that Roger was being much more protective of his pretty young stepmother than Chase appeared to be of his wife.

"Are your father and Miranda having trouble?" I moved toward the wet bar in the arbor and fished a club soda out of the refrigerator.

"I'd certainly be furious with him if I were her." His face flamed as he realized how that sounded. "Oh, God, don't take that wrong. And I guess I understand now. But ever since last month Dad's been a beast to her." He pulled a handkerchief from his pocket, patted his moist face. "Goddamn weather's like a sauna. He's acted so funny—I mean, he can't possibly think that Miranda—that's nuts, really nuts. No, that can't be it. I know he didn't tell her about the poisoning because he didn't want to scare her. She's just a kid really. She doesn't know about ugly things."

I kept my face blank. It's always a mistake, I could have told him, to confuse innocence with age. There are children who are preternaturally wise and old folks who see with angel eyes.

I dropped into a webbed chair. "Tell me about Miranda."

"There isn't much to tell. Like I said, she's just a kid." His chair creaked under his weight. "Lyle hired her. He figured it would fit in with Dad's back-to-the-basics editorial stuff. Youth. Innocence. An anchor without that sleek New York fashion-model look. Dad agreed." He grinned but without malice. "Obviously. I understand from Lyle that Dad asked to meet Miranda because he was impressed with her work. Two months later they got married in St. Thomas."

"It's a rather striking age difference." I kept my voice neutral.

But Roger took it as criticism. He pulled his chair closer to mine and said earnestly, "It's not the way you think it was. People just assume Dad's a cradle snatcher. I know for a fact— Lyle told me—that Dad was impressed with her, but that would have been the end of it. Except for Miranda herself! Lyle said she fell for Dad like a ton of bricks. He didn't go after Miranda at all. It was Miranda who went after him. But if you know anything about her past . . . Her mom died when she was just a little girl—younger than I was when my mother died and that's tough—and Miranda's dad raised her. I guess he must have been a great father. Poor kid, she lost him, too. Last year. Anyway, when Miranda met Dad, it was like somebody tossed stardust in her eyes. She was obsessed with him. And, hell, how could any man turn her down? I wish I had just a little of Dad's magic. Whatever it is."

I could have told him. I met Chase when I was her age and Chase was young and vibrant with the unmistakable, seductive aura of a winner. But it wouldn't have made Roger feel any better.

"You don't seem to mind."

"Mind? Mind what?"

"Having such a young stepmother." I reached over to drop the soda bottle in a wastebasket.

He gave me an endearing smile. "Henrie O, I like Miranda

—and I want Dad to be happy." His eyes darkened. "The only problem Dad and I have is that we don't agree on anything about how he runs his papers. God, he could do so much *good*. But we all know they belong to him. Not me."

He seemed oblivious to the obvious next step. "They will be yours someday, won't they?"

"Oh, yeah, but Dad's in great shape. He's—" His eyes narrowed. "Oh, now, wait a minute. You think I'd poison my own dad, shoot him down so I could control the editorial policies of his newspapers? No way. I'm not into patricide. Not for any damn reason."

I left him looking after me with an expression of hurt. I know the conclusion I was supposed to draw: This good fellow, this right-thinking agreeable son, was too open, too disarming, too earnest to be considered a suspect.

Maybe. Maybe not.

I knocked on the French door.

No answer.

I knocked twice more, then turned the handle.

The drawers to the dresser were yanked open. Negligees and blouses, silk slips, panties and bras poked over the edges of the drawers, were strewn atop the puffy bedspread. Two open suitcases were propped against the pillows. The Prescotts' decorator would have cringed at hearing the elegant piece of furniture described as a dresser. It was actually an English Colonial commode of lemonwood and ebony. It glistened in the light of the crystal lamp.

Miranda swung about to face me. Her heart-shaped face was ashen. She looked like a bereft child.

I had come into the room in no mood to console, ready to snap a terse "Grow up."

But this was a personality that was so fragile, so near dissolution that instead I asked, "What are you doing, Miranda?" in a mild, soft voice.

"I want to go home." The words were tiny breaths. Blindly she grabbed a handful of rainbow-hued lingerie from the top drawer.

"Where is that?" I stepped quietly closer.

Her head swiveled and anguished eyes focused on me. "Chase hired you?"

"Yes."

"You aren't lovers?" Her mouth quivered.

"No." Now I understood her shock when I'd first arrived. She'd been convinced her husband was inviting a lover to the island. I must have come as quite a surprise. But now her distress was dreadful. It was akin to seeing a kitten mauled by dogs.

"I thought . . . I thought . . . but the folder you had, it was all business."

Now I knew who had looked in my purse, rifled through the dossiers.

"Yes, all business."

Some of the pain seeped out of her face. "You don't lie, do you?" It was the trusting voice of a child, high and thin.

What a sad, guileless question. But, for now, there was only one answer to give, no matter how false. "No."

"Tell me— Tell me why Chase doesn't come to me. Why has he shut me out? Why has he been so distant, as if he didn't love me anymore? Why has everything been so wrong? It has been wrong. For weeks now. He isn't himself. He's . . . His eyes are wild. Wild!"

I crossed the room and led her to the wicker chairs near the windows. She came obediently and sat down, still holding a lavender camisole tightly in her hands.

"Sometimes," I began gently, "we have to remember that people—even people very close to us—act in strange ways because of difficulties they're facing. The way they act may not have a single thing to do with us. Now, you admire Chase—love Chase—because he's strong. Isn't that right?"

Her eyes clung to mine. Her hands gripped the lovely silk camisole as if it were a lifeline.

"Look at it this way, Miranda. Chase has been very kind to you, very gentle. Am I right?" I reached out, loosened those talon-tight fingers, pulled the camisole away, shook it out.

"Oh, yes, yes. Always." Her hands trembled. She clasped them tightly together.

"How gentle would it be to tell you that someone wanted to kill him?" I folded the camisole, laid it on the bed.

She winced as if I'd struck her. "Do you mean . . . It isn't because he thinks . . . thinks . . ."

"That you tried to poison him? Shot at him? Of course not. Now let me help you put these things away. First I'll bring you a cool cloth . . ." As I talked I walked briskly into her bath, found a clean washcloth, and dampened it.

When I handed it to her, she accepted it with a shy smile. "You're right. I know you are. I've been so selfish! Just thinking of myself and not about Chase at all and how terribly upset he must be. Oh, how awful to realize that behind a face you know there is so much hatred." She pressed the cloth against her face for a long moment, then jumped up, suddenly bright and vivacious. It was disconcerting to see her mood change so abruptly. "Quick, we'll put everything back. I don't know what I was thinking of. How could I have been so stupid? But, you see, I care so much," she said nakedly. "I can't live without him."

"Don't say that," I said sharply. If ever age teaches any truth, it is that we must accept life as it happens, no matter what the pain, no matter what the loss. And loss always comes. Loss is the price of love. "We don't make those decisions, Miranda."

It took only a few minutes to restore the handsome room,

to put away the scattered lingerie, to return the expensive luggage to the back of a huge walk-in closet. As we worked, Miranda talked, her voice as high and light as the chatter of starlings: how wonderful Chase was, how handsome, how strong, how fascinating, how exciting. . . .

Roger's observation had indeed hit the mark. Miranda was obsessed with her much older husband. Despite her youth and her delicate, childlike beauty, there was a powerful sense of hunger, avidity, overwhelming determination. Was she so obsessed that if she felt him slipping away, she would rather see him dead than lose him? She had cried that she couldn't live without him. Did she mean instead that she would not permit him to live without her?

As for Chase, no matter how delightful at first—the possession of that no doubt exquisitely youthful and lovely and passionately responsive body—wouldn't her constant outpouring of adoration become oppressive? Had he tired of Miranda?

As we walked out of their wing, into the main hall, she impulsively stood on tiptoe and soft lips brushed my cheek. The scent of Giorgio tickled my nose. "Thank you. You're so kind. I feel so much better. I believe I'll go out to the gardens now, cut some roses. Chase loves red roses."

I watched her walk down the hall, so young, so graceful, so lovely.

And so deadly?

I don't have an emotional response to kitchens, but even a noncook like myself could admire Rosalia's immaculate domain, with its sparkling tile work surfaces, white-ash cabinets, and a redbrick floor, and take delight in the wonderful aromas. A hint of cayenne seeped from the bubbling stewpot and the sharp smell of fresh yeast from the flour mixture she was kneading on a marble cutting board pervaded the orderly room.

The housekeeper paused, her hands clutching the dough, and watched me with frightened eyes.

Was it I who frightened her, or was she terrified because someone had made an attempt on her employer's life?

I took a low-key approach. "Rosalia, I'd like to visit with you for a little while, if it's convenient."

"With me? But I was here in my kitchen. I know nothing." Shrillness sharpened her voice. She dropped the dough and wiped her hands on her apron. She was as immaculate as her kitchen. Her white uniform was fresh and starched, and her white leather shoes glistened with polish. Her black hair was tucked in a tidy coronet braid. She wore no makeup on her smooth ivory skin. I knew that she was forty-seven, that she had married Enrique when she was nineteen, that they had no children. Both she and Enrique were born in Havana and came to the United States as teenagers after the Cuban missile crisis, their families settling in Miami. Enrique had worked at various marinas, eventually becoming the all-purpose handyman for a wealthy yacht owner. Two years later Chase purchased the yacht, and Enrique had come with the boat. On longer trips Rosalia had accompanied them as cook. Chase was so pleased with their work, he had hired both to serve his household, wherever it might be. So, for almost three decades, Enrique and Rosalia accompanied Chase and his family from home to home, including, finally, Prescott Island.

There should be a wealth of knowledge here if I were skilled enough to mine it.

"Rosalia, tell me something of your duties as housekeeper."

She wiped her hands again, but some of the tightness eased from her thin shoulders. I listened patiently as she softly described her daily and weekly duties, which were complex indeed, involving the ordering of food, creation of menus, and overseeing of cleaning at six residences. "And Enrique, he is in charge of all else—the cars, you know, and the boat, and the machines. Whatever must work, he makes sure that it does so. And if the boat must be caulked or the roof repaired, why, Enrique tells Mr. Prescott and, quick, quick, it is done."

Repairs, corrections, events—whatever—do seem to march at a brisk pace for the very rich.

"You and Enrique have worked hard for Mr. Prescott for many years. I know you've learned a lot about Mr. Prescott and his family over that time. What kind of man is he?"

She reached down, began to work the dough again. "It is not for me to say." There was great dignity in her voice.

"Rosalia, they say no man is a hero to his valet. I need to know what kind of man Chase Prescott is to his housekeeper. Don't you see, if I can have a true picture of him, I can better see who might be angry or hurt or greedy or cruel enough to try to kill him?"

"A true picture?" She shook her head and her hands moved with increasing sureness, kneading, plumping, smoothing. "I tell you, lady, you are looking for simple answers where there are none. So what do I say?" She did not look at me as she settled the mound of dough and covered it with a damp cloth. "Mr. Prescott, he was always a nice man to Mrs. Elizabeth, his first wife. Yes, I say this to you. A very nice man." She wiped her hands on her apron. "But I know that he—"

"Rosalia." Enrique spoke quietly, but the sound of his voice stopped her as effectively as a shout.

There were four entrances to the kitchen: one from the main hallway, and that was the way I'd come, a second on the north, probably leading to a wash area, a third that led directly to the dining room, and a fourth to the outside.

Enrique stood in the second doorway.

As I looked toward him I caught the tiny, almost imperceptible movement in the doorway into the dining room.

But the door didn't continue to open.

I looked at Enrique while keeping that just barely opened dining-room door in my peripheral vision. "Enrique, I'm glad you've come." I wasn't going to admit defeat without a fight. "As you can see, I'm trying to get a better picture of the relationships between Mr. Prescott and members of his family. And staff. I know people who work for Mr. Prescott have probably visited often enough that you can help there, too."

He continued to look at his wife, his coal-black eyes hard.

I had underestimated this man. He was a type I knew— lean, tough, muscled, usually a soldier of some kind, often a guerrilla. His pockmarked face was impassive, but he radiated a particular kind of arrogance, the machismo that sees women solely as objects, either of veneration or lust, but never as partners and companions. This was a man who would do what he had to do to survive, and he would do it without compunction.

"As you were saying, Rosalia," I encouraged, "about Elizabeth Prescott, Roger's mother."

She lifted her eyes, and there was stark fear in them. Her voice was high and unconvincing. "Mr. Prescott took her to many, many clinics, many doctors, but the cancer, it was too big. They found it too late." Her hands made a shape—a cancer the size of a grapefruit?—and her eyes implored me.

I knew with the certainty of stone that this was not what she had begun to say when her husband intruded.

She picked up a spatula and a spoon and carried them to the sink. "It was such a hard time, so much pain for Mr. Roger."

"And for Mr. Prescott?"

"It is difficult for a man to lose his wife." Enrique's eyes glittered. He folded his arms across his chest. "It was very hard for Mr. Prescott."

Had that door to the dining room moved just another fraction?

"How soon did he remarry?" I met Enrique's steely gaze.

Our immediate and complete antipathy couldn't have been stronger had we engaged in a shouting match.

Neither of us gave an inch.

Rosalia looked swiftly toward her husband. She seemed to shrink inside her dress as she stood there, her body drawing in upon itself, tightening.

My eyes challenged Enrique's for a measure longer, then I turned to her. "I imagine you remember when a new mistress came in."

Enrique turned his angry face toward his wife.

Rosalia didn't look at him. She murmured, "The funeral was in April. And the wedding was in October." She gave me a lightning-swift look.

I thought I understood her intent. I wasn't certain. But, for now, I dropped that line of inquiry. Instead I concentrated on Enrique.

He didn't overtly resist, but his eyes glowed with anger at being questioned by a woman. Every answer was a bland reiteration of a theme: Chase Prescott was the finest of all employers, Mr. Prescott's family was nice, Mr. Prescott's media employees seemed to be very outstanding.

"What do you think about Mr. Stedman?" The door to the dining room was still ajar.

"Mr. Prescott doesn't hire me to talk about people who work for him." His folded arms said it all.

I gave him a frosty smile. "To hear you tell it, Enrique, working or living with Mr. Prescott is idyllic. How do *you* account for three shots and poisoned candy?"

"It isn't—"

"—your job to figure that out. Right. I got you the first time. But, as has been said in another context, those who aren't with me are against me. Which makes me wonder very hard how it would benefit you, Enrique, if Mr. Prescott should die."

I could read his response without any problem. He was controlling a powerful impulse to hit me.

"Think about it, Enrique. I'll check back with you later. I expect some specific responses about the people who are here and what you know about them and Mr. Prescott." I paused at the swinging door into the hall, still acutely aware of that telltale crack into the dining room. Someone stood there listening. Why? "If you are still in a see-hear-say-no-evil mode, we'll have a little talk with Mr. Prescott."

I stepped out into the central hall to a suddenly shocking assault of sound. A Chopin mazurka was being played with an intensity that bordered on violence. It was the first time I realized that the door into the kitchen was sound-proofed.

It delayed me just an instant, then I turned and ran lightly across the hall and opened the doors to the dining room. I could see across the dim room—the shutters were closed and the immense chandelier dark—to the door to the kitchen. It was no longer ajar. I stepped into the dining room, pulling the doors shut behind me, and skirted the table to reach the door. Had I imagined it? I eased it open a breath—and saw Enrique sliding his leather belt through the loops of his trousers.

I couldn't see Rosalia.

I didn't need to.

Anger raced through me.

I kicked open the door and plunged into the kitchen. I walked past a cowering Rosalia until I stood a scant foot from her husband.

"No."

His face flushed an ugly dark crimson. A pulse throbbed in his throat.

For an instant I knew he was going to strike me.

"Listen closely, Enrique. If you hurt Rosalia—now or in the future—you'll go to jail. I'll make sure of it."

He glared at me. His hands fell slowly to his sides. "I don't know what you are talking about, Mrs. Collins."

My eyes dropped to the belt in his hands. "Put it back on. Keep it on."

I swung around. "Rosalia, I'm going to find Betty now. She will stay with you. She will help you move your things to one of the rooms near mine."

Rosalia's lips quivered.

Enrique blazed, "She is my wife!"

"She will do as I say. I will speak to Mr. Prescott about this as soon as he returns."

Enrique shot his wife a look that made my blood run cold. Then he whirled and slammed through the doorway.

Tears seeped from beneath Rosalia's closed lids.

"Do as I say, Rosalia. Betty and I will protect you."

Slowly her eyes opened. The tears couldn't hide the terrible hopelessness.

"I'll send Betty. If he returns, run away. Come where there are people. I won't let him hurt you again."

I hated leaving her alone in the kitchen. Would Enrique return? Would it be worse for her because I'd intervened? Or would the fear of Chase's response stay his hand? I could only hope that Rosalia would do as I'd directed. But it is hard to break the shackles of fear and dominion.

I stepped back into the dining room, through the door eased open by the unseen observer. It took only a few steps and I was outside, stepping through French doors onto a bricked terrace. To my left was the line of willows screening the terrace from the outer buildings. I glanced toward the empty tennis courts and the tangle of willows close to the track.

I didn't expect to see anyone and knew, if I did, that too much time had elapsed to connect the sighting to the listening presence in the dining room.

Instead, I stood thoughtfully for a moment, aware of the

ominous clouds banking up in the south and of the Calcutta-like heat. A storm was coming. I didn't need the unmistakable, un-erring ache of my bones (as accurate as any barometer and more impossible to ignore) to tell me that. But it was simply one more uncertainty in a situation so murky that I couldn't be sure what mattered and what was totally irrelevant.

Did it matter that Enrique beat his wife?

What had Rosalia meant to tell me about Chase? Was it important in finding out who wanted to kill him?

Who had pressed against that slightly opened door to listen to my questions to Enrique and Rosalia?

Was it the killer, nervous at my efforts?

Or was it a suspect, craven with fear of a false accusation?

I couldn't know. I only knew that I was plunged into an atmosphere dense with suspicion and dislike, and that all of the contradictory, ill-understood relationships had to be sorted out.

And I'd damned well better hurry. I had less than twenty-four hours now.

But first . . . I found Betty in the laundry room. When she saw me, she stopped short, her eyes widening in alarm.

I told her what I'd said to Enrique and Rosalia and what I expected of her. There was no surprise in her face. But she looked uncertainly at the half-loaded laundry basket.

"Let it be. I'll explain to Mr. Prescott. Go to the kitchen. Stay with Rosalia."

She walked back to the house with me. At the kitchen steps she said only, "Enrique will be like a madman."

"I can handle that."

"Yes, ma'am." I thought I heard satisfaction in her voice.

I wiped the sweat from my face and used the French doors to enter the house. When I reached the hallway, the crashing chords from the piano resounded with furious passion. The pi-anist attacked the music with a ferocity that I couldn't ignore. I ran swiftly up the stairs.

The decor of the music room offered a fitting setting for the dramatic performance. A huge black concert Steinway, two walls sheathed in crimson velvet, a third wall of mosaic—I recognized a replica of the central figure that adorns Barcelona's Palau de Musica—and a fourth wall of stained glass with glittering glass fingers of sunlight pointing to angelic faces, clearly patterned after the enormous circular central skylight of that opera house.

The pianist came to a thunderous conclusion, then rested her hands, the fingers powerful and graceful and tipped with scarlet nails, on the ivory keys. The huge mirror facing the piano reflected the woman and the instrument.

"Ah, the bitch." Icy blue eyes met mine in the mirror. "I've been expecting you."

A pale rose and cream Dresden clock chimed a melodious three o'clock.

She twisted on the seat to face me. "Do you like being a hired gun?" Her voice was laden with contempt.

I crossed to a green silk Victorian settee and dropped into it. "You interest me. Do you approve of murder?"

Valerie gave a short, dry laugh. "Perhaps of Chase's."

"Then you won't mind telling me who you think would like to kill him and why?" I moved uncomfortably on the settee, wondering if it still contained its original horsehair stuffing.

"My dear, SRO." She trilled a tattoo on the keys. "Or it would be if we weren't stuck on this asinine island. His enemies are legion. And well deserved." Lifting her chin, Valerie declaimed, "As it is, 'we few, we happy few, we band of brothers.' "

" 'For he today that sheds his blood with me / Shall be my brother. . . .' " I smoothed some lint from the settee. "You have it rather backward, don't you?"

"No." Her merciless face might have been carved from ivory. "Every person he touches withers. Did you know that?

He's like phosphorus, a brilliant glitter but it burns at the touch. Everyone on this island has been damaged by him. Because he doesn't care for anyone but himself." She fingered the heavy gold links of her bracelet. "He married Elizabeth for her money. He was unfaithful to her from the very first. It doesn't take a woman long to know. I wonder how long after she found out that the cancer started to grow."

"That's scarcely fair —" I began.

"You *listen* to me." Her eyes glittered with hatred. "How do I know? Because my baby sister fell in love with him — and he was still a married man. I told her and told her, but she wouldn't listen. Then Elizabeth died and Chase asked Carrie to marry him. But it wasn't because he loved her. Mr. Chase Prescott wanted a mistress for his big, expensive houses, a stepmother for Roger. He didn't really care about Carrie. When she finally realized that, she turned into a frenetic, driven woman, never satisfied with one place. She went down in a charter airplane. They shouldn't have taken off, not in that kind of weather. But she insisted. They found the plane the next day, after the storm ended. The pilot was still alive, but he died before they got him to the hospital. Now there's the new little wife, and maybe it's going to be hardest of all on her."

Surely I caught a hint of gentleness in Valerie's voice. "Funny, isn't it? Everybody always acts like it's men who lose their senses over women, but that's not the way I've seen it happen. He's gone through life taking whatever he wanted and never giving a tinker's damn — and now the bill's come due. Well, I'll tell you straight, I hope he pays in full." She swung back to the piano.

I didn't know the music, but it was slow and heavy, the beat of a dirge, solemn and funereal. In my mind I could see black-draped horses with black shaker plumes, moving ponderously, pulling a coffin-laden bier.

Sweat stung my eyes, filmed my face and arms. No-see-ums swarmed me. Chinch bugs rose from a mound of rotting grasses. Transparent-winged dragon-flies looped and circled like Sunday-morning aviators. In the tangled underbrush on either side of the narrow path unseen insects hummed like violins warming up.

I stopped and looked at an old, old live oak. Live oaks aren't especially tall as eastern trees go. The biggest live oaks reach only forty to fifty feet. But this tree's venerable age was evident because its gnarled branches reached out so far, some butting groundward for further support. On a sloping branch I glimpsed a corn snake, its vivid red splotches bright against its tan body.

Corn snakes go after moles. But this one was climbing, inching higher and higher.

Some animals know when earthquakes are coming.

Some—like snakes—know when it's going to storm. Snakes are extremely sensitive to movement. They are deaf, but their capacity to analyze vibration is extraordinary.

The corn snake was seeking safety, high above the ground.

I picked my way carefully on the rest of the path through the forest. I didn't want to obstruct a snake. Snakes, contrary to their reputation, do not aggressively attack. They bite only when they feel threatened. But disturbing a snake is surely grounds for a swift response.

The thick, moist air was difficult to breathe. I was huffing by the time I came out of the woods. A weathered-gray board-walk led to the dunes. I couldn't see the ocean yet, but I heard the thundering crash of surf.

The dunes were magnificent.

I stopped for an instant to hold that picture in my mind. I was looking at one of the few pristine beaches left. The only trace of man was the boardwalk. No dune buggies had wreaked their havoc here. No heedless walkers had trampled these dune plants underfoot. Delicate bright yellow flowers topped the prickly pear cactus. Sturdy, thick-leaved sandwort, sea rocket, and saltwort thrived. Seaside morning-glory vines spread over the sand like veins in marble. Jessamine, chickasaw plum, wax myrtle, and beach pea flourished, offering subtle and gorgeous touches of rust and rose, tan and gold.

These were dunes as dunes were meant to be.

As I hurried along the boardwalk, bent against the increasingly stiff wind, I realized that the roar of the surf was not an accompaniment to the beach; it was a clamor.

I reached the crest of the dune.

The surf that rolls in to the South Carolina coast is small beer compared to the waves off Hawaii or Australia. It's a surf that usually provides a perfect playground for children, little breakers, nothing too forceful. But the waves I saw this afternoon were awesome. Harbingers of greater to come, they hurled themselves ashore, six to seven feet tall, curling and cresting, foaming and churning.

Haskell buffeted his way out, the surfboard pushed before him.

I caught my breath. Dear God, that wave . . .

A mountain of water curled above Haskell, poised to descend with the rumble of an avalanche, the force of a thousand fire hoses.

Somehow—was it skill or foolhardiness or blind luck?—Haskell buoyed up, up, up and then his board curved over the spume, teetered for a heart-stopping instant on the edge of a watery green abyss, then triumphantly merged into the curling lip to ride the pounding, thunderous, churning surf toward shore. All I could see in that dangerous explosion of foam was his sleek, dark head, held high, and his fierce, sly smile.

I try not to engage in envy. It is perhaps the least attractive trait of homo sapiens. Of course, we share it with other mammals, from gorillas to chimpanzees to house cats.

I've never wanted to trade my existence for that of any other soul, from the most brilliant academic to the wisest philosopher to the most gifted athlete. But, just for an instant, I wished that I was young and wild and free, that I could hurtle through time and space daring life and death with such glorious abandon, a part of the wind and waves and water.

Abruptly, the board upended in the whirling maelstrom of foam and Haskell was gone.

I ran toward the beach.

For a long, long moment I searched the water crashing ashore. And then he came, tumbling, rolling, struggling. Another wave flung him down. Again he disappeared. Then his dark head came up and he flailed toward shore, weaker now. Another wave crashed over him.

I staggered out in the water, wary of the surf, and reached out a hand to help him.

He tried to get up, fell, swore.

"Hurry. Another big one . . ."

We made it just in time.

Haskell dropped to the sand. His chest heaved. I sat down beside him, breathless.

"You're a damn fool," I remarked conversationally when I could speak.

He tried to roll over, muffled a cry of pain. He massaged his right knee. "Banged it."

"You're lucky you didn't break your neck." I tried to sound stern.

His eyes blazed with excitement, though his face was pale. "I'll tell you something." He still pulled breath deep into his lungs. "I'll tell you something—now I can fucking well *die* happy."

I grinned at him. Dammit, I liked him. He was untamed, perhaps untameable. I hoped he didn't have a murderer's heart, because I liked him.

I gave one last look back at the high surf as we walked up the boardwalk together. Those waves and the heavily overcast sky and the snake seeking sanctuary meant that the huge storm south of us was sweeping this way. I would talk to Chase when he and Trevor returned. This was a tiny island that could easily be washed over in a hurricane. We'd better get out while the going was good. No later than tomorrow, and perhaps tonight if the hurricane warnings were already hoisted.

Haskell and I didn't talk as we walked back through the gloom of the forest. I waited until we had reached the pool and he'd toweled off and was comfortably sprawled in a deck chair, his mouth still curved into a tiny bemused smile of exaltation.

"Haskell, who do you think shot at Chase?" I opened the wet-bar refrigerator, lifted out two Heinekens, and handed him one.

"Oh, yeah. Thanks. Great." His dark hair was plastered in ringlets close to his skull. He looked very young and, as always, sensually attractive with his olive skin, long-lashed brown eyes, and full lips.

I thought he wasn't going to answer.

He shrugged. "Ouch." He rubbed his left shoulder. "I kind of ache all over." It wasn't a complaint. He gave a more restrained shrug. "Who the hell knows? Maybe a little green man from Mars. Shit, I don't know."

"Or care?" I tipped up the cool, water-beaded bottle and welcomed the sharp taste.

For once he looked at me without mockery. "Naw. I don't . . ." He frowned, shook his head. "I don't like anybody to die. I *hate* that. Death." He gulped more beer. "They made me go to the funeral home. For my mom. She was . . . nothing. Just flat and white and . . . dead." His hand tightened on the bottle.

"I'm sorry."

Slowly his vise-tight grip on the bottle relaxed. He gave me a crooked grin. "You're okay, really. I mean, you sound tough, but you feel things, don't you?"

"More than I want to," I admitted. I looked at the pool and saw that the wind was high enough to ripple the clean blue water.

"Yeah." His face crinkled in a perplexed frown. "It doesn't do any good to pretend you don't care, 'cause underneath it just hurts more. But when I go fast, then I don't think about anything, I just feel good. Faster and faster and faster. God, it was great on that wave. It was *great*."

I could have told Haskell that no matter how fast he ran, he couldn't outstrip his feelings. But it's kinder to let each generation climb that mountain unknowing. If we knew at twenty what we know at sixty, it would make the climb that much harder and more harrowing.

"Okay, so you don't want Chase dead, even if it means the fastest powerboat money can buy." I watched him carefully. I'd swear that just for an instant he thought about a boat and what it could mean and how much he would love it, but almost immediately he pushed the thought away, dismissed it. Inside, I felt a moment of joy, but I kept my voice matter-of-fact. "Help me out, Haskell. You're smart. You notice things. Who's tried twice to kill him?"

He finished his beer and struggled up, still favoring his knee and shoulder, to get another from the wet bar. He took his time, uncapped the bottle, then cautiously resettled in his chair. "I don't get it. No way do I get it. Look who's here—Valerie? Well, I mean, how crazy can you get? She might break a damn fingernail."

I laughed. It *was* difficult to picture Valerie slinking through the pinewoods, lethal pistol in hand. I would have thought she'd be too afraid of snakes even to step into the woods.

"As for Miranda, Jesus, she worships him." There was an odd note in Haskell's voice, not quite jealousy, not quite disdain.

My smile slipped away. Once again I balanced it in my mind. Adoration or obsession, which was it?

Haskell tipped the bottle to his mouth and swallowed greedily, then continued ruminatively, almost as if talking to himself. "Take old Lyle. He's a true-blue shit. But murder? I mean, he's got the inside track, he's the fair-haired boy. Is he in that big a hurry? Not if he's as smart as everybody says he is. And Roger, he may thump his chest because Chase sneers at his bleeding-heart sob stuff, but he's really fond of his dad. Last Christmas Roger sent off to Africa—to Kenya—for this carved cheetah for Chase's wooden-animal collection. Have you ever seen Chase's collection? He's got it in his office in Atlanta. It's super-fantastic. Rhinos, elephants, zebras, lions, antelope . . . Anyway, there was this particular cheetah. It was a hell of a lot of trouble, took months. Roger was so excited he almost threw up when the damn thing arrived. Came by air. Scratch Roger, I don't care what anybody thinks. And who does that leave?"

"Trevor. Burton. Enrique, Rosalia, and Betty." I finished my beer and waited. I knew Trevor had an alibi that definitely wasn't faked, but I wanted Haskell's opinion of him.

"I don't like Trevor." Haskell put the beer bottle on the flagstone. "So damn charming." He made it sound like a disease. "Like a politician. He's got that kind of smile, all shiny white teeth. I wouldn't trust him as far as I could throw him. But why blow away this rich guy who thinks he's the greatest lawyer in the country? That would be stupid. Right?"

I nodded.

"Well, old buddy Trevor may not be Abe Lincoln, but he's not dumb. Oh, I guess Roger would probably keep him on, at least for a while, because Trevor knows everything about the business. But Trevor would just be trading one boss for another. What's the benefit?"

I couldn't see one either. And there was no perceptible rift between Chase and his favorite lawyer.

"As for Burton, pardon me while I puke. He wouldn't have the guts to *think* about a murder. He's a drip." Haskell spoke with the intolerance of the young and strong for the weak and hapless.

"Our murderer keeps a very low profile," I reminded him. "Hiding poison in candy and shooting from behind a tree don't argue lots of guts."

He grunted. "More than Burton's got."

"I'd say Enrique has a full complement." I drained the last few drops from the bottle, considered another, decided against it.

"That's a dangerous dude." The words might be those of someone young, but his tone wasn't. He spoke with utter conviction.

You don't have that kind of conviction without knowledge.

I put my bottle down on the side table. "Come on, Haskell, let's hear it."

He shot me a troubled look, then shrugged. "Hell, what can it hurt? I was a little kid. Nine, maybe. We were on a cruise down in the Caribbean. Me and Mom and Chase. You know it can get tough down there—drug runners decide they need a new boat, what the hell, stop some rich guy's yacht, bump everybody off, sail on their way. It happens. It almost happened to us. It was Christmas Eve."

I could tell that it still hurt him.

"Christmas Eve. I woke up to hear somebody shouting. It was a couple of guys—I saw them in the lights from the saloon. Like anybody down on the beach. Tanned. Blond. Beards. Khaki shorts. The kind of guys who might be on the boat next to yours at the marina. They both had thirty-eights pointed at Chase. The bigger one ordered him and Mom to walk toward the stern. Anyway, all of a sudden, pow, pow, and these guys doubled up, like in slow motion. They had *holes* in their chests." He shifted in his seat, winced, and reached down to massage his knee. "Enrique stepped out of the shadows. He looked at Chase and they moved together and picked the guys up, one at a time, and tossed them overboard. Like they were garbage. There was blood everywhere. So Enrique hosed down the deck."

No, I hadn't overestimated Enrique.

Haskell put it in perspective. "Yeah, Enrique's a tough dude, but why kill Chase? Chase told me one time he pays Enrique fifty thou a year because he'll do anything Chase wants him to do."

"And Rosalia does everything Enrique tells *her* to do?"

"Oh, yeah. He knocks her around, I'm pretty sure. I told Chase once. He told me to mind my own business."

I'd wanted facts. There was a fact.

A harsh and ugly one.

I wanted to protest, to say that Chase wouldn't have said that, wouldn't have ignored that kind of abuse in his own home. But I knew in my heart that it was more important to Chase to have Enrique as a fiercely loyal employee than to protect Enrique's wife.

But I wasn't as young as Haskell, and Chase would have to respond to me.

Haskell lifted his head, listening, then stood and shaded his eyes to gaze out across the sound. "Here comes the *Miranda B.*"

The sky was an angry red to the south. Splashes of crimson streaked the gunmetal-gray clouds.

". . . sailor take warning."

Haskell grabbed his towel and got up.

I stood, too. I knew I had only seconds left and one more question, an important one, to ask.

"Didn't I see you out back last night, Haskell? Late last night?"

He looked at me blankly. "Out back? Out back where?"

"Near the servants' quarters. You and perhaps Betty?"

He didn't even have to speak; his face made his answer so plain: astonishment was followed by a look of pure outrage. "Hey, what do you think I am? Do you mean . . ." He shook his head in sheer disgust. "Look, I don't have to get sex like that. No way. I've got plenty of girls. *Plenty* of them." And he strode away.

I might as well not have bothered making up a welcoming committee of one out on the pier.

Chase stalked by me, his face purple with fury. He did manage a curt "I'll talk to you later, Henrie O."

I stood by the boathouse, my hands on my hips, and I suppose my irritation was evident.

Trevor Dunnaway, his blond hair awry from the wind, his face red from too much sun, dropped onto the boards and ambled wearily toward me. He threw out his hands. "I'm in the doghouse. You got a job for an ex–corporate counsel?"

"He's fired you?" The wind whipped my clothes against me.

"Oh, no. Not quite. He probably will tomorrow," Trevor said gloomily, jamming his hands in the pockets of his madras shorts. "As you may or may not know about Chase, he doesn't like for the hired help to disagree after he's given what he considers the final word."

I fell into step with him. "I gather you lodged a dissent."

"A couple of them." He heaved a sigh. "Like the unwisdom in keeping recalcitrant houseguests in captivity. I can just see the lawsuit Val will file next week. I pointed that out. Didn't make me popular. And I told him I intended to fill you in on a certain insurance policy. Chase and I absolutely disagree about how it could figure in all this. Made him furious. And to cap it off"—another heavy sigh—"I insisted we keep the radio on, get the weather reports. Now he's evenly divided between being royally pissed off at me and at God. There's a hell of a storm coming out of the Caribbean. Hurricane watch issued at noon. Hurricane Derek. Winds in excess of eighty-two mph and building. Already knocked the stuffing out of Cuba. Widespread flooding. Landfall could come as early as tomorrow evening. Somewhere between Miami and Savannah."

Savannah wasn't that far.

So we would get heavy rains, at the very least. And by tomorrow night the surf striking the island could wash right over those beautiful, unspoiled dunes. But that was tomorrow night.

I was more concerned with tonight. "Let's go a little faster, Trevor."

He groaned but kept pace.

I didn't want to let Chase out of sight. We were even with the pool when Chase yanked open the French door to his quarters. He looked back and yelled, "You're off duty, Dunnaway. My wife's here." And slammed the door behind him.

The lawyer sighed. "Yeah, Dunnaway, your goose is cooked." He reached up to touch his face tenderly. "Literally and figuratively. Christ." He looked wearily around, then pointed to some chairs beneath an awning. "I don't need another dandy solar ray. Come on, if you'll get me something cold to drink and murmur soothing reassurances about the future of my gilt-edged career with Prescott Communications, I'll tell you all about Chase's will, damn him, and a particular insurance policy."

At his direction I fixed him a scotch and soda, heavy on the scotch. I handed him his drink.

He grabbed it, drank half. "You will put in a good word for me, won't you?" His voice was forlorn. He wasn't kidding.

"Sure. I'll remind Chase that you know more about his financial affairs than anyone except him and his accountants. He'd keep a spraying skunk on his staff if it were to his advantage." I dropped into a chair, also in the shade. I'd had enough solar rays myself.

Trevor winced. "There's something about that analogy I

don't like. However, to business, then I can crawl off ignomini- ously to my room and hunt for something to put on my face. It feels like raw meat."

"Looks like it, too." He was going to be lucky if he didn't have some blisters.

He turned sun-reddened eyes toward me. "All right. You want to know about the will. It's pretty straightforward. The entire estate is valued at eight hundred million. Chase and Mi- randa have a prenuptial agreement. She receives approximately twenty-five million. Roger receives all the rest except for some minor bequests: fifty thousand dollars each for Enrique, Rosa- lia, and Betty, and five hundred thousand for an old friend—"

I was afraid I knew what was coming. I could feel the muscles in my face tightening.

"—Henrietta O'Dwyer Collins."

Fury swept me. Chase couldn't do this to me. I would not permit it.

"I see."

There was a long and fairly awkward silence. Trevor obvi- ously hesitated to speak. And I didn't intend to discuss this development.

"All right, Trevor. I'll take care of that bequest as soon as I see Chase. But tell me the rest. What about Haskell?" My words were clipped.

Trevor was grateful to find neutral ground. "He comes into control of his mother's money. It's enough that he can tell Chase to take the office and shove it."

So the motives continued to pile up. A young woman with twenty-five million could look forward to a lifetime of attention and pleasure. Roger would control the editorial output of a media empire. Haskell could have his pick of the world's fastest —and finest—speedboats. And though small in comparison, the bequests to Enrique, Rosalia, and Betty could seem immense indeed to them.

"And then there's the insurance policy."

I was listening but still fuming—until Trevor's words finally registered and knocked everything else out of my mind. I stared at him, aghast. "Trevor, that's crazy! Talk about asking for trouble!"

He was defensive. "It wasn't the least bit crazy at the time. Look, the IRA put a price on Chase's head—his British papers waged all-out war against the IRA—and he'd just extended his loans, bought a major newspaper in New York. This was—God, time goes fast!—this was more than ten years ago. Closer to twelve now. If anything'd happened to Chase then, Prescott Communications would have gone down faster than the *Titanic*. The policy reassured some damn nervous investors."

"Okay, let me see if I've got it straight. This was a variation on the old double-indemnity policy, but this particular policy—"

"Lloyd's." He drank deeply.

"—pays double to the company in the event Chase is murdered. A clear one hundred million, right?" I was sitting bolt upright, which isn't easy in a pool chair.

He downed the rest of his drink. "Right."

I leaned forward. "So the answer's simple. Cancel that policy. Get back to the mainland and a phone and cancel it tomorrow."

"Yeah. Well, you can talk to him. I've talked till I don't give a damn." He sprawled back in the chair, a man who had endured too much sea, sun, and Chase.

"I'll talk to him." I had, in fact, quite an agenda in mind. "Why didn't he tell me about this?"

"He says it's irrelevant. He says why the hell would anybody want to enrich Prescott Communications?" Wearily, Trevor pushed out of his chair, crossed to the bar, and splashed more scotch in his glass. No soda this time. "I said, 'Chase, stop acting like a goddamn ostrich and look around.' But he made me spell it out. It's so clear a blind person can see it. Finally I told him that Lyle Stedman is a cold-eyed, greedy, ambitious bastard with the soul of an anaconda. I did my good deed of the day, I told Chase Prescott the honest-to-God truth, and you know what?"

I waited for the bitter voice to continue.

"He told me to go to hell."

I poked my head in the kitchen door.

Rosalia's head jerked my way. A thin breath whistled through her teeth.

"Has Enrique been back?"

She and Betty shook their heads, but the fear in Rosalia's eyes didn't lessen.

"It will be all right." Betty tried to sound cheerful. "I've moved our things into the room next to yours, Mrs. Collins. Are you sure—"

"Positive. Thank you for taking care of it." I started out, then paused and said casually, "Oh, Betty, we need you upstairs for a minute. In the music room." I led the way.

When we reached the music room, I motioned for her to enter. I followed her inside and closed the door. "This won't take long." Again I was opting for a reassuring voice. I pointed at the rose petit-point chair. "Please sit down."

The maid looked around the empty room, realized she'd been decoyed, and stared at me, her eyes anxious. She tried to edge past me to the door. "I'm sorry, ma'am. I've got to set the table for dinner . . ."

"I won't keep you long."

"I need to get back. Enrique'll be there pretty soon."

Betty was closer to fifty than forty, with a pudgy abdomen, too-broad hips, and a face that might once have had a candy-box prettiness. But now lines of fatigue clustered at the corners of her eyes and her mouth had the permanent sag of lips that had forgotten how to smile.

Not a sexy woman. Especially not to a young man like Haskell. What had prompted Chase to suggest a tryst between Haskell and Betty? It was ludicrous. But it had occurred to Chase when I told him someone had hidden in the shadows late last night and refused to respond to my call. It made me wonder about Chase's perceptions of his stepson. And of this woman!

She was obviously wary of Enrique. Surely his rule of force didn't extend to her. No, that was unlikely. But it's easy enough for a powerful personality to cow underlings. If I'd had more time, I would have pursued it, asked how he treated her, what kind of overseer he was. Because I intended to become a big monkey wrench in Enrique's future. But right now I didn't have time for side excursions.

"Betty, I want you to relax." I could see both of us in the mirror behind the piano. Betty stood rigidly, her arms tight to her side, her eyes flared wide. I had a genial smile on my face and so, hopefully, looked more like a mother hen than a swooping hawk. She continued to stare at me mutely. A nervous tic fluttered her left eyelid. So much for my effort to soothe.

Okay. I knew how to play it. Easy questions first.

"Betty, how did you find your job with Mr. Prescott?" This should put her at ease. It was a long time ago and had nothing to do with the attacks on Chase. I remained between her and the door.

"I came to work for Mrs. Lee when Haskell was born. She brought me with her when she married Mr. Prescott."

She was nervous about taking the time, darting occasional glances at the porcelain clock on the mantel, but I had truly touched the right chord. She was eager to say how lovely Carrie Lee Prescott had been and to tell me about Haskell as a little boy.

Which made Chase's suggestion all the more outrageous and puzzling.

I heard about Carrie's beauty—"Why, you'd never know she and Miss Valerie were sisters, they looked so different. Mrs. Carrie had dark brown hair and the most beautiful skin you ever saw. Mr. Haskell looks just like his mother"—and Haskell's superiority at sports—"He can swim like a fish, Mrs. Collins. And he's a wonderful tennis player"—and how dreadful it was when Mrs. Carrie's plane went down. "I was the one had to call Paris to find Mr. Haskell."

Then I asked a simple question. "Now let's see, Betty, where did you grow up?"

Panic flared in her eyes. She opened her mouth, closed it. Finally, grudgingly, she muttered, "Waynesboro."

"Does your family still live there?" I smiled.

She watched me with sick fascination. It seemed forever before she nodded, jerkily, not saying a word.

I knew I'd uncovered something. But there was no point in pushing her. If only I had a telephone that really worked . . .

I shifted away from the personal. "I suppose it's been exciting being a part of Mr. Prescott's staff, getting to travel and meet famous people." Once again I was as genial as a talk-show host.

"Yes, ma'am." She looked longingly toward the door.

"As you know, Mr. Prescott asked me to try to find out who's behind the attacks on him."

She licked her pale lips.

"And he wants *you* to help me."

She blinked at that. "Me? Mr. Prescott wants me to help?"

"Yes. Because you have been a part of his household for so many years, and you may have seen people do things or heard them say things that could tell us if they were really very angry or upset with him."

"Oh, no, no." Betty shook her head violently. "Not me. I

don't pay no attention. I don't care how people do. I just clean up. And straighten. And put things where they go. I don't pay no attention."

With that she moved roughly past me, her hands scrambling for the door, and then she was through it and running heavily toward the kitchen.

Obviously, she had paid a great deal of attention.

I skidded into my room in a hurry. I can shower and dress in seven minutes. I had twenty minutes before dinner.

The singed book was still in place, secreted among the folders.

I carried it to the table and settled down to scan.

It didn't take long to figure out why Chase loathed this unauthorized biography. Jeremy Hubbard had a talent for unearthing the unattractive, including the accusations that Chase had brilliantly engineered a meeting with his first wife, Elizabeth Warren, and pursued her solely because of her father's substantial media holdings; that Chase had deliberately forced Elizabeth's brother Aaron out of the business and refused to help him later when he was in financial trouble; that Chase had been responsible for a market rumor that had dropped a competitor's stock price until Chase was able to amass a controlling interest at an incredible bargain; that Chase was ruthless in jettisoning older employees no matter how long and how loyally they'd served him.

But the meat of the book—to my mind—was a series of ugly revelations about Chase's personal relationships:

Chase never visited Elizabeth when she was hospitalized.

Chase delegated his secretary to select birthday presents for Roger.

Chase went to Europe on business when Carrie was hospitalized for a miscarriage.

Chase had no time for friends other than those who could help him in a business sense.

Chase didn't attend Roger's graduation from college.

There was more in the book, of course: questionable stock deals, rapacious mergers, unjustified dismissals.

Hubbard was clearly a clever, skilled writer. He'd pieced together a series of facts and the result was a damning portrait.

I showered quickly, thinking about the revelations in the book and about all the conversations I'd had.

I knew so much.

Why couldn't I put a face to Chase's attacker?

As every newspaper reporter knows, there comes a moment when the facts fall into place, when it is clear what matters and what doesn't. Then the story writes itself: The lead focuses on the most important element, the follow-up paragraphs support the statement made in the lead, and the body of the story amplifies and explains subsidiary information.

I'd counted on learning a lot from conversations. I had.

I'd counted on learning a lot from the book I'd retrieved from the incinerator. I had.

But nothing jelled. The mass of data I'd acquired was as formless as a spilled deck of cards.

I couldn't point a finger.

Say I opted for Lyle Stedman as a power-and-money-hungry executive intent on taking control of Prescott Communications.

A poisoned chocolate piece?

Shots from behind a tree?

From this type-A guy with an international reputation for naked ruthlessness?

Weren't these two attempts much more likely to be efforts by a young woman whose passion for a man had turned from love to obsession?

Neither of the attacks on Chase, when you studied them,

seemed designed to succeed. Wasn't that perhaps the result of conflicting motives in Miranda's subconscious, the desire to possess warring with a lust to hurt?

For dinner I chose a royal-purple cotton damask coatdress. I like bold colors. But I wished it didn't remind me of tonight's sky. Though the storm building on this island in the half-glimpsed, not-quite-understood relations among its visitors might well erupt long before tomorrow's storm.

I clipped on oversize pearl earrings and a two-strand pearl necklace to match the faux-pearl front buttons.

I gave myself a last glimpse in the mirror: My hair was smooth—upswept tonight—and my makeup even.

Only my eyes reflected the turbulence in my mind.

It was as if we were all bit players awaiting our cues. Only our host and hostess were absent.

His sunburned face obviously painful, Trevor slumped morosely in a club chair, a drink in his hand, ignoring everyone. Valerie's lips were pinched. The actress's eyes kept darting toward the doorway. She was looking for trouble, it was evident in the glitter in her eyes, the rapid drumming of her crimson nails on her chair arm. Roger leaned against a bookcase, his back to the room. He held an oversize volume open in his hands, but he never turned a page. Burton stood stiffly by a huge Oriental screen, as if he were not a part of the gathering in the room. The secretary looked ill at ease and even weedier and less impressive than ever. Haskell paced by the French doors and occasionally opened them to step out onto the terrace. Each time he returned to the room his frown was darker. Lyle Stedman's fiery red hair was still faintly damp from his shower. He leaned back in one of the club chairs, seemingly at ease, but his eyes watched us all warily.

Since that revealing—and personally upsetting—talk with the sunburned lawyer, I certainly appraised Lyle in a new light. At the track that morning—and didn't that seem like a decade ago?—Lyle had indicated deep concern over Chase's confidence in his ability to refinance the huge outstanding loans. Prescott Communications would certainly have no difficulty at all in refinancing—if that Lloyd's of London policy on Chase's life paid off.

The French door clicked again. Haskell closed it behind him. Roger reshelved the book—an atlas?—and turned to face the room. Valerie toyed with the heavy gold chain at her throat.

Of course, if that enormous policy paid off, it would only enhance the worth of the ultimate estate . . . to the benefit of almost everyone in the room. How many of them, I wondered, knew about that policy? Actually, I was quite certain that had any persons wanted to know—and were knowledgeable about corporate life—they could easily have discovered it. That kind of information is included in annual reports and would most certainly have been included because that was the whole point —to reassure investors.

The sullen quiet was becoming oppressive, unnatural. I had just resolved to break it when brisk footsteps sounded in the central hallway. Chase and Miranda swept into the room.

It was an entirely different Chase, affable, smiling, exuding good humor with a touch of embarrassment.

If he was changed, Miranda was transformed. Her face glowed with happiness and contentment, her pretty eyes sparkled.

"For God's sake," Chase cried, his voice deep and vibrant, "we aren't holding a wake, people. Here, now, everyone have a drink. Val, do you want sherry? Henrie O, a gin and tonic?"

When a logjam breaks, there is a rush, a surge of logs, crashing and tossing and buffeting one another.

In just that instant the two of them ignited conversation and it was almost as if the dreadful interlude of the morning had never occurred.

I accepted my drink—marveling again at what Chase had discovered of my likes and dislikes after so many years—and observed the suddenly invigorated gathering, Roger in lively conversation with Trevor, even Burton unbending enough to accept a drink from Enrique. I was impressed anew with the power of Chase's personality, his charm, his persuasiveness, his intensity, and ready, when I had a chance, to tangle with him. Leave *me* a bequest! Not if I could help it. But his ebullient good humor made me smile, irritated as I was.

The only nonresponsive face belonged to Haskell. He looked toward the French doors, then squared his shoulders and approached his stepfather. He waited patiently until Chase finished talking to Lyle.

I strolled close enough to hear.

"Chase, we need to get the hell off this island. I checked the weather again—from the *Miranda B.*—and they think the hurricane's picking up speed. Right now it's heading for Miami. But you know how quick that can change."

"I know, I know." And still Chase's tone was good-humored. "Everybody, everybody—" He held up his hand.

The conversations died away. Every face turned toward Chase.

I will never forget him as he stood in that elegant room that evening. His blue blazer was a perfect fit, of course, and his white slacks a dramatic counterpoint. He never looked better, an aristocratic face—sharply defined, classic features, a firm chin, full lips. His dark hair had just enough silver to qualify as distinguished, his dark eyes were commanding—but, tonight, pleasant.

There was no sense of anger or urgency, and certainly none of fear.

"Some of you—those of you who are old salts—can't have helped noticing the deterioration in our weather. My stepson's been monitoring the progress of the storm on our ship radio, as has Enrique. The upshot is, we'll leave the island after breakfast tomorrow and return to the mainland." His face hardened. "This morning I indicated we'd stay here until we knew the truth of the shots that were fired." He paused for a long moment, his mouth compressed, then managed a wry smile. "This afternoon my legal counsel convinced me that was an unwise decision. Further, I became aware of our weather situation. And finally, I decided I didn't like the idea of continuing as a sitting duck. So the decision's been made. Let's enjoy our dinner and our evening. Tomorrow morning we leave."

Dinner was almost festive. Sometimes the laughter seemed forced. But there was certainly an undercurrent of relaxation. Chase was making every effort to charm. He went out of his way to speak genially to Trevor and even restored prickly Valerie to good humor, promising to look over her play. "It would be fun to back a show again. Give Miranda and me an excuse to spend more time in New York." And he gave Valerie's arm a friendly squeeze.

I was glad, truth to tell, to have the burden of this investigation lifted from me. And perhaps I could get myself deleted from an official list of suspects, if the investigation was handed over to the police. After all, I'd been nowhere near Chase's New York brownstone when the poisoned candy killed the dog and Trevor and I had been standing together when this morning's shots were fired. I held tight to that hope. Perhaps I could slip away unnoticed, unheralded. Because if the jackals started digging into my past . . .

I felt almost relaxed. I foresaw my own escape from the turmoil of Chase's problems. However, I still intended to get out of Chase's will. And I certainly had much to say to him about Rosalia. But all of that could be handled easily enough. Then I could return to my life, free at last of Chase and his grip on my past. I had come when summoned. I hadn't accomplished Chase's objective, but I felt that I had gone a long way to pay an old debt.

In any event, I was no longer involved.

But, as we walked out of the dining room, Chase leaned toward me and said, "Come to my study. In half an hour."

9

Chase leaned against the mantel above the unlit fireplace and waited for me to answer his request, a request I definitely wanted to reject. He was frowning, as he always frowned when it appeared he might not have his way. But his presentation tonight had lacked the force and fury of our previous encounter. He was determined, yes, but tonight he no longer looked driven and feverish. His face was calm. He smoked, but he lifted the cigarette to his mouth almost absentmindedly.

I sipped the aromatic and sinfully delicious chocolate liqueur and felt the emotional shackles slipping around me again. He had launched so swiftly into his plea that I hadn't even had a chance to bring up the will and the bequest to me. I would, no fear of that. But first . . .

"Chase, you can't keep treating this like a private problem. Attempted murder is a crime. Contact the police." This was what I had said at the very beginning; this was what I knew must be done, even as I wondered how to distance myself from public notice.

"Do you want headlines?" His dark eyes were unreadable.

Fury flamed through me for an instant. What right had he to drag me back into his life, to make me vulnerable to exposure?

But I knew the answer to that.

There are rights and rights, and I had not always accorded Chase what belonged to him.

"Henrie O"—suddenly he was all warmth and charm, focusing a magnetic smile on me—"you're wonderful when you're mad." His mouth curved in a rueful, forgive-me smile. "I'm sorry. I'm so obsessed with what's happened to me that I forget that this isn't your life, that you have work and deadlines and goals that have nothing to do with me." He rested his arm along the mantel. His fingers absently turned the base of a marble statuette, one of a pair. "The thing about it is, I have to find out. Because it's poisoning my life. I look at my son—and Roger and I have had our problems. He's a visionary, like his mother. He wants the world to be good, but he hasn't learned that you can't force people to be good. I look at my son, and I wonder, 'Is it you? Are you the one?' I reach out for my wife and suddenly the whisper's there in my mind. 'Are you the one? Are you trying to kill me?'" He gripped the statuette. "Or I'm talking to Lyle. Lyle. God, I can't tell you, Henrie O, it's like being born again. Can you understand that? He's what I was when I was young. Smart. Fast. Six jumps ahead of the crowd. He knows he's going to make it. He's got that desire that won't be quenched. And he's going to take Prescott Communications into the next century. He's going to make Prescott Communications the most important media conglomerate in the world. In the world, Henrie O, not just America or Europe. I've felt twenty years younger ever since Lyle came. I look at Lyle, and I think, 'Was it you? Was it *you*?'" Chase stared at me. "I've got to know. And the hell of it is, I know the police won't figure it. It's going to take the kind of instinct they don't teach at police academies. It's going to take the kind of instinct you've got, Henrie O."

I looked at him over the rim of the crystal liqueur glass. The poignancy of his cry touched my heart.

Was it you? Was it you?

How terrible and ultimately how destructive of trust and love to look at a familiar face and hear that dreadful question in your mind.

Chase's eyes gleamed. "Henrie O, you will stick with it, won't you?" The relief in his voice laid another burden on me. He couldn't hide his delight. "God, I knew I could count on you. When we get back on the mainland, you can get your own information on everyone. You'll have an unlimited expense account, of course, and anything I can do to help, I will."

He stood triumphant in front of the fireplace, head high, hands jammed into the pockets of his blazer.

I stared at him grimly. Was I acquiescing because he needed me? Or was I taking another desperate step to keep this investigation out of the public eye? "If I'm to do it, Chase, I will certainly need your help. More help than you've given so far. Why didn't you tell me about the Lloyd's of London policy?"

The eagerness seeped out of his face. Once again he was confronting the reality of murderous intent behind a familiar smile. "Lyle." That was all he said. "I don't want it to be Lyle."

He gave me a half-woeful, half-amused look. "But then I don't want it to be anybody. And I still keep thinking, This is nuts, this is crazy, this can't be happening. But it is. And I think about Miranda. She's . . . she's so lovely, so young. She thinks I'm wonderful. I can't help liking that. No one can. It's better than the most powerful narcotic. But, the truth is, and I guess she knows it, deep down, I don't love her the way she loves me. I'm sorry. God, I'm sorry. I would if I could, but the truth is"—and he paused, searching for words, trying himself to understand—"I guess I'm not a person who's ever been able to focus on love. I've fought and battled and struggled all my life. I've tried to be good to everyone. But I've never really loved . . ." Now he did look at me, and the emotion in his eyes was unmistakable. "Except once, Henrie O, once when I was young and the world still held magic."

"But we are no longer young." I made it crisp. "Looking back is an exercise in futility. The mistakes we've made—all of us—are written in stone, Chase. We have to live and die with them—and forgive ourselves, if we can. The point, my dear, is not to make mistakes now, if we can help it. So I'll try to help you find who's behind the false face. But from this moment on I want you to be absolutely honest with me."

He regarded me for a long moment, then gave an abrupt nod. He pulled a straight chair close to me and sat. "All right. What do you want to know?"

"A lot. Let's start with the book, *The Man Who Picks Presidents*. You hired a private detective. Who did he investigate?"

There was a flash of appreciation in his eyes. "Burton. Valerie. Haskell. Roger. Enrique."

What a revealing list.

"Not Miranda?" The liqueur rolled so easily, so deliciously over my tongue.

"Miranda?" His voice rose in sheer surprise. "She wouldn't." His confidence was total. "Besides, most of it she couldn't have known about—the stuff about Elizabeth and Carrie and Roger."

"That stuff. How much of it is true?"

"It's twisted, Henrie O, twisted. Sure, I was gone a lot. Dammit, I was *working.* Elizabeth understood that. The bastard took true things and made them look ugly."

That was a start on what I needed to know. How did Chase view the biography? What stung the most?

"Okay, Chase. Hubbard goes after you in all arenas. Family relationships. Work ethics. Business practices." I didn't spare him. "What made you mad enough to file a lawsuit?"

He found his pack of cigarettes, lit one. His voice was hard. "The damnable part was about my family, an outright claim that I married Elizabeth for her money, that I stayed away from her when she was sick because I . . . because I couldn't stand to be around anyone seriously ill, that I never had anything to do with Roger." His face was rigid with anger. "Dammit, I had *work* to do. That was a tough period, very tough. We were fighting for survival, an antitrust suit, the editor of our Atlanta paper had a fatal heart attack, the guild struck for six months. It was a hell of a time."

I gave him a minute to calm down. But his answer made it clear. He knew that the leaks came from someone who knew him well, someone very close to home.

"What did your investigator find out?" I looked regretfully into my glass. Almost empty.

Chase's anger fled, supplanted by genuine amusement. "The damnedest things. Would you believe old Val has a live-in boyfriend, emphasis on boy, a twenty-three-year-old guy named Billy with long blond hair? And Burton had a formal burial with a granite stone for his cat, Cherie, when she died?" He took a last drag on his cigarette, stubbed it out. "Haskell serves dinner at a soup kitchen twice a week, then drops at least a hundred bucks on Saturdays at the races. Roger's on every

liberal mailing list in the country—if not the world." He shook
his head. "The bottom line is that nobody's got a fat new bank
account here or in Switzerland, nobody's rented a safe-deposit
box, nobody looks to have pocketed a penny from any unknown
source, and this guy I hired is one of the new brand of computer
dicks who specializes in finding stray bonds or hidden assets."

I could see how Chase had figured it: damaging insinua-
tions had been traded for money.

But perhaps money hadn't been the motive.

"Burton could be the one. He's what we used to call malad-
justed." Every decade has its pseudo–social science lingo. I
knew Chase would remember the gray-flannel-suit days when
the epitome of success was to be well-rounded, a figure of
speech as revealing of its times as any I've ever heard.

Here at least Chase and Haskell were in strong agreement.
"Burton's a wimp." Chase's tone was dismissive. "He would
p—" He paused, and I was amused when I realized he was
rephrasing to avoid offense. "He's scared to death of me. He's
so afraid he'll be blamed for anything that goes wrong that it's
pathetic. Sure, I know he's resentful. He looks at me and thinks
I'm a rich bastard who gets to do anything he wants to do while
he has to work his guts out for pennies. That's true. It's the
difference between talent and mediocrity. And I know he's tickled when something like that damned book comes out. He loves
to see me squirm. But he'd never take the risk himself."

I took the last sip of liqueur. "Enrique takes risks."

Chase looked at me warily. "So you've picked up on that."

"Yes. Feeding information to a writer wouldn't bother him
a trifle. After all, a man who beats his wife wouldn't stick at
selling information about his employer."

There was a strained silence.

Chase's eyes shifted away from mine.

I felt very tired. "Chase, you know how that man treats
Rosalia, and you haven't done a damn thing about it."

He shrugged. "All right, sometimes I'm a bastard. I never said I was perfect. But why the hell does she put up with it?"

It didn't surprise me. He had the arrogant confidence of a rich white male who had never been dependent, never in his life. No one had ever physically hurt him or threatened him. The world belonged to him and to men like him. They had a trigger-quick disdain for anyone who wouldn't fight back. They didn't believe in a victim's resigned acceptance of abuse, the victim's pitiful sense of punishment deserved.

"She puts up with it . . ." I began. Then I shook my head. "She's scared and cowed and emotionally crippled. But you aren't, and you've got the chips. You'll remedy it?"

He shot me an exasperated glance, then quickly said, "Oh, hell, yes. I understand—you're making that a condition. I'll see to it."

I didn't leave it at that. "What will you do?"

"Oh, she has a sister. I'll send her to visit and arrange for some counseling. I'll talk to Enrique, make it clear he's out on his ass if it ever happens again."

"I will talk to Enrique, too." And he'd listen. If he wanted to keep his job, he'd listen. Hating every minute of it, fingers itching to strike out at me, Enrique would listen.

"Enrique." Chase fumbled for another cigarette. "Frankly, I'd be delighted if it was Enrique. He's a hired hand. He's not my wife or son or stepson. But I can't see why the hell he'd do it. He likes money, sure, but would he take a chance on losing his job? I pay handsomely, more than he'd ever make anywhere else. No, I don't see him as the source for that garbage in the book. I had him looked over because I don't trust him. He'd do anything that would advance himself, but he's not stupid."

"Maybe he'd like to get his hands on what you've left him and Rosalia." I reached up and unclasped an earring that was beginning to pinch.

Chase's face was fully illuminated by the bronze floor lamp

behind his chair. I studied the dark hollows beneath his eyes, the straight, patrician nose, the firm jaw and determined mouth. I saw the swift appraisal in his eyes, followed by almost instant negation.

"If I were fool enough to broadcast the contents of my will, yes, Enrique might be tempted. But no one knows what's in that will, Henrie O, except my attorney, myself—and now you."

"But that isn't true of the infamous insurance policy, is it?"

"No."

"As for the will itself, family members have no reason to assume they aren't included, right?"

"I guess that's right." It was a grudging assent.

He knew it was right.

Any rich man's will can provide a motive for murder if there is a legatee greedy enough to trade a human life for money or power. Chase's will was no different. Under it, every person on the island—including myself—might have good and sufficient reason from the police's point of view to commit murder. And Chase's statement to the contrary, none of us could prove we were unaware of its provisions or, at the very least, unaware of the likelihood of receiving some kind of bequest. Especially the family members.

Chase had certainly put me in the soup—if anything happened to him—along with all the other legatees.

Now was as good a time as any to bring that up.

"I wish to be removed from your will, Chase. Immediately."

The stubborn resolve in his face answered me.

"No." His answer couldn't have been simpler or less equivocal.

I tried to keep my temper. "I don't want your damn money."

"I know that. But I shall decide who receives a part of my estate—a part of *me*, Henrie O. I have that right."

I didn't want to talk about rights.

Chase knew that.

He regarded me steadily. "Henrie O, now, after all these years, I want an answer. Why did you run away?"

I didn't want to look back. It reopened wounds that I had thought long since healed.

"Whenever I see an Indian summer day, Henrie O, I think of you and what you took away from me." There wasn't so much anger as great sadness in his voice.

I clasped my hands together and stared down at them, but I was seeing the office, jammed with desks, typewriters, a tele-type. We had worked for a news bureau for a midwestern daily, and we had covered Capitol Hill. It had been the most exciting, demanding, exhilarating, passionate year of my life, and the most heartbreaking.

"The House Un-American Activities Committee. That college professor from Connecticut. A Hollywood actor claimed he was a Communist. It was the height of the witch-hunt. Before McCarthy took on the army—and lost. The professor's wife came in." I could see her as if it were yesterday, a woman in her early thirties with anxious eyes and a shaking voice. "She begged you not to run the story, said it would ruin her husband. He was up for tenure. She said he'd only gone to a couple of meetings when he was in college, that it didn't amount to anything. But you wouldn't listen."

I looked at Chase, at his intelligent, determined, puzzled face.

He didn't remember.

But I'd never forgotten.

"Agnes Moran, Chase. Her husband was Thomas Moran."

The name kindled no recognition.

"She was terribly upset." How paltry the words were. Even now—more than forty years later—I remembered so vividly the desperate fear in her eyes, the slight, musical voice ravaged by urgency. "She'd found out that you were going to break a story on her husband. She begged me to help persuade you not to do it. She said his career would be ruined. She swore that he'd never done anything to hurt his country. I asked you to talk to Moran, get his side of it."

Chase squinted, then smacked his fist against his palm. "Oh, yeah, Moran. He was one of those saps that got mixed up with the Reds when he was in college. Hell, I had letters he'd written to some Russian official. I don't remember the details now, but he was so glowing about the new world order, that kind of thing. Oh, God, that was hot stuff then. That was the series I did that first caught Elizabeth's dad's attention. That series set me up."

The series had resulted in a subpoena to Thomas Moran. That had gotten lots of headlines. His college had refused him tenure. The day Moran was to answer the subpoena, he had driven to Arlington National Cemetery and the Tomb of the Unknown Soldier and put a bullet in his brain.

Chase didn't remember that part of it.

When I reminded him, he merely looked surprised.

"I covered the funeral." The maples had blazed like fire, the oaks had been as brilliant as dollops of gold. "His widow saw me. She pulled away from the family, and she told me that you and I had killed him. She said she hoped we were satisfied to see a good man destroyed for no reason."

"I wrote a story. The facts were true." There wasn't an iota of regret in Chase's voice.

"Moran was served up like a fatted calf to satisfy the paranoia fanned by the malevolent senator from Wisconsin." Even after all this time I was angry, angry at the warping of freedom, the mind-jacketing the McCarthy years had begun.

Chase shrugged. "Moran should have had the guts to defend himself."

"But you didn't care whether he was innocent," I continued steadily. "All you cared about was a big story—no matter what it did to him or to his family."

"Big stories." He smiled faintly, and his eyes challenged me. "That's my business, Henrie O. I thought it was yours."

Big stories. Yes, I'd had more than a few. And so had my husband, Richard. But neither of us had ever—knowingly—broken a story for our own advancement or broken a story when we knew the official attack was politically motivated. Yes, we had had to cover those kinds of stories when they became news, but we had never originated them. I had no Willie Horton stories on my conscience.

I'd left the cemetery that long-ago morning and gone to my apartment and packed. I had made up my mind. I couldn't love a man who sacrificed human lives for his own advancement.

Chase sighed. "I suppose I should have known. You've always had a quixotic streak, Henrietta. But I thought—hell, I thought you'd been seeing Richard, decided he was the man for you. And I wasn't going to come after you—if that's the way you felt."

I shook my head. "No. That's not what happened. I went back to Kansas, to my mother's sister. Richard followed me. He tracked me down—and he asked me to marry him."

I had been honest with Richard when he came. He had still wanted to marry me. I had said yes, and it had been the best decision I'd ever made.

"I called and called your apartment." Chase sat up straight and leaned toward me, his eyes blazing. "Finally I knew you were gone and not coming back. Nothing's ever hurt me that much."

He was so close to me, close enough to reach out and touch. He still radiated that animal energy, that high, intense enthusiasm for life and success and power. He was still extraordinarily handsome with his high-bridged nose and deep-set eyes and full lips and firm chin.

Different indeed from my equable, steady, honorable husband, Richard. Richard's face had been broad and open. He had had reddish-brown hair and hazel eyes and a crooked grin. And he had been a loving husband and father.

Chase slumped back in his chair. "You never knew it, but I kept track of you through the years, you and Richard and Emily."

I didn't answer.

"The three of you made quite a team."

"Yes. Yes, we did."

I had made a choice years ago.

I stood and so did Chase.

We looked at each other without pretense.

"I came here, Chase. I will do my best for you. But that is all I will do."

He walked with me to his study door.

As I started to leave, he reached out, caught my hand. "I wish," he said softly, "that I had been Richard."

I managed a smile though I felt close to tears. "Oh, Chase, it wouldn't have been the right kind of life for you. Richard and I never had a dime. Richard and I never owned a newspaper or a television station. We had a lot of laughter, but we scrimped from payday to payday."

"You had fun."

"Yes. But then, be honest, Chase. So did you."

He grinned at that. "By God, so I did. And I built an empire. An empire, Henrie O." It was almost as if a trumpet sounded behind his words.

I slept fitfully, images of past and present intertwined: the agony in my heart as I'd packed so long ago and caught a train to Kansas City; Richard's face when he found me the next week; Emily as a newborn, so tiny and delicate and dark; the many,

many years and many, many journeys. I was in an airplane, a propeller-driven twin engine, and it bucketed and banged its way through the sky. Rain streamed against the windows, and there was an odd, harsh thumping sound—

I came awake abruptly. Somewhere a shutter banged in the wind, and rain splashed steadily against the windows.

I twisted and turned, wishing for the thick, black, comforting curtain of sleep but miserably aware that it would be hours before sleep would return.

Finally I gave up and snapped on the lamp next to the bed. Three-thirty. With a sigh I got up and went to the alcove. I made some decaffeinated tea and found a fresh, small loaf of pumpkin bread. At least I would always remember Dead Man's Island for its exemplary hospitality.

I got a pad from my purse. I'm fond of To Do lists.

To Do

1. *Obtain extensive background information on Betty.*
2. *Search for evidence of instability in Miranda's past. Drugs?*
3. *Why wasn't T. Dunnaway among those C.P. had investigated re the leaks to the unauthorized biographer?*
4. *Is Burton Andrews really the wimp other men judge him to be?*
5. *Talk to Roger again. Who would have better reason to be bitter about Chase's—*

Explosions shattered the night.

First a series of rapid, harsh cracks in quick succession, then an enormous, concussive burst of sound. That horrendous boom rattled the windows, assaulted the eardrums, a huge, tearing, roaring, mind-numbing detonation.

By the time I reached the window and flung aside the shutters, the blaze was far beyond anyone's control. Not the

finest fire-fighting equipment in the land could have saved the
Miranda B., captured in a round and glowing ball of flame. The
lovely yacht writhed, blackening in her incendiary prison as
tongues of fire fed by diesel fuel sparked high in the night sky
and swiftly spread from the shattered boathouse to the pier. As
I watched, the skeletal frame of the boat collapsed inward.

The rain fell. Not an especially strong rain, just steady and wet
and dispiriting. This wasn't the rain that would come with the
hurricane but the product of the peripheral clouds associated
with that storm. Even so, it was damp and unpleasant on the
breakfast patio. But we all stood there, most in varying states of
nighttime disarray, and watched our means of escape from the
island disintegrate within the curling, quivering, devouring
flames.

We waited in silence and grim foreboding as Chase and
Enrique came up the path, returning from their fruitless journey
to the steps of the pier. That was as near as they could go to the
blaze. In the glow from a garden light Chase's face was rigid
with anger. Enrique's dark eyes flickered uneasily.

Miranda, childlike in a short pink and white cotton nightie,
darted out in the rain and caught Chase's arm. Her voice was
thin and high. "Chase, Chase, I'm so frightened. What happened to our boat?"

Her husband put his arm around her, pulled her with him
toward the porch. "Come out of the rain, my dear." His tone
was gentle. When they stepped beneath the roof, he looked at
the rest of us, his face harsh.

Valerie's exquisite silk negligee was in odd contrast to her
haggard and witchlike face.

Roger's blond hair stuck out in tufts on his head, and his
face was swollen with sleep. He had the rumpled look of a teddy
bear.

The thick mat of dark hair on Haskell's chest glistened in the light. Wearing only red-plaid boxer shorts, he stood with his hands on his hips, staring out at the flames, his arrogant face somber.

Lyle's hastily tied seersucker robe bunched unevenly around his waist. He, too, was barefoot and barelegged. His dark red hair lay sleekly on his skull. His mouth was closed in a tight line.

In wrinkled khaki slacks and a creased knit shirt, Trevor stood with his arms tightly folded across his chest, his mouth turned down in a heavy frown.

Burton clung to one of the porch pillars, his face ashen. He was the only man on the porch in a pair of pajamas, pale blue cotton shorts and top.

I was dressed. I can dress in seconds, and my walking shorts and a shirt were at hand. Tennis shoes took but a moment, and I smoothed my hair up in a bun and pinned it as I ran downstairs.

Betty and Rosalia, both in long cotton gowns, waited just inside the French doors, not comfortable with joining us, too frightened not to stay near.

"I can't believe . . ." Chase began violently. Then, as Miranda shivered in his embrace, he took a ragged breath. "There's no point in standing out here getting wet. Let's go inside."

He led the way to the living room.

We trooped silently after him.

Chase led Miranda to a couch, then turned to face us. "One of you is a goddamned fool."

That loosened tongues.

"It's your boat," Valerie snapped. "Who else would know how to blow it up?"

Roger turned on her. "Don't be an idiot. Why would Dad do that? It's nuts!"

"Why did he invite us here to start with?" The actress's voice rose, dangerously near hysteria. "Talk about nuts—"

"Shut up, both of you." Lyle's voice was ugly. "Something damn crazy's going on, all right, and we've got to figure it out."

"But nobody would destroy the boat deliberately. Would they? Would they?" Miranda's frightened eyes sought Chase.

I decided to toss in an observation. "Dynamite."

That was all I said, but the quiet it evoked was instantaneous.

Every eye turned toward me. Even Chase's.

"Dynamite. Three sticks, I'd say. Those explosions ignited the fuel."

"Christ, that *is* what it sounded like." Lyle looked at me sharply. "Who the hell here would have dynamite?"

If there was an answer, none of us knew it.

"That's not the point." Haskell strode to the center of the room. "It doesn't matter—not now—who blew it up or why. But we've got to get the hell off this place."

Miranda smoothed her flimsy nightgown down closer to her knees. "We have plenty of food, and we thought everyone was staying until next Thursday anyway. So . . . I know it isn't pleasant . . . the way things have turned out, but it will be all right. . . ."

She and Haskell were so close in age, but his face was old when he looked down at her. There was pity and affection and a desperate sadness in his gaze. "Randy," he said gently, "the storm. There's a big storm coming. A hurricane. And it will wash right over this island."

Her eyes widened. Huge and dark and terrified, they moved from Haskell's face to her husband's. What she saw there brought her hand to her throat. "Chase . . ."

Chase lifted his head, listened to the drum of rain against the windows. "Right now we're all right. And the storm may veer inland into Florida. This may be all the storm we'll have, but . . ."

The rest of us understood.

Hurricane Derek—the last we heard, the last we knew— was heading for a landfall between Miami and Savannah. If it struck Savannah—a full-force hurricane—this island would be just like Dead Man's Island so many years ago.

Except this time the lifeless bodies hanging in the trees would be ours.

10

Chase worked like a man possessed. His intensity galvanized us. There was much to do. The upstairs central portion of the house was chosen as the likeliest to survive the battering waters—if they came. Of that area Chase chose the music salon, an interior room, as our headquarters.

We all helped, bringing food, water, bedding, an extra supply of life jackets Enrique found in the storage building, flashlights, some medical supplies—and anything we thought would

float. I carried my mobile telephone with me, dialing and redial-
ing, one time after another, alternating 911 with the number of
the Savannah Coast Guard air and rescue station. I didn't have
much hope, but there was a chance, even though the line crackled with incessant static. The call might be received and enough
of it understood even if I believed there was no response. And
there was the hope, certainly my strongest hope, that the message would be overheard by a ham-radio operator monitoring
the air for Mayday calls from vessels in distress. I kept it up
until I was hoarse, intoning over and over: *"Mayday. Mayday.
3250.5 north, 8055.1 west. Party of twelve marooned on sea island. Boat
destroyed."*

When my throat was dry and scratchy, I handed the phone
to Valerie. I wrote out the numbers and the message, and she
took over, sitting cross-legged on a rose velvet sofa in the corner
of the room, her platinum hair spilling down around her pale
face, her crimson-nailed fingers punching the buttons with savage determination.

At one point Chase looked around, his face haggard.
"Where the hell's Haskell? Why isn't he helping?"

Rain slapped against the poncho. My tennis shoes squished
through an inch or more of water on the path. The rain splashed
down with no letup, saturating the ground. The runoff flooded
the path. My feet were damn cold.

I heard the steady crack of the hammer as soon as I pushed
open the main door to the storage building.

Haskell knelt beside a pile of two-by-fours. A life jacket lay
on the floor next to a plastic thermos. He didn't even notice the
spray of rain as the door opened behind him. He worked at a
furious pace, grabbing the boards, slamming them in place,
pounding in the nails swiftly. Makeshift, yes, but already recog-
nizable as a raft.

I hurried across the cement floor. "Haskell, no."

He looked up—such a young face, so handsome and appealing. No trace lingered of the languid, sulky youth I'd met at tea that first afternoon. His eyes were scared, but he managed a grin. "Hell, I lost my surfboard. Gotta make a new one."

I knelt beside him. "I've got a mobile phone. We're sending out a call for help every few minutes. Someone will hear and alert the Coast Guard. This"—I pointed at the platform of shiny new wood gashed by hurried hammer strokes—"is foolish. You wouldn't stand a chance."

He reached for another board, maneuvered it into place, began to pound. As the steel head struck home, Haskell spoke jerkily. "Yeah. A chance. Maybe the only chance. I've got to try. That phone's a joke in this kind of weather. And the connections never have been any good out here."

I reached out, gripped that warm, muscular arm. "Haskell, dammit, you'll *drown.*"

"Maybe. But nobody's going to answer that phone, Henrie O. Not even E.T." The weak grin touched his face, then was gone. "The deal is, I'll damn sure drown if I stay here—and so will everyone else." He used the back of his hand to wipe sweat from his glistening forehead. "Listen, you'd be surprised what people hang on to in a hurricane and live to tell about it. Mattresses. Parts of roofs. Tree limbs. Logs. My raft'll be okay. And I'm going to use some rope, make some handholds. The only thing is"—he looked at me steadily, acknowledging the risk, knowing what he was about to do—"it depends upon the currents. If I get a current into shore, hey, then I've got a chance. And if I can get to land, reach help . . ."

"Haskell, that storm may turn inland well south of here. Your chances of surviving are better if you stay here." Dear God, I wanted him to stay.

"But if the storm comes here"—his voice was remarkably calm—"nobody will make it. Unless I get help before then."

I looked into dark brown eyes filled with courage and fear. He knew and I knew what would happen if the hurricane struck here—horizontal winds with the force of freight trains, winds and rains no man could stand up against. Waves twenty stories high. A wall of lethal water sweeping the island. But the raft was a wild man's gamble.

A brave man's gamble.

He lifted the hammer, attacked another nail. "I can do it." He struggled to his feet, favoring his right knee. "I've got to find rope."

"No. I'm going back to the house to get Chase. You mustn't do this, Haskell."

He was pulling down a coil of rope from a hook, talking to himself. "Shears, where the hell did I see those shears?"

I ran all the way to the house and up the stairs and, breathless, called to Chase. It took a moment to make it clear, then he raced down the steps and out into the rain, thudding and splashing down the path to the storage building. I followed.

Chase stood in the open doorway. I came up beside him.

The hammer lay near the pile of unused boards. Pieces of rope were scattered around.

The raft was gone.

And so was Haskell.

Toward dawn the rain slacked off. But purplish-black clouds bunched over the sky like mailed fists, somber auguries of what was to come.

When I saw that I could not be of much help—most of the provisions were now in place, the lower and upper walls in the central section braced with more hastily hammered two-by-fours, the windows covered with plywood sheets, the phone manned, this time by a hollow-eyed Trevor—I set out in search of Betty.

I found her in the kitchen, helping Rosalia fix breakfast. Breakfast.

It seemed insanely normal after the night we'd spent.

"Rosalia, we need Betty upstairs for a few minutes. Can you spare her?" I helped myself to coffee, poured in milk, even added sugar.

Rosalia turned from the oven. "Certainly, Mrs. Collins. And please tell Mr. Prescott that breakfast will be ready at seven."

I looked up at the kitchen clock. A few minutes before six.

Rosalia opened the oven door and the delicious scent of baking muffins—blueberry?—wafted toward me.

I gulped the wonderfully warming brew and realized I was ravenous. "Yes, of course. It will be good for all of us." I tried not to think of Haskell plunging up and down on that uncontrollable raft in churning, unforgiving water.

I finished the coffee and opened the kitchen door. I waited for Betty to precede me, but as soon as we were out in the hall, the door closed behind us, I pointed toward the dining room. "Let's duck in there for a moment. No one will disturb us."

Betty stopped dead. She would have darted right back into the kitchen, but I barred the way.

"It's all right, Betty." I flashed her an approving smile. "I know that you are very careful, very thorough with your duties. I want to ask for your help. Now you unpacked my clothes when I arrived Thursday." I made it a nonthreatening statement.

Hesitantly, Betty nodded. I wondered if she realized how her hands were twisting as she watched me.

"Wonderful. Come, then, let's go relax for a moment in the dining room." We passed the huge ebony-framed hall mirror. Once again I saw our faces, mine intense and determined, hers mute with expectant misery.

She wanted desperately to escape from me. But she could

see no way to do so. Her feet dragging, she walked with me into the dining room. I flicked on the lights.

I wondered absently how long we would have that luxury. The beautiful chandelier glittered. All the gold appointments — the gold-threaded drapes, the gilt-framed mirrors, a pier table with gold-plated caryatid legs and dolphin feet — glistened as brightly as the day they were created. They would be as anomalous awash in seawater as the luxurious cabins of the *Titanic* had been.

I gestured for her to sit on the white upholstered sofa. But she shook her head and stood nervously beside it. Her hands twisted and twisted.

I leaned casually against the sofa, trying a little body language to relax her. "Betty, I just want you to think back a little bit. Since you unpack for the guests, naturally you're generally aware of what is in their luggage. Now, were there any wrapped parcels about this long?" I spread my hands a foot apart. "Like a package of candles."

"Candles, ma'am?" Almost immediately, understanding flickered in her eyes, confirming my judgment that Betty was both intelligent and observant. Her hands stilled. "Is that how dynamite is shaped, Mrs. Collins? Like candles?"

"Near enough. An inch or a little over in diameter. Eight to twelve inches long. Like inch-round sticks a foot in length. They're yellowish with a waxy feel. They look like a mixture of oil, sawdust, and clay. Straight dynamite has an almost sickening-sweet smell."

It didn't escape me that when she was confident the questions had nothing to do with her personally, she relaxed enough to sit on the edge of the sofa. Her hazel eyes stared off into space. When Betty's face lost its subservient cast, the thoughtful, measuring look in her eyes was clear to see.

I didn't try to hurry her.

Finally she gave a little sigh of disappointment. "No. But I didn't open three pieces of hand luggage. One was yours. Mr. Dunnaway has a briefcase. Mr. Haskell brought a gym bag." Her mouth quirked. "I smell real good. I didn't smell anything sweetlike."

"So you're pretty certain that none of the other guests could have had sticks of dynamite with them." So how the hell did it get on the island?

"I don't see how. There was nothing like that—nothing— in any of the cases I unpacked. And how else could something like that get on the island? We don't get any mail here. All our supplies are opened and put away by Enrique. Anything a guest brings goes directly to the room. You can check with Enrique and Mr. Andrews to be sure. I unpacked everything but those three things. I smelled rose petals in Miss Valerie's things and spicy soap in Mr. Dunnaway's. But nothing sweet."

I hadn't been too hopeful, but this was an avenue I had to pursue. Because someone had managed to come up with explosives somehow. "Okay, Betty. How about the storeroom here on the island. Do you know if there's ever been any dynamite around? Maybe to blow up tree stumps, something like that?"

Although if Chase had chosen this island for its solitude and quiet, as Burton Andrews indicated when I arrived, certainly it would have been more agreeable to dig out stumps than to explode them. But Chase and his entourage wouldn't have been here when construction was under way.

"Nothing's ever been blown up—not when we've been on the island." Betty was quite definite. "And I've never seen sticks like you described. But you should talk to Enrique."

Gusty winds tugged at my clothes, scudded magnolia leaves across the ground, rattled the palm fronds, whipped the somber cypress. Wind sighed through the live oaks with the eerie sound of zithers mindlessly strummed. It was a hostile world, the dark sky lowering overhead, branches cracking, the air heavy with moisture.

I almost turned toward the maintenance building. Light streamed from the open door. But instead I ducked into the maritime forest.

I wanted to see the ocean.

I went as far as the first dune.

If the person who had detonated that dynamite, stranding us here, had taken the time to walk across the island and look at the boiling, churning, explosive surf, surely the explosion would not have occurred. Not if that person had any idea of the vulnerability of this low-lying piece of land.

If Haskell didn't reach the mainland . . . If our desperate calls on the mobile phone weren't answered . . .

I had no doubt of our fate.

The signs were too clear.

The tide surge could be measured. I estimated at least fifteen feet.

The interval between the waves was longer than it had been yesterday. Much longer. An unmistakable portent. And the waves were awesome, lifting tons of water up against the purplish sky, up, up, up. Foaming crests curled over to crash with explosive thunder. The dune plants rippled as if yanked by a giant's hand. The mist from the thunderous surf drenched me in seconds.

How could anyone have been fool enough, or desperate enough, or angry enough to subject all of us to this indifferent, unstoppable force?

Was someone willing to die to see Chase dead? Or was Chase not even the main focus anymore? Had anger so possessed some soul that all humanity was gone, replaced by the kind of vicious violence that was willing to die to deal out indiscriminate death, like the sniper in a campus bell tower or the gun-laden attacker in a shopping mall?

If that was the case, my dogged pursuit of information was pointless. Rational investigation is incapable of explaining irrational acts.

But I must find out what I could.

I hurried back along the sodden path, wet tendrils of ferns slapping against me. I caught myself just in time from stepping on a black snake seeking higher ground.

I moved carefully but even faster. There would be more and more snakes if the rains started again.

As they would.

And when they did, it wouldn't be the straight, unremarkable rains of the peripheral storms. No, the next rains would streak from the sky, pummel the waterlogged earth, cascade into standing, ever deepening pools of water.

As I came out of the forest and turned toward the maintenance building, I saw that the door was shut.

I hesitated.

Enrique was probably back in the main house.

But it wouldn't hurt to take a quick look through the building myself and to look more closely than I had before.

I opened the door and stepped inside.

Enrique had left the light on. Perhaps he expected to return soon. Perhaps it was simply an acknowledgment that there was no longer a reason to conserve electricity.

If the storm swamped the island, this building would be swept away, and with it, of course, the generator.

Why not leave the light on?

I tried not to look at the remnants of Haskell's desperate work. I still carried with me in my head the howl of the frenzied ocean, a roar so deep and pervasive, so inhuman and incalculable that it numbed the mind. To be adrift in its midst would be so terrifying, so dreadful . . .

Concentrate.

I opened cupboards, closets, boxes.

I didn't have time to search every possible hiding place. But I wasn't looking for a hiding place. I wanted to know if dynamite had been stored here, for whatever reason. If it had, that fact could be known by those who regularly used the maintenance building. That would include Enrique, the cleaning and work crews that visited the island every week, and, possibly, Chase.

I found no trace of dynamite anywhere.

"Dynamite?" Burton's voice broke in a squeak. "I don't know anything about dynamite. Why would I? I'm a secretary, not a workman." His face no longer appeared boyish. But the faint stubble of fair beard on his cheeks looked seedy rather than masculine, like a downy duck caught in a windstorm. He caught my wrist in a grip of surprising strength.

"Are we going to get out of here? You know things. Is it all right? Is this just some kind of hideous joke someone's playing? To scare us? The island won't disappear in the water, will it? Will it?" His eyes bulged. Hysteria wasn't far distant.

I tried to be reassuring. "It's hard to say what might happen, Burton. A lot will depend on where the storm strikes. If it's close, we might be in trouble. But hurricanes are odd. It could turn and streak out to sea, or it could veer to the west, sweep over Florida and move into the gulf."

"Mrs. Collins"—his voice was a husky whisper—"do you think somebody's insane?"

Enrique's shirt had pulled out of his trousers. His sleeves were rolled up past his elbows. Sweat streaked his swarthy face. Blood welled from an angry scratch across the back of his right hand. He hammered with swift, competent grace.

For a moment I thought he wasn't going to answer. Then

he paused to wipe his face with his sleeve. "Dynamite? On the island? No." He turned, grabbed another board, slammed it into place. As the hammer thudded, he swore in a monotone, one hostile obscene phrase after another, describing the antecedents, life-style practices, and intelligence of whoever had ignited the explosion aboard the *Miranda B.*

I didn't doubt his sincerity.

I found Chase pacing the upstairs balcony, looking out at the mist-swept sound and the jagged peaks of white foam. The wind had eased considerably, but I knew better than to take comfort. This was simply a lull.

He swung around as I stepped out onto the balcony.

"Any word? Have we got through yet? Made any contact?" He was still angry and, I think, astonished, at what had happened, at the fact that someone had dared to taunt him like this.

"I don't think so. I'll check with Trevor. I've been nosing around. Trying to figure out who could have set the explosives." I shivered in the wind. I was wet through from my walk.

He shook his head impatiently. "That doesn't matter now. God, we've got to get out of here. If there were something, anything . . ." He swung around, strode to the railing, and gripped it.

I came up beside him.

"Come downstairs, Chase. Rosalia said breakfast will be ready at seven." *The condemned man ate a hearty breakfast.* Yes, I'd written that once, years ago. The only formal execution I ever covered. I still feel a sour curdling in my throat when I remember it.

"Breakfast." He repeated it as if it were a word he'd never heard. He let go of the railing, jammed his hands in his jacket pockets. He wore a crimson and navy nylon warm-up that seemed incongruously cheerful.

"We need the nourishment. Come on, Chase." I started for the doorway.

He stared out at the sound again. "I don't know what to do." Frustration and anger harshened his voice.

"We're doing all that we can," I said quietly. I looked up at him, his fine-boned face now taut with anxiety, and thought that he was—perhaps for the first time in his life—caught up in circumstances that not even one of the richest men in the world could control.

It galled him.

"Chase?" I managed a smile. "Do you want my take on it?"

Some of the tension eased out of his body. His eyes brightened. "Sure. I remember press parties when you'd wrap a red kerchief around your hair and put on huge gold hoop earrings and tell everybody's fortune. Have at it, Henrie O."

I'm afraid my smile wavered for an instant. I, too, remembered those parties—and the time I held his hand, so tightly, and told him a dark young woman would be his wife and his helpmeet for life. But we all know how much stock to place in fortune-tellers.

I began to talk rapidly, both to drown out memory and to be heard above the freshening wind.

"A free prediction, won't cost you a cent." I lifted my voice in a reedy singsong. "Listen to a Gypsy who's traveled this sea. The storm will pass by, we'll heave a great sigh. Sure as pirates love pieces of eight, tonight we'll gather to celebrate."

He gave me an odd smile.

I felt absurdly pleased to have lightened his mood, even if only for an instant.

"Pieces of eight." His eyes had a faraway shine. "Funny how romantic it sounds—and it's only money. Money. Sometimes it isn't enough." He looked back toward the water. His face hardened. "And sometimes it is. Come on, Henrie O. Let's go downstairs. What the hell, you may be right." At the foot of the stairs he paused for an instant, then said, "Go on out for breakfast. Let's keep to a regular schedule. It will encourage everybody. I'm going to check on Miranda, then I'll swim."

Lyle worked the telephone. He paused long enough to shake his head at the offer of food. "Just coffee, okay?" His savagely red hair bristled in unruly curls. He hadn't shaved and thick red stubble covered his cheeks. He wore khaki shorts and a T-shirt. He hunched over the phone, dialing, talking, cutting the connection, dialing, talking. . . .

I was pushing open the door to the dining room when I heard the change in his voice.

"*Savannah?* Coast Guard Group Savannah? Stranded party of eleven seeks rescue. Sea island 3250.5 north, 8055.1 west. Stranded party of eleven . . ."

I swung around, hurried back to him.

He gave the message over and over. The hope in his voice lessened with each repetition. Finally he stopped, breathing deeply. "I heard something. I think we had a connection. Just for an instant. I don't know if it was long enough. But, by God, it's something. And if it happened once—" He punched the buttons exuberantly.

Hope is so much better than despair.

I was a little surprised when I entered the dining room to find it empty. Rosalia had promised breakfast at seven and it was now a few minutes past. Then I saw through the French doors that Enrique and Betty were setting out the serving dishes on the sideboard on the patio.

I opened the doors and smelled bacon and sausage and cheese grits—and the sweetish, heavy, wet-foliage scent that follows a drenching rain. A glum, grimly quiet group occupied the two tables.

I wondered briefly why on earth breakfast wasn't being served in the dining room. It would certainly have been far more cheerful than to be outside on an overcast, sultry morning like this. The wind had lessened, though the palm fronds still fluttered. But I supposed in the aftermath of the explosion no one had taken time to direct Rosalia to change the location — and of course that wasn't her decision to make. Miranda wasn't among those on the porch. It should have been her call. Or Chase's.

"Good news," I said briskly.

Every face turned toward me.

The men started to rise. I motioned them to keep their seats. "Lyle just made momentary contact with the Savannah Coast Guard station. He doesn't know how much they got, but they got something. And now he's continuing to call. And he'd love some coffee, Betty." I crossed to the first table, grabbed up a coffee thermos, and poured the hot, steaming brew almost to the brim of a crimson pottery mug. Usually I add two generous dollops of milk. This morning I wanted it black, hot, and strong.

Rosalia hadn't changed the site of breakfast, but she had switched the breakfast dishes from delicate china to brightly hued pottery.

"Hey, that's great." Roger's face creased in a delighted smile. He had shaved, nicking his left ear. A spot of blood stained his yellow polo shirt. "Best news I've had in a hell of a long time." He splashed maple syrup liberally over his waffle. "Come on and have some breakfast, Mrs. Collins. Maybe the Coast Guard will get here before we finish." He twisted to look out across the waterlogged gardens at the whitecap-laced sound.

I looked, too, but at a sky laden with knobby clumps of purplish-black clouds. To the south, lightning flickered behind the bulges of cloud that stretched from horizon to horizon, looking as if they'd been gouged out of slate.

I took a huge gulp of the coffee. God, it was hot.

Trevor spooned sugar into his mug. "Momentary?" he repeated. Oddly, he was the least altered in appearance from the previous days. His curly blond hair was neatly brushed, his face smoothly shaven, his pale pink sports shirt crisp and fresh. But his voice was tight and sharp.

"You mean he didn't really talk to the Coast Guard, don't you?" Burton demanded shrilly. "So why get our hopes up? Nobody's coming. I know nobody's—"

Valerie twisted suddenly and slapped Burton hard. "Shut up, little man." Shocked, we fell silent as she continued with withering contempt, "See if you can't at least pretend you're a man. Don't you know, if the ship's going down, we might as well enjoy a last good breakfast." She reached for a blueberry muffin. "At least the food's damned good."

Burton pressed a shaking hand against the red welt her ring had made. Tears glistened in his eyes.

I lifted my voice. "The point is, we do have a chance."

Valerie lifted an elegantly penciled eyebrow. "Come this way again sometime when you've got more good news." She poked through the roll basket, picked out two miniature cheese-topped sweet rolls.

"My pleasure," I responded over my shoulder with a flicker of a smile. I like spirit.

I walked swiftly toward the pool. I could have waited until Chase finished his workout, but he would want to know immediately.

I stopped at the shallow end of the pool. The sweet, smooth sound of "My Isle of Golden Dreams" contrasted sharply with the intermittent but rapidly increasing growls of thunder.

Chase knifed through the water, his arms slicing like pistons, his head turning and drawing air in as his legs thrummed the water in a four-four beat.

As he neared, oblivious to my presence, ready to make his flip turn, I yelled, "Chase. Chase!"

He pulled up, stood, his chest heaving, water glistening against his skin, his face ruddy with exertion.

"Chase"—I couldn't keep the joy out of my voice—"brief contact with the Coast Guard. Lyle doesn't know how much they heard, but it was something. Our first break."

"Good," he said simply. He locked both hands and slammed the water. A plume of water geysered up and splashed over me.

"God, I knew it." This was Chase at his most confident, his voice deep and full of excitement. "They'll come. They're smart bastards, Henrie O. They're probably scanning the area for our signals right now. They'll find us." He looked up at the sky, his eyes intent. "Helicopters. I'll bet they're here within a half hour."

"Chase, Chase, it was just a contact. Nothing that definite." But his sudden confidence made me smile.

He was revitalized, his dark eyes flashing, a triumphant smile lighting his handsome face. He gripped the pool edge, pulled himself up, and stood beside me, lithe and strong. "*Okay.*" He looked down at me, an odd mixture of pleasure and pain in his eyes. "I'm always lucky when you're around, Henrie O."

I caught the intent in his eyes just in time and took a backward step to escape his exuberant embrace. Out of the corner of my eye I saw Miranda standing in the French doors of their quarters.

"Well," I said lightly, "if they're going to be here in half an hour, you'd better get dressed, Chase. I think I'll have some breakfast."

"Yeah." He grabbed a towel from the back of a deck chair. "Great idea." He shivered, hesitated, then said briskly, "But I'm going to get warm first."

Lightning splintered the sky. Thunder boomed.

It was closer now.

Not here yet.

But close.

Chase started up the path to the hot tub.

I almost called out to him. A hot tub wouldn't be my choice with an electrical storm coming. But I've never succumbed to maternal instincts with men.

I wondered if we'd have time to finish breakfast before the rains began. The saccharine Hawaiian music was now sullenly counterpointed by an almost constant murmur of thunder.

I pulled out a chair to join Roger's table.

Chase hurried up the wooden steps of the hot tub and jumped into the frothing water.

He didn't scream.

It was more of a yelp, a sudden stricture of the vocal cords. His body arched, an unmistakable, violent, shivering contortion. With that single strangled sound he slid smoothly beneath the churning, gurgling water.

11

"Don't!" I cried. "Don't go
near it. Don't!" My voice was terrible, a rasping, desperate cry.

It stopped them. Miranda, arms outstretched, halted only a
few feet from the redwood tub.

"My Isle of Golden Dreams" continued to play.

Chase's body broke the surface and bobbed facedown in
the foamy water. A dead man's float that wasn't a summertime
joke.

"Don't touch anything," I shouted. "Miranda, for God's

sake, don't!" I whirled to Enrique. "Quick. The power source. Get it off. Quick. Quick!"

"Chase." Miranda's cry was a whimper, lost in a closer, harsher crack of thunder. Slowly she crumpled.

Enrique half-turned toward the bathhouse, hesitated, then swung around and bolted off the patio, splashing through puddles to disappear around the side of the house.

The generator, of course. That's where he was headed. God, yes. There was likely a fuse panel in the bathhouse, but Enrique wasn't going to take any chances.

Smart.

Valerie shoved back her chair. "My God, what's going on here? What's happened to Miranda? Is she dead, too?" She clutched her napkin, her eyes bulging as she looked frantically around, as if expecting death in some unknown, unknowable guise to wrap his arms about her next.

"She's fainted," I snapped. I whirled. "Roger, circle around the tub. Stay the hell away from it. Take Miranda into the house. Don't let her come back out here. Trevor, help him."

Trevor Dunnaway's face looked like old linen left out to mildew. Numbly, he nodded and pushed back his chair.

I didn't bother to ask Burton to help. He hunched at the table, a half-eaten muffin crushed in one hand, staring in horror at the hot tub.

"Dad," Roger said thickly. He was on his feet, his face slack with shock, his eyes glazed with horror. "Got to get him out of— Mouth-to-mouth. Got to—"

"If you touch that water, you'll be dead, too." Roger's hands trembled in mine, like an old man with palsy. "Roger, listen to me. It's too late. Only a cardiac defibrillator could get his heart started again. We don't have one. There's nothing we can do. Nothing." Of course, Chase's death could have resulted from instant asphyxia because of damage to the brain stem rather than heart failure. It depended on how the current ran, leg to arm or foot to head. But there was no way to bring him back from brain-stem damage either.

Don Ho's voice broke off in mid-lyric. The lights around the hot tub and on the patio flickered and then were gone.

The silence was almost more grotesque.

I stood between Roger and the tub until Enrique strode back to the patio, his dark face masklike.

"Is all the current off, Enrique? Every bit of it?" I had to be sure.

"The generator is turned off. There is no current on the island." His dark eyes flickered toward the hot tub.

I took a deep breath. I felt old and tired. More than that, I was stung by grief and anger. Chase had trusted me, and I had failed him.

But if I could not save Chase, I would avenge him.

The French door was flung open. "Hey, the lights—" Lyle stopped short, looked across the patio. "What the hell's going on?"

Valerie reached out to grip the back of her chair, and I knew she did it to keep from falling. "Our little vacation from hell has just provided its first death." Her voice was thin and ragged.

I looked at her sharply. Did she . . . could she think this was an accident? But there wasn't time now to deal with Valerie.

I gestured to Lyle. "You can help. We have to get Chase out of the tub. He's been electrocuted. Valerie, Miranda's stirring. Go see to her. Get her in the house."

Lightning exploded. The jagged silver-white spear was brilliant against the pitch-dark clouds. The boom of thunder followed immediately.

The storm was almost upon us.

Miranda began to sob, heavy, choking sobs. Valerie, her voice gentle, said, "Come with me, honey. We have to go inside. There's nothing we can do for him. Come with me."

At the hot tub the men—Lyle, Roger, and Enrique—worked to get Chase out of the water. The limp body slipped from their hands once. Roger gave a guttural moan. Trevor gently pushed him aside. "Let me."

It took Lyle standing in the tub finally to push the body up where Trevor and Enrique could pull it over the side. Roger reached up and vainly tried to cushion his father's fall to the ground.

There would be some bruising after death from this rough handling, but other than the scrape on his left arm from the awkward hoisting over the tub's wooden edge, Chase's body was unmarked.

Lyle sloshed down the ladder.

The smell of chlorine eddied around us. I would always remember that odor and the muttering rumble of incessant thunder and the unending flicker of lightning.

Chase's face, slack in death, appeared utterly at peace. We looked down at him, the Chase we knew in form but with that fierce spirit forever quenched.

Roger fell to his knees beside his father, gripped one flaccid hand, and began to cry, great tears that rolled silently down his cheeks.

"All right," I said quietly. Tears are sometimes a luxury that cannot be afforded. "Lyle, let's use the chaise longue over there"—I pointed across the pool—"as a stretcher, and take Chase—"

"Wait a minute." Lyle yanked on his khaki shorts, soggy with tub water. His wet T-shirt sagged against his chest. "How the hell do you know so much, lady?" His eyes were hard.

Burton jumped to his feet, pointed at me. "She said Mr. Prescott was electrocuted. How did she know that?"

I was impatient. "Because I can think—and because I was awake on Thursday night when the power went off. I should have paid attention to my own instinct. I was out on the grounds when the lights came back on, fifteen to twenty minutes later. I heard someone coming from the direction of the generator. But when I called out, no one answered. Why not? Anyone abroad on an innocent errand should have responded."

No one interrupted. Lyle leaned forward, his hostile buccaneer's face intent. Roger had picked up a fallen towel and was gently drying his father's hair, smoothing it. Trevor stared stolidly at the hot tub, determinedly keeping his eyes away from Chase's body. Enrique rocked back on his heels, wary and suspicious. Burton hung back on the patio, his face white with fear.

"I told Chase what had happened. I urged him to be careful in view of the poisoned candy he'd received. But when someone shot at him yesterday, I suppose we both were more concerned with a direct attack. I thought as long as he was with someone else, he would be safe. I should have kept on thinking about those lights going out—and why someone might have wanted the power turned off."

"Okay." Lyle's agreement was grudging, but he no longer sounded accusatory. "I get you." He turned toward the tub. "But how the hell did it happen?"

"I suggest"—I raised my voice over a clap of thunder— "that we find out." The wind was rising, raising goose bumps on Lyle's skin, tugging strands of my hair free, fluttering the napkins on the breakfast tables. "Burton."

The secretary started.

Maybe my voice was a little sharp, but I was in a hurry. The rain would be upon us soon. "Get a notebook. Quick. Then get back down here and take notes of every single thing that we do."

Burton hesitated.

"Pronto." My voice was whip-sharp.

He darted a glance at Roger, then turned and scurried off the patio.

I didn't waste time.

"Enrique, how is this tub emptied?" I stepped toward it.

"There is a drain, there, near the bottom." He squatted on his heels and pointed.

A high, clear voice announced, "I wouldn't touch that thing for all the cocaine in Bolivia." Valerie crossed the lawn toward the pool. Her face was the color of old putty. She gave the tub a wide berth. She cradled a pale pink comforter in her arms. "Miranda wanted me to bring this out—for Chase."

Roger pushed up from the ground and took the comforter. He laid it gently over his father.

Valerie looked down, abruptly made the sign of the cross. But the blue eyes that turned to me were not grieving. "Miranda's in bed. Valium and hot tea. I told Rosalia and Betty about Chase, and I told them to stick together. You should come inside, too, Roger. It won't do any good. To stay out here with . . . him."

Roger shook his head. "I can't leave him here." He looked down at the damp towel in his hands, then abruptly flung it away.

Thunder exploded overhead.

I looked impatiently toward the house. Where was Burton? "All right, we've got to hurry. Roger's right. We mustn't leave Chase out here. Trevor, will you and Lyle please use that chaise longue, the one that straightens out all the way . . ."

I didn't have to explain.

Lyle and the lawyer, their faces set and white, were awkward at their unaccustomed task, fumbling when they tried to pick Chase up. One dead hand kept slipping free to dangle over the side of the webbed chair. Roger reached over to tuck the comforter under his father's body. Lyle and Trevor slid the

shrouded bundle onto the webbing, then picked up the im-
promptu stretcher and looked at me.

"I think the storage area." I looked toward Enrique. "The
refrigerated room."

After an instant of hesitation the makeshift cortege started
off. Roger stood uncertainly for a moment, then followed, head
bent.

Valerie and I watched them carry the holiday furniture
with its macabre burden around the corner of the house.

The actress shuddered. "Going to put him in an icebox.
Jesus."

I ignored her and approached the hot tub. I circled it,
moving a few inches at a time. It was difficult to see in the
murky light. I wished I had a flashlight. I ran my fingers lightly
along the wood.

I found what I expected, next to the wooden steps that led
up to the rim of the tub. The cord was brown, just a bit lighter
than the redwood, caramel against cordovan. It was taut against
the side of the tub. I looked at the ground, poked aside a mound
of oyster shells with the tip of my sneaker, and spotted the
electrical tape that fastened the cord tightly to the bottom of the
tub.

Valerie followed me, looking uneasily around, taking care
not to touch the tub.

The flagstoned path to the hot tub was bordered by vigorous stands of monkey grass. Lights fashioned like luminarias
ran on both sides of the path, spaced about four inches apart.
These were included in the system that afforded music around
the pool.

The cord disappeared into the monkey grass.

Lightning exploded. The explosive crack sounded so near,
Valerie and I cringed. She gripped my arm, her fingernails
sharp against my skin. "God, that was close. We'd better get the
hell—"

Burton reluctantly edged out onto the patio. "The lightning's too close. Just because you're crazy doesn't mean I have to—"

"Bring the notebook here," Valerie ordered. "Then go hide your stupid head."

His face resentful, Burton dashed out to us, shoved the notebook and a pen into her hands, and turned and ran back to the house.

Valerie took the thick-tipped pen and began to draw, her eyes measuring, her hand surprisingly swift. In a few, economical strokes the hot tub, its steps, and the cord took shape. She held the drawing up for me to see. "Stage design" was all she said.

I pulled back a sheaf of monkey grass.

No expense had been spared in installing this wiring system. The metal-sheathed pipe supporting the luminarias also contained extra outlets every few feet.

I pointed to the first outlet.

Valerie sketched the cord leading up to it and the innocuous brown plug inserted in the outlet.

I borrowed her pen, eased the plug out of the socket.

The first drops of rain, cold and hard, spattered down as the men came around the side of the house. Roger was in the lead. He broke into a heavy run. The others followed suit, and they all passed him. Valerie and I hurried to the patio.

"Cover the drawing," I directed.

She grabbed up two cloth napkins and wrapped them around the notebook.

"Hurry," I yelled at Enrique, "drain the tub."

He looked out at the rain, then shrugged impassively. Pulling a pair of canvas work gloves from his back pocket, he ran to the tub and crouched beside it.

The wind gusted, and rain billowed onto the patio.

Lyle, shivering, his arms tight to his body, watched impatiently for a minute. "Yeah, this has to be done. But it won't matter a damn if we don't get some help. I'm going back inside, get back to the phone." He hesitated, gave me a stark, abrasive look, then turned to Roger. "If you want my advice—and you may not—but here it is. Watch like a hawk. Make sure you know what's going on, what's found."

He turned without waiting for an answer and strode toward the French doors.

Roger looked after him, his kindly face puzzled.

"It's good advice," I said dryly. "Even if it's directed at me."

"Or perhaps," Valerie volunteered tartly, "a good offense makes the best defense. I for one don't trust anybody on this bloody island."

Enrique straightened. He hurried back to the patio and shook himself like a wet dog. "The water's out," he announced.

"Thank you." I turned to Valerie. "I want you to come with me and watch, then you can sketch what we find." Lightning glittered overhead; deafening thunder erupted.

Valerie looked up. The bones of her face shone in sharp relief in the unearthly glow from the sky. But she didn't refuse me.

I held out my hand. "Enrique, the gloves, please."

"They are wet."

"That doesn't matter."

He stripped off the gloves, which were very damp but not sodden, and handed them to me.

Valerie put the notebook on the table, using a plate to anchor it against the wind.

We reached the hot tub and climbed the steps.

Roger and Trevor were close behind us.

But that was all right. The more who saw, the better we could report to the authorities.

If, of course, we survived the onslaught of a hurricane against a sea island.

I wouldn't have taken odds on that.

But taking odds wasn't my job at the moment.

Looking down into the rain-splashed hot tub was.

Roger drew his breath in sharply. "Oh, my God, look at that!"

I pushed open the swinging door to the kitchen with my knee, clutching a damp cardboard box in my arms. I was wet through and cold, but I had work to do before I dried off and changed clothes.

Rain slammed against the windows of the darkened kitchen.

"Rosalia?" I called as I stepped inside.

My eyes widened.

The meat cleaver in Rosalia's hand wobbled. She held it over her head, poised to attack. Betty stood behind her, pressed against the side of the refrigerator.

"It's all right," I said quickly. "I just want to talk to you, Betty. I need your help in trying to find out who killed Mr. Prescott."

The lights in the kitchen flickered, then came on.

I hadn't told Enrique to turn the generator on, but he'd obviously decided to do so. Good. Our situation was frightful enough without the added discomfort of dark and shadowy rooms.

Perhaps it was the lights that reassured Rosalia. The kitchen once again was an oasis of normalcy, the sparkling cleanliness of the tiled workspaces, the shiny copper bottoms of the pans hanging above a central workstation, the homely famili-arity of a suds-filled sink. Here, it was hard to believe a man had been murdered a thousand feet away. Slowly Rosalia lowered her arm.

"I do not know what to do," the housekeeper began apologetically. "Tengo miedo. Who will come, what will happen? What took Mr. Prescott? Enrique say he jump into tub and die. But that is not right. Mr. Prescott is not a young man, but he is a strong man. And someone shot the gun at him. I am afraid."

"We are all afraid, Rosalia, and you are wise to arm yourself. You and Betty must stay together. That will keep you safe." I put down the box on the central workstation.

Her jet-black eyes regarded me sorrowfully. "Mr. Prescott, he wasn't alone."

It was a twist of the knife in a wound that might never heal.

No, Chase hadn't been alone, and I had been so confident he would be safe so long as he was in sight of others.

"No." I managed to keep my voice even. "He wasn't alone, but he was the victim of a trap, a very clever trap planned and put into operation Thursday night. Let me show you." I gestured for them to come close.

They approached hesitantly.

I rested my hands on top of the box. "This is very important. I want you both to look—and especially you, Betty—and tell me if you've ever seen this before." I opened the box.

It was not a remarkable portable hair dryer except for its size. I travel with one that is scarcely larger than my hand. I hadn't used it here because the guest bathroom contained a hair dryer. That, too, was a small one. This one, made of pale gray plastic, was huge, the motor casing a good five inches in circumference, the nozzle four inches long with a two-inch diameter. Its only distinguishing mark was a hairline crack that ran from a wedge-shaped chip in the rim to midway down the length of the nozzle.

Rosalia spoke immediately. "No. I have never seen it, Mrs. Collins."

Betty stared at it with a sick fascination. "That is what killed Mr. Prescott?"

"Yes." I glanced around, spotted a pad by the telephone. It was easier to explain with a drawing. I drew the hot tub and its interior steps. "The hair dryer was taped against the right side of the interior steps"—I marked an X there—"then the cord, taped at five-inch intervals—waterproof tape, of course—came up the side of the tub, curled over the top, and ran down the redwood siding in the shadow of the exterior steps. The tape was tightly fastened at the bottom, then hidden under the monkey-grass border until it was plugged into an outlet."

The wet dryer reeked of chlorine. Would I ever smell chlorine without a sickening lurch of memory?

"The bubbles," Betty said faintly.

I understood what she meant and once again recognized the working of a shrewd mind.

Rosalia stared at Betty, puzzled.

"That's right," I agreed. "Mr. Prescott didn't see the hair dryer down there—no one who used the tub saw it—because the water jets kept the surface moving." Bubbles, lots of bubbles. I would never listen to Don Ho's champagne music again with pleasure. "I don't know if the hair dryer would have been noticed, even with the jets turned off, because this is a deep tub —five feet, I think—and the steps probably cast a shadow. In any event, he obviously didn't notice."

Betty's fingers picked at her polished-cotton uniform skirt. "I can't say for sure. But I saw a hair dryer just like this one. Gray and big. I left it in the suitcase because we have hair dryers in all the bathrooms."

God, was it going to be this easy? I couldn't believe my good fortune. "Whose suitcase, Betty?" I asked quietly.

Her hands clenched. She knew how much this mattered. Her answer was almost a whisper. "Mr. Dunnaway's."

Thunder boomed.

I passed Lyle in the upstairs central hall, sprawled in a crimson silk loveseat. He still worked the phone, his red hair still unbrushed, his bony, unshaven face intent. He ignored me as I walked by. I saw no one else.

Eerily enough, in contrast to the cataclysmic roar of the storm, the creaking and groaning of the house, the clatter and bang from outside as trees crashed and debris hurtled through the air, the inside of the house—all the lights blazing—was totally quiet. When I reached my room and stepped inside, I felt like a ghost returning to an ages-distant haunt. My covers were thrown back, just as I'd left them when the banging shutter awakened me early that morning. There was the notebook—with its list of information to seek—that I'd dropped when the *Miranda B.* exploded.

I placed the box with the hair dryer on the desk and picked up the pad.

Now I could never ask Chase why Trevor Dunnaway wasn't among those his private detective investigated in regard to the vicious gossip supplied to the author of *The Man Who Picks Presidents.*

Betty had identified the deadly hair dryer as Trevor's.

But Trevor and I had stood together and heard the shots fired at Chase on Friday morning.

Surely we weren't dealing with two separate murder plans —the shooting and the electrocution?

I couldn't believe that.

Though they certainly were entirely different methods. Weren't they?

I pulled off my soggy clothes, draped them in the bathroom. I looked longingly at the shower. It would be wonderful to get warm.

Like an echo in my mind, I heard Chase saying: "I'm going to get warm first."

I yanked a towel from the heated rack—oh, God, the luxuries on this island—and briskly rubbed the warm, soft cotton against my chilled body. I took time to dry my hair, then hurried back into the bedroom, slipped into a fresh blouse, slacks, and socks. But I put my soggy tennis shoes back on. They might be wet, but they afforded a good deal more traction than leather-soled shoes. They would work better if I had to scramble into a rescue helicopter or boat. Not that a boat or helicopter could reach us now. No transport made by man could survive these battering winds.

But all of this merely occupied the perimeter of my mind. I was trying to sort out what had happened and what I should do. But I couldn't get past the fact that nothing jibed.

I picked up a brush, swiftly brushed my hair, and began to pin it up.

If the murderer had put the hair dryer in the hot tub on Thursday night, why hadn't Chase been electrocuted when he jumped in the tub on Friday morning?

Had the hot tub been intended merely as a backup plan in case the shooting at the point failed—as it had?

How did the destruction of the *Miranda B.* fit in?

Its sole effect—so far as I could see—was to maroon everyone on the island with a hurricane approaching.

Surely that was the act of a madman. Was there a single person on this island who didn't understand the gravity of remaining on this sliver of low-lying land in the path of a huge storm? Was killing Chase worth risking the murderer's own life?

Could the shooting on the point and the booby-trapped hot

tub have been independent efforts? Murderer One and Murderer Two? And how about the poisoned candy? Who got credit for that?

As a young police friend of mine would urge: *Get real.*

But weren't these efforts so different that they argued independent origins?

I jammed a last pin into my upswept hair, reached for my lipstick.

I shook my head at my reflection in the mirror. My eyes narrowed. "No." I said it aloud. "Hell, no. Candy and a gun and electricity. But they all have one common denominator: an effort to remain unseen and unknown by their object."

That still didn't explain to me, though, the greatest anomaly. Why hadn't that deadly hair dryer been plugged in when Chase jumped into the tub Friday morning?

If I understood that, I knew I would understand everything.

The house shook. The wind thudded against it like the frenzied hoofbeats of a thousand runaway horses.

I looked at the windows, opaque with rain. Yes, I would understand everything . . . except the thought processes of the murderous person who had stranded us on this island.

How long would Chase's beautiful house withstand this inhuman battering? I pictured Haskell's tiny, insubstantial raft, caught in a maelstrom of foam and spearing rain. *Oh, Haskell, dear God I hope you've made land. Please, God.* But it did no good to imagine his fate.

I turned, grabbed up the soggy cardboard box. While there was time left, I would use it.

Even over the roar of the storm I could hear the crashing chords from the music room when I stepped into the hall. I wondered if Valerie was trying to drown out the shriek of the wind, or if she was simply determined to spend what might be her last hours immersed in the transcendent glory of Rachmaninoff, caught up and transformed beyond fear, avidly sucking out of her life its last creative endeavor.

I stopped at the door closest to the central hall and knocked.

I was lifting my hand to knock again when the door opened.

I looked up at Trevor Dunnaway.

There was only a trace of the cosseted, comfortable, self-assured man I'd met at tea two days before. His thick blond hair was neatly combed, his pale pink sports shirt crisp, his white cotton slacks immaculate, but he stared at me hollow-eyed, his handsome face slack with heartsick fear.

It told me one fact, and I was hungry for facts: This man hadn't blown up the *Miranda B.* This man knew what could happen in hurricanes.

I smelled bourbon.

I looked at the glass in his hand.

He followed my glance, held up the tumbler, half-full of amber liquid. "Want some?" His voice was just a little slurred.

"No, thanks. Can we talk for a minute?" I shifted the box to my hip.

He blinked, then shrugged. "Sure. Come on in. What do you want to talk about? Modern art? Communications in the next century? The wonders of electricity?" He shook his head violently. "Not funny, Trevor. Goddamn not funny." He stumbled to a linen-upholstered settee with a green and tan background of marshland and geese flying overhead. He hunched in one corner and lifted the glass.

I crossed to the couch and plumped the box down beside him.

He swallowed the bourbon and choked a little.

I flipped open the lid. "Take a look."

The lawyer wouldn't turn his head. He held the tumbler in both hands and stared at the scant half-inch of bourbon remaining. Abruptly, he downed the rest of it. "I don't have to look at the goddamn thing. I saw it in the goddamn hot tub."

"I want to know if you've ever seen it before."

Slowly he lifted his head. "You'd make a great little prosecuting attorney, lady. And if I were my client, I'd tell me to keep my goddamn mouth shut. But what the hell difference does it make? We're all going to die." He looked toward the windows. "I wonder what will break first, the wings or the central part of the house? Maybe it's time we went to our nice hidey-hole with the food and the flashlights." But he made no move to go.

I wasn't going to be deflected. "The hair dryer. It's yours?"

"Mine all right. I recognized it. Stupid little crack on the nozzle. I dropped it when I was in San Francisco last week. Cracked it. Still worked fine." He looked faintly sick. "God, yes, it works. Worked. Killed Chase, didn't it?" His mouth quivered. "Somebody took it and used it to kill him. God, a hair dryer." He wasn't too numbed to be indignant. "Why me? Why the hell me?"

"When did you see it last?" The window behind the couch rattled like castanets.

He blinked. "Damned if I know. I've been trying to think. Maid unpacked my stuff. I didn't need it, got one in the bathroom. The hell of it is, I don't know. I never looked in my suitcase—not till I came back here from that damn tub and went to the closet and it wasn't there." He blinked again. "I knew it wasn't there, I'd just seen it. But I had to be sure." Without warning, he lurched to his feet and shambled across the room. He picked up the open bottle of bourbon on the dresser, poured another slug. He drained the glass and stared at me owlishly. "Why take *my* damn hair dryer?"

It was a good question. But not the most important question that needed answering.

The second-floor hallway was deserted. I saw the mobile phone lying on the crimson silk loveseat. I wondered where Lyle was. I knew what he would be doing: thinking, struggling, working to devise a means to survive. I never doubted that. Lyle was a man determined to prevail—just as Chase had been. Finally, Chase had not prevailed. Was Lyle the reason why?

I stood there, trying to decide in which direction to go. Thoughts glimmered in my mind with the swiftness and incalculability of goldfish darting deep in a summer pond. I listened for a moment. Valerie had left Rachmaninoff for Debussy, and I took some comfort from—when the notes could be heard above the shrieking of the storm—the elegant strains, played with great delicacy.

I hadn't liked her when we met. I wished now we'd had more time. I still might not like her overmuch, but there was more to Valerie than her sleek veneer suggested.

I wished, too, that in what looked to be the waning moments of my life I had a hand to grasp, loving eyes to look into. But perhaps it was better to reach the end while engaged in the pursuit of a task. Certainly that was the way I'd spent my life. "Work for the night is coming"—that verse by Annie Walker has been my touchstone. I could have done worse.

It was much too late to waste time now.

I was beyond worrying about niceties such as entering rooms uninvited.

When no one answered my knock at the first bedroom in the opposite second-story wing, I opened the door. The bed was unmade, of course. Betty hadn't followed her usual housekeeping routine. Not this morning. But the untidiness went further than rumpled covers. A sandy beach towel was flung carelessly over a chair. Damp swim trunks lay on the floor halfway between the door and the bath. A half-empty soda bottle and a crumb-littered plate were on the bedside table. Two boating magazines lay beside them. There was a bronze picture frame on the dresser. I picked it up. The young woman with curly black hair laughed into the camera. Her arm lay easily around the shoulders of the sturdy little boy. He held a basketball in the crook of one arm. Haskell's mother had been a very beautiful young woman. I put down the frame and said, once again, one more time as I had so often this long morning, a prayer for the safety of her son.

I knocked at the door across the hall. Again no answer. I

opened it. Except for the unmade bed, this room was immaculate. Betty wouldn't have had to do much cleaning here. When I checked the closet, I knew it was Burton's room. The clothes hanging there were too small and too inexpensive to belong to any of the other men. I took a couple of minutes to prowl through his things, looking in the obvious places. I lifted up the apparent bottom lining of his large suitcase and saw a lurid magazine cover featuring a blindfolded, naked woman, her back bloodied with welts, her hands chained. So much for Burton's boyish appearance. I wondered what Chase's response would have been had he realized his secretary's preoccupation with brutal, exploitive sex. Distaste? Disinterest? But if Burton's ugly little hobby hadn't affected Chase personally, he wouldn't have cared, would he?

He hadn't cared about Rosalia.

I moved quickly, more to put that thought behind me than with any expectation of learning much. Burton's checkbook revealed a balance of two hundred and thirty-six dollars and eight cents. But a secret income—say for the juicy tidbits provided the author of Chase's unauthorized biography—would certainly not be reflected in the secretary's everyday bank account. Burton wasn't a fool, and he knew all about Chase's efforts to discover the source's identity.

Burton, defensive, unconfident, sullen. Had the little man already taken refuge in the music room?

I doubted it.

If Burton didn't like women—and I was certain of that now—he would avoid as long as possible being at close quarters with an overpowering personality like Valerie's.

But he might want company. Maybe he'd gone down to the kitchen. The day I arrived flashed into my mind. I remembered the contempt with which Burton had treated Frank Hudson, who had brought me across the sound. No, the secretary saw himself as above the staff. Not quite a guest, but certainly better than a house employee. No, he wouldn't be in the kitchen.

When I opened the door of Chase's study, Burton was at the desk, shoving folders into a couple of briefcases.

"What are you doing?" I suppose the surprise was evident in my voice. I wouldn't have expected Burton to be thinking about his job.

The glance he gave me was hard to decipher, a combination of discomfort and smarmy self-assurance. His face was unshaven. He held up a folder for me to see. "I thought I should get the papers. About the refinancing. Roger will need them."

Why didn't I believe him?

I walked over to the desk. As he opened folders, flipped through the papers, I could see figures and letters, so it all made sense. But there was something about his expression—it reminded me of Richard Nixon responding to Watergate.

"Exemplary of you. Continuing to give your best effort for your late employer, despite the difficult conditions. Heroism under fire, so to speak."

"I thought I should," he snapped, his voice reedy with indignation.

"Fine. Exemplary, as I said. But while you're working, let's talk for a minute." I took one of the easy chairs by the desk. "You've been here to the island with Chase and Miranda a number of times, right?"

He hefted a yellow folder, checked the tab, eyed the almost-full briefcase, shook his head, returned it to the desk, and selected another. "Yes." He crammed this file into the second briefcase.

"Tell me about Chase's schedule." The exquisite comfort of the chair only emphasized the weariness of my body.

He gave me a blank look. "What difference does it make now?"

"A lot. I take it he had a regular schedule here. Or didn't he?" I moved to the edge of the seat. The depths of this chair were too tempting. I wanted to sink back, let it all go, but my journey wasn't finished.

The secretary poked and prodded at the folders. "Yes, he did. Every morning he got up at six-thirty, swam for half an hour, then . . . then he relaxed in the hot tub for ten minutes or so. He got out and toweled off and came to the patio. He always had granola and yogurt for breakfast. After a shower and dressing he'd go to the point—if the weather was nice—and paint until lunchtime. In the afternoons he'd work for a while, then he and Mrs. Prescott would go out in the *Miranda B.*"

I fingered the smooth linen of the chair arm. "So you could count on Chase being in that hot tub every morning about seven o'clock?"

Burton's head jerked up. "What do you mean *I* could count on it? Listen, I didn't have any reason to murder Mr. Prescott. I'm not going to be blamed for—"

"Burton, cool it." I didn't bother to hide my irritation.

He broke off, his cheeks flushed.

"I didn't mean you in particular." I kept it brisk and impersonal. "I meant anyone who'd ever visited this island—including you—would know that Chase would be in that tub at seven A.M."

"Yeah." His glance slid sullenly away from me.

"Okay. Who of the people here this weekend have been on this island before?"

He didn't have to think about it. "Why, everyone—except you."

Everyone. Haskell, too.

"Did anyone else ever get in the hot tub?"

Burton tried to pull the second briefcase shut, but it gaped open at least an inch. "I didn't pay any attention. I think Roger did a couple of times."

"In the mornings? With his dad?"

Burton shook his head. "I don't think so. Nobody else was into exercise first thing in the morning. Except Mr. Stedman. But he jogs. I don't think he ever came to the pool early. Haskell used the pool the most. In the afternoons."

I would check with everyone, of course. But only Chase used the hot tub first thing in the morning. So anyone could have crept out late at night after everyone else was in bed, plugged in the hair dryer, and felt confident Chase would be the victim.

But if everything was in place on Thursday night, why had the murderer waited until Friday night to plug in the hair dryer?

Why instead had the murderer tried to shoot Chase on Friday morning?

Why, why, why?

"The gunshots." I said it aloud, my voice vexed.

Burton's body tensed.

I knew as clearly as if it had been branded on his forehead that Burton knew something about the shooting.

"Okay, Burton, what did you see?" If it was not the voice of judgment, it was close enough.

He gripped the edge of the open briefcase. "I told you. I already told you. I wrote it all down, and I told you. Why are you always riding me?"

I got up, walked to the desk, put my palms on it, and leaned toward him. "Burton, if you saw who shot at Chase, you'd better tell me before the killer comes after you."

Burton yanked with all his strength, the briefcase closed, and he faced me with a defiant smirk. An *amused* smirk. "You think you're so smart." He didn't try to hide the soul-deep hostility in his voice. "You know the answer to everything. Well, you're not as smart as you think you are. I've already told you — I didn't see anybody shoot at Chase." He grabbed the two briefcases and hurried around the desk. He opened the door. I had one last glimpse of his taunting eyes.

They reminded me of the eyes of a little boy on a schoolground, sticking out his tongue at the hated teacher.

However, I know the truth when I hear it. Burton had not seen the gunman.

But he knew more than he was telling about that attack on Chase.

If he hadn't seen the person shooting at Chase, what could it have been? A sound? A smell?

I would have to check my notes, but, as I recalled, he was one of the first to arrive on the scene.

What did he know?

And how could I—

The lights went out.

The study was plunged into a somber dimness. The storm howled. I thought for a moment that it had worsened, then I realized that for the first time I was merely hearing it without the masking background hum of the air-conditioning.

I walked across the room, pulled aside the heavy velvet drapes.

The rain undulated against the windowpane, making it as cloudy as an inches-thick sheet of plastic. I pressed my face against the cool glass and looked and looked. It was like viewing the world through thick-lensed glasses, nothing quite in focus, but I could make out enough to know that the minutes were running out. The gardens were gone. No trace remained. Where there had been roses and azaleas and vine-laden arbors, now there was only an oily gray swirling mass of water puckered by the frenzied, wind-driven rain. Italian cypress, uprooted by the wash of waves, bobbed in the water, along with deck chairs and jagged chunks of wood from the splintered buildings that had stood on the lower-lying land behind the main house.

The roar of the wind sounded like lost souls crying for sanctuary.

A square, lantern-style flashlight rested on the piano, spreading a cone of light over Valerie. The actress stared at the ivory keys. Her fingers delicately touched them and the notes were a tiny ghostly melody scarcely audible over the storm, more imagined than heard. Brahms Lullaby. I wondered what untroubled memories it evoked, what solace it provided. In the dim illumination her elegant bone structure and unblemished skin looked young. I caught for an instant a glimpse of how lovely she'd once been.

I glanced around the music room. Enrique hunched by a boarded-up window, his head cocked, listening, listening. Rosalia and Betty sat against the wall in the corner nearest that window. Rosalia held a rosary in her hands. Her eyes were closed; her lips moved soundlessly. Betty's arms and head rested on her bent knees. But where were the others, Roger and Trevor and Lyle and Burton and Miranda? Certainly it was time and past time for everyone to seek refuge here.

"Damn!"

I swung around.

Lyle Stedman swore again. "Damn it to hell!" He grappled awkwardly, halfway through the door, with a sheeted mattress. One end of the mattress caught a bronze stand. The stand toppled over. A Chinese dragon vase crashed noisily to the floor.

Valerie's fingers never faltered on the keyboard. Rosalia jumped to her feet. Betty lifted her head to watch, but Enrique, his head bent, continued to listen.

"Let's try to get the damn thing on its side." Roger's flushed face appeared in the doorway.

The men shoved and heaved and the mattress quivered and

slid, then flopped heavily onto the parquet flooring, knocking a magazine stand over.

Lyle moved quickly, shoving a chair and a side table out of the way. "Come on, Roger, let's start a stack here."

Roger bent and picked up his end. Lyle grabbed the front, and the two men maneuvered the mattress up against the wall.

Lyle grunted, "Okay. Come on," and headed back out into the hall.

"Lyle, what are you doing?" I called after him.

He paused in the doorway. "Whistling 'Dixie,' Mrs. Collins." His rawboned face looked gaunt but composed. "I've heard the damn things float. So what the hell, why not?"

Betty pressed her hands against her lips and stared in mute misery at the mattress.

So Lyle and Roger hadn't given up. Well, neither had I. "Enrique, we need to round everyone up. Find Trevor and Burton, tell them to come here." I picked up a flashlight from the several collected on the coffee table. "I'll go down for Mrs. Prescott."

Enrique looked toward me. His face had a greenish sweaty look.

The wind screamed and roared and thundered now, louder than a thousand freight trains, a sky full of bombers, a killer avalanche.

"No." It was all Enrique said. He turned back to the window, reached up, held tight to the two-by-fours buttressing the sheet of plywood.

I didn't have time to deal with him. I knew he could not be bullied, not like Burton. Both were hostile to women but in such different ways. Enrique was dangerous. If I had a weapon—I felt a jolt as the realization struck me. Oh, Christ, a weapon! How could I have forgotten?

Betty struggled to her feet. "I'll go, ma'am."

But I was already running. I didn't even bother to answer.

I was midway down the main staircase when the house shuddered, a slow, wrenching, grinding reverberation.

I could feel it in the soles of my feet. The stair treads trembled. The wall to my left canted away from me. The now useless chandelier that hung over the main entryway swung, back and forth, back and forth. The oblong crystals struck one another over and over, a cascade of sound, windchimes gone mad.

"Miranda?" I stood midway down the staircase, clutching the leaning banister, and shouted.

Where was she? God, she was so young. And this morning she'd been so distraught. This was wrong. Dead wrong. She should long ago have been upstairs in the secured area. Miranda and the weapon I'd stupidly forgotten.

I switched on the flashlight and hurried down the leaning staircase, frantic with worry. Why hadn't I thought of her sooner? Chase would have wanted her protected. *Oh, God, let Miranda be all right.*

I held the light out in front of me, chest high. Its thin beam scarcely penetrated the gloom. I collided with a knee-high jardiniere that had slid to the middle of the foyer. I winced and turned to my right, sweeping the cone of light along the floor. God, it was dark. I wished I'd asked Roger or Lyle to come with me. But I couldn't take the time to go back now.

I refused to think about time, and how little time might be left.

I plunged down the hallway, calling her name. "Miranda! Miranda!" My foreboding grew. Why didn't she answer? But perhaps she didn't hear me. The wail of the storm was an assault on the mind and heart, an unending, almost unendurable, gut-deep howl.

I half-limped, half-ran down the hall.

The door to Chase and Miranda's suite was closed.

I twisted the doorknob.

It turned. Thank God, it turned.

I pushed the door open.

"Miranda!"

Not a sound or a movement except for the tumult of the storm.

I darted the flashlight's beam swiftly around the room.

Miranda lay on her back in bed. Her head, the black hair curling sweetly, rested against the white satin pillow. Her eyes were closed. She looked like a child, vulnerable and appealing, deep in sleep.

It took all my strength to approach that bed and grasp a limp hand. Such a small and dainty hand. I uncurled the fingers, lifted up a small brown plastic vial.

Valium.

I tucked the bottle in the pocket of my slacks, then held her wrist and searched for a pulse.

Nothing.

I pressed a finger against the carotid artery beneath her right ear.

It was so hard to tell, with the roaring noise that surrounded me, pressed against me, and the shifting, quivering moan of the walls.

I thought I felt a tiny, almost imperceptible quiver.

I swung around, reached across to the dresser, and grabbed up an ornate silver-backed mirror. I held it close to Miranda's lips.

Faintly, ever so faintly, the mirror clouded.

I dropped the heavy mirror, slewed around, and ran, the beam of the flashlight swinging madly in front of me.

"Roger! Lyle! Roger! Help! Help, help!"

"Henrie O? Mrs. Collins?" Lyle was midway down the stairs.

"Hurry!" I screamed. "Miranda's ill. I need your help."

Lyle thudded down the stairs, Roger on his heels. They slowed enough to let me lead the way with the flashlight.

In the bedroom I swung the light toward the bed. Lyle took one look and grabbed the slight form up in his arms.

"Bring a pillow and some covers," I told Roger. As they moved, I swiftly searched the warm-up suit Chase had discarded early that morning when he decided to swim, searched it and found nothing. I looked frantically around. The blue blazer Chase had worn the day before . . . I ran to it. No gun in the pocket. I danced the light over the chests, the tables. No gun. No gun.

"Come on," Lyle shouted raggedly. "Come on!"

Time to search had run out. Was the gun in that room? Or had someone taken it after Chase died?

But I could look no longer. I took the lead, shining my flashlight up the shadowy hallway. We were almost back at the central hallway, almost there, when the front door sagged inward.

There was no especial noise, or perhaps it simply couldn't be heard above the hurricane-force winds.

One moment we were hurrying forward, only a few feet away from safety; the next a waist-high wall of water rushed inside with greedy sucking noises, sweeping us off our feet, slamming us against the walls.

I went under.

The water was cold. My shoulder struck something hard. A hot, quick pain shot down my left arm. I lost my grip on the flashlight. I struggled to regain my footing, swallowed water, came up choking.

A strong hand grabbed my shirt and lifted me up.

"Hold on to the stairs," Roger sputtered.

I grabbed a baluster, and he turned away and went splashing off into the darkness.

"Oh, Christ, help me," Lyle called, "I've lost her. I've lost her."

I saw an eerie glow deep in the water.

I took a deep breath and ducked down. My fingers closed around the flashlight just as another big surge of water swept in, lifting it and me. When I broke the surface, sputtering, I paddled a few feet and was back to the stairs.

I swung the light swiftly around the entryway.

Vases, picture frames, and satin sofa cushions bobbed in the water. A straight chair, almost upright, floated close enough to touch. I jerked out of the way as a grandfather clock loomed out of the darkness to crash into the stairs, easily snapping that portion of the banister.

Lyle and Roger fended off furniture as they dove down and down, frantically searching for Miranda.

I pointed the beam at the water. There, toward the back of the hall, a glimmer of white . . .

I held the flash steady. "Lyle, Roger, there she is!"

They both went down and came up together, supporting her between them.

Miranda moaned. She was still alive!

I pulled myself up and over the banister and flopped onto the steps. I was halfway up the steps, but they were already awash.

Holding Miranda and trying to reach the stairs, Lyle fought the deadly current. Roger swam alongside, fending off the bigger pieces of flotsam. The noise was all around us.

I kept the light steady.

At last they reached the stairway. His chest heaving, Lyle came up out of the water, still cradling Miranda in his arms. He clambered up the steps. Roger, breathing heavily, an angry scratch on his face, was close behind them.

We were almost to the top when the entire staircase shuddered beneath us. With a rending crack the bottom two-thirds of the stairs crumbled away from the wall.

Where we had been there was nothing but swirling water and jagged, jabbing pieces of wood.

Betty stood waiting for us on the landing. Whimpering, she stared past us at the sucking, hissing, foaming water.

"Betty." I was so glad to see someone who would help. "We've got to hurry. Mrs. Prescott is very ill. We need to get her warm. Could you get some towels and a couple of blankets?"

I wished I knew what more to do. Should we try to induce vomiting? But she was unconscious, and there would be a danger of choking. What was needed—if it wasn't already too late —was a stomach pump and possibly a blood-cleansing apparatus. All we could safely do now was keep her warm.

We carried her into the music room. Trevor was sprawled on a long sofa. He lurched to his feet. "My God, what now?" He smelled like whiskey, but his voice wasn't as slurred as it had been earlier and his movements were assured.

"An overdose." I shooed the wet and bedraggled men over to a corner. Trevor poured mugs of broth for them. I wondered if I'd ever have a chance to tell Rosalia what a good job she'd done in bringing up supplies.

When Betty came in, carrying a good half-dozen towels, Valerie and I stripped off Miranda's sodden nightgown and gently dried her off.

"We've got to wrap her in something warm." I started for the hall.

"Don't go out there," Roger cried. "The whole wing may go anytime."

"I'll hurry." I threw it over my shoulder. I dashed through the upper central hall and ran down the corridor—the sloping corridor—to my room. I grabbed a cotton robe for Miranda and some dry clothing for me. Back in the music room we slipped my robe around Miranda and tucked her into a blanket on one of the mattresses Lyle and Roger had brought.

It was nice to have a task to cling to, something to think about besides the pounding of the rain and the slam of the winds against the house and the gun that I should have found. With each surge of water the central part of the house shuddered.

How much more could this wounded structure withstand?

It wasn't until we had Miranda as comfortable as possible and I had ducked into a dark corner to dry myself off and redress that I paid any attention to the room and its occupants.

Rosalia knelt at the foot of Miranda's mattress, her hands gently smoothing the blanket. Valerie sat beside the mattress, holding one of Miranda's limp hands in hers. Enrique remained hunched by the window. His eyes were closed, his arms crossed tightly across his chest. Trevor leaned against the piano, but his head was up and he was listening. I could feel his fear all the way across the room. Roger and Lyle huddled under blankets. Each held a mug in his hands.

God, yes. Something hot to drink, to fight the chill that bit deep into my bones. I was halfway across the room to the table with its array of thermoses when I suddenly stopped.

"Burton. Where's Burton?" I looked at Betty.

"I hunted for him, Mrs. Collins. Just like you told me to. I went to his room"—she pointed toward the other wing—"and I checked Mr. Prescott's study, but I couldn't find him anywhere. I called for him and then I was going to go downstairs. I didn't know where he could be, but I wanted to find him and ask him to come here like you told me to and I got to the top of the stairs. That's when you were bringing Mrs. Prescott up the steps. If I hadn't waited for you to come up the stairs, I would have gone down and I would be in the water."

Damn Burton. He wouldn't be any help, but this was by far the safest place to be.

"I can't see any reason why he would have gone downstairs," I said briskly. "So he's up here somewhere. We've just missed him. I'll go to his room. Why don't you take another look in the study? Did you have a flashlight with you?"

Betty shook her head.

I gave her a flashlight.

It only took a minute to cross the hall—at a greater slant now—and check the secretary's room. When I opened the door, I knew immediately that he wasn't there. A window had blown in, shattering glass across the bed. Waves of rain swept inside, drenching the spread and the carpet.

My flashlight beam danced from the bed to the dresser to the desk. I walked that way and saw the briefcases he'd stuffed with folders sitting open on the desk. They, too, were wet, the luxuriant leather sodden.

As I watched, a black snake curled over the lip of one briefcase. The reptile lifted its head, looked toward me.

I stumbled backward. The light flickered from the desk to the windowsill. A cottonmouth oozed over the sill. I aimed the flash down between the bed and the window. A tangle of snakes quivered, a dark shivery mass on the floor. A water moccasin, with that identifiable pit-viper mouth, slithered from beneath the bed.

I whirled around, ran toward the door.

The snakes were fleeing from the flood, seeking sanctuary wherever they could.

I could imagine them crawling over the house, under the eaves, onto the roof.

I hurried out the door, slammed it behind me.

And that's when the scream rose, high and hideous.

13

The tip of Burton's tongue stuck out between his teeth.

I saw that first.

We arrived at the study at the same moment and clustered in the doorway—Roger, Trevor, Lyle, and I—our flashlights aimed at the motionless figure sprawled on the floor between the desk and a bank of filing cabinets. The top drawer in the middle cabinet was pulled out.

Betty huddled against the wall, just inside the door, trembling. "He must have been there all the time," she whimpered, raising terrified eyes to us.

I looked at my watch. A quarter-past ten. I'd set out to look for Miranda and sent Betty in search of Burton for the first time about an hour earlier.

The maid pressed back against the wall. "Last time I just poked my head in the door and called. Nobody answered and it was all dark. Then I heard you calling for help, Mrs. Collins, and I didn't even think about him again." She looked down at the flashlight in her hand. "But this time I had the light and I saw his feet."

She swung the cone of light to the highly polished brown leather tassel loafers, then along Burton's body to his face. He was lying chestdown, but his face was turned toward us, resting on his right temple and jaw. So the poked-out tongue, blood thick at the tip where he'd bitten himself, was easy to see. But this time it wasn't a taunt. When Burton's assailant struck him down—and the bloody misshapen swelling behind his left ear was easy enough to see—the blow had jolted Burton's head forward and the reflexive movement of the floor of his mouth had thrust his tongue between his closing teeth.

"Oh, God," Trevor moaned.

I was the first to break out of our frozen tableau.

In a couple of strides I reached Burton. I knelt by him and with a ghastly sense of déjà vu picked up a limp hand to seek a pulse.

Lyle followed. His flash revealed the drops of blood spattered on Burton's downy stubble of blond beard.

"He's still alive." But his pulse was slow and erratic. I wondered how far the hematoma had spread, how much pressure was being exerted on the brain. Burton needed medical care immediately.

"If the Coast Guard comes . . ." I didn't finish. Any reasonable chance of rescue had ended when the storm struck.

Roger dropped down beside me. "Could he have fallen, hit his head on the desk?"

I gave him a level look. "How? What do you suggest? Practicing a backward flip without a pool? Levitation gone wrong? Look at him. He's lying in the wrong direction to have fallen and struck anything."

Roger's face reddened. "I thought maybe he lost his balance, something like that."

I didn't bother to answer. Instead, I swept my light in a gradually widening circle around Burton.

Nothing is ever new under the sun, of course, but I thought this might qualify as a highly unusual means of attack, the kind of weapon that would delight even jaded police reporters.

The slender marble statuette of Aphrodite had been flung away. A white gash scarred the gleaming parquet floor. The artwork had skidded, scoring a several-inches-long path, then lodged against the clawfoot of a spider-legged table. Blood and flesh and hair clumped on the three-inch-square bronze base.

I remembered watching Chase's hand close around the base of a statuette. I lifted the light, swept it across the mantel. The statuette was one of a pair. Its twin was still in place.

But the most telling evidence of all, the most meaningful, was the unstained beige cotton washcloth, thick and fluffy, lying a scant inch or two from Burton's polished loafers. I understood its significance immediately.

Roger pointed at the statuette. "Oh, God, look at the blood."

Lyle looked instead at the still, crumpled slight figure. "Why him? Why the hell go after him? Chase, yeah, somebody might have a reason."

As you did, I thought, *as you did*.

"But Burton? That's weird."

"Yeah, somebody's crazy, crazy as a loon." Trevor's self-control cracked. "Listen, don't anybody come near me." He was backing out into the hall. "Do you hear, don't anybody come near me!"

He was close to collapse, the collapse of a man who'd never in his life faced danger or horror. I turned toward him. I could only dimly see a shape behind the shaking flashlight. "Trevor, we're all going to stay together from now on. Don't worry. We'll take care of one another."

"Oh, yeah, just like we took care of Chase. Somebody damn sure took care of Chase. Listen," he said feverishly, "I don't know anything. I don't know who killed Chase. I don't know anything about Burton. Hell, I was with you when the bastard shot at Chase. I don't know a damn thing."

"Then you should be quite safe. Why don't you escort Betty back to the music room, Trevor? We'll all be along in just a moment."

"Yeah, yeah, sure." The lawyer turned and headed up the hall. He didn't wait for Betty.

She hesitated.

"Go with Mr. Dunnaway, Betty. We'll take care of everything here." I was glad to see them go. I couldn't watch everyone at once, and I needed to be quite certain that I didn't miss a thing when it came time to move Burton. The odious little man might die, but I damn sure didn't want to give his attacker another crack at him. It wouldn't take much: pressure on one of the carotid arteries, a handkerchief stuffed in his mouth, his nostrils pinched shut. . . .

Someone was going to be devastated to know that Burton still lived. I wished I'd had the wit to look swiftly about when I announced he was alive. But I hadn't.

From this moment on I had one priority: to protect Burton.

"When the going gets tough . . ." Lyle drawled. He didn't bother to hide his disgust at Trevor's behavior. "First thing I'm going to do when we get back to Atlanta is fire that jerk." There was an instant of silence, then he slanted a look at Roger. "If that's okay, boss."

Roger stood very still. He wasn't smiling. His gaze locked with Lyle's. "Yeah, Trevor's a jerk." He spoke thoughtfully. "Dad thought he was a hell of a lawyer. I don't know if physical courage has to be included in a lawyer's job description. But we're a long way from having to worry about that right now, Lyle. Right now we need to worry about Burton and whether we can keep him alive until help comes." He shook his head. "Burton! I can't believe anybody'd deliberately try to hurt him."

Perhaps I'm cursed—or blessed—with a cynical mindset. It seemed to me that both Roger and Lyle were being more than a little disingenuous in their exclamations of surprise that the unctuous little secretary was a victim. The guilty person would be delighted to convince everyone that it must be a crazed killer, thus discouraging speculation about what Burton might have done to invite violence.

Because I suddenly felt confident that I knew the reason behind this attempted murder.

It all went back to the flurry of shots fired at Chase on Friday morning. I was sure of it. I didn't say it aloud. But I would have bet a Coast Guard rescue vessel I was right.

"As you say, Roger, we'll worry about what happened to Burton later. Right now I want to—"

The house shuddered, then gave a screech of agony like a living thing dismembered.

The floor beneath us tilted.

"Oh, Christ, the house is going, she's going!" Lyle shouted.

Time expands when the mind confronts mortal danger.

It has happened to me before. Once when a guerrilla lifted a submachine gun to fire at a party of journalists; once when a hijacker grappled with a pilot and the airplane plummeted out of control; once when a gunman darted from a crowd, his pistol aimed at the President.

Time and distance were meaningless, as if each instance would last forever.

And this moment.

The images in my mind and heart were always the same: Richard's laughing face and the touch of my mother's hands and Emily's bell-like laughter.

Those experiences convinced me that nothing matters— nothing truly matters—in life except people. Not money, not fame, not challenge, not despair, not hatred, not power—only the people who have loved you and whom you love.

The floor stopped heaving. A last tremor rippled through the wood.

I don't know how long we crouched where we had fallen— yes, the jolt was that strong—before Roger spoke. "Good God, what do you suppose that was?"

Lyle swung his flashlight toward the door.

Water lapped over the doorsill.

"The south wing. It's gone." I managed to keep my voice even, but I couldn't keep the shock out of it though I had covered Camille and knew too well what hurricanes could do— knocking off this portion or that of a hotel, destroying one house, leaving the one next door untouched. There is a capriciousness, an unexpectedness about hurricanes that makes them that much more terrifying. "We've got to get back to the music room." I didn't tell Lyle and Roger about the snakes. Maybe we'd be lucky. At the very least we should have a few minutes before the desperate reptiles clinging to the central portion of the house found this new raw wound to enter.

I didn't have to urge the men to hurry. It took only minutes to fold a card table, gently lift Burton's battered head, and slide him onto it. Roger and Lyle carried the table while I held Burton's legs up and as straight as I could manage. We could only hope that Burton hadn't suffered a neck or spinal injury. But we had no choice. We had to move him to the safest area.

I pointed the flashlight toward the floor. It helped Roger and Lyle see their way. It helped me watch for snakes. So far, so good. But I didn't breathe easily until we'd cautiously maneuvered our burden down the hall and into the music room and closed the door behind us.

Lyle's mattresses, intended for use in a desperate last-ditch effort to survive, were piled three deep along the south wall of the music room, an interior wall. Miranda, as unmoving as the dead, lay on the top mattress, securely wrapped in a cream-colored wool blanket. Valerie still sat beside her, holding a limp hand.

Betty moved forward quickly to help. Valerie laid that slack hand on the covers and stood, looking toward us.

Lyle hesitated, shifting his hands for a better grip. "We need to get a mattress out from under Miranda's."

"No," I said quickly. "There's room for Burton on the top mattress. We can ease Miranda over and put him next to her."

It made sense. It was easier. But my objective was to keep them together. I must watch out for both at the same time.

One of us had slammed that statuette onto Burton's skull.

Had Miranda swallowed that bottle of pills of her own accord? Distraught with grief over Chase's murder or undone by guilt, it was possible, but I was in no mood to take chances.

Betty and Valerie gently moved Miranda, snug in her blanket, to the interior of the mattress, close to the wall.

Lyle and Roger shifted Burton onto the mattress. Fresh blood stained the ticking beneath his head. I checked his pulse. Still erratic, perhaps a little weaker. His left cheek felt clammy beneath my fingers.

"A blanket, please."

Betty brought a light wool coverlet.

As I gently drew it over Burton, I decided to make sure the head wound was all we had to deal with. I handed my flashlight to Betty and carefully eased a hand under his body and inside his blazer. I felt the crackle of an envelope in an inside pocket. My immediate instinct is always to investigate. I didn't hesitate. I pulled the envelope out.

The plain white envelope was full of crisp fifty-dollar bills. It was quite a stack. This was a nice sum, perhaps as much as five thousand dollars.

Roger looked over my shoulder. "Oh, that's probably a stash of cash from the safe. Dad always had plenty of cash with him. I guess Burton was bringing it along in case the house was completely washed away."

There wasn't even a note of suspicion in Roger's voice.

I hoped Roger had the benefit of tough advisers when he took control of his father's empire. Otherwise, it would be broken up and swallowed by predators faster than vultures devouring a road kill.

Because my take on that envelope was entirely different. Burton was stealing the money. I knew it as certainly as I know that Santa's jolly ho-ho-ho is cynically designed to make cash registers ring. Now I understood why it had surprised me to find Burton hard at work this morning salvaging files, why the episode had had a counterfeit feel. That had been his excuse, his cover, to get his fingers on cash that nobody might ever ask about. A nice, safe, cautious little crime. If the house went, who would ever know or question what had happened to the valuable contents of that safe?

If the house went . . .

I lifted my head, looked toward the boarded-over windows. Somehow they still held against the unceasing, demonic attack of the wind and rain. Water was beginning to seep inside and trickle down the walls.

I handed the envelope to Roger.

Without comment, he folded and stuffed it into a back pocket of his shorts. He followed my gaze and stared at the windows, listening to the banshee scream of the storm.

A heavy thump shook the wall that once had faced the tennis courts. A good-size something, a tree limb or a drowned deer perhaps, had struck the house.

Every eye watched the wall, but miraculously it held. Each in his or her own fashion welcomed the extra minutes or perhaps even seconds of protection afforded us from the killing storm outside. Who could hope for more?

I was once a prisoner of government forces in El Salvador, along with three leftist guerrillas. We had expected to die at dawn. Indeed, we most certainly would have except for a fifteen-year-old boy who had led us to safety while our captors slept from the drugged wine he'd brought them. On that night I had felt the unmistakable touch of death's bony fingers, on that night and during this long day.

Waiting helplessly to die engenders a somber quiet. It pulls the muscles of the face, plants frightful phantasms in the mind, recalls to the heart a lifetime's triumphs and failures.

But I wasn't going to sit here and wait to die. I still had a task—to discover Chase's murderer and Burton's attacker—and I intended to see it through. If I could.

But first I looked around the room. Trevor was lying, pillows propped behind him, on the couch next to the opposite wall, just past the piano. His right arm shielded his face; he had withdrawn. I glanced from one face to another, stopped finally at Rosalia's. She once again sat on the floor in the southeast corner of the room. Her hands held the rosary, her lips moved, her eyes were closed.

"Rosalia."

She lifted her head.

"Will you come here, please, and sit beside Mr. Andrews?"

Rosalia hurried across the room.

Valerie, still standing beside the mattresses, stretched and yawned. After breakfast she'd put on green linen slacks and a cream cotton turtleneck. Her golden hair was pulled up in a ponytail with a saucy green bow. Her clothes were cheerful; her face was not. Deep lines bracketed those cherry-red lips, her skin was ashen, dark shadows made her eyes huge. "I don't have designs on the little man, but if Rosalia suits you better, that's fine with me." She turned and walked to the piano, slid onto the seat, and touched a key. The note was almost lost in the howl of the wind.

I followed the actress with my eyes. No one could ever say Valerie had slow thought processes.

Rosalia came up to me.

"Why don't you sit here?" I patted the mattress, next to Burton.

The housekeeper darted an unhappy look at me but obediently took her place, perching gingerly on the mattress's edge.

"Would you like something hot from a thermos?"

She started to get up.

"No, please. I want you to stay with Burton. If anyone comes near, watch carefully. Shout if anyone tries to touch him." I spoke loudly enough so that all in the room could hear, even over the storm.

Rosalia's fingers clutched the rosary. Her wide eyes clung to my face.

That done, I moved to the table in front of the fireplace. It was laden with thermoses, bottles of water, and several covered plates. I poured a mug of coffee for Rosalia and for myself. I lifted the cloth from the first plate and snagged a ham sandwich. I've never tasted anything as good as that sandwich: the ham had a sweet-sugary Virginia-smoke taste, the mustard was just hot enough, the French bread was flaky and fresh. It took only four bites to devour the sandwich. Then I took Rosalia's coffee to her and gulped some of mine.

And looked around our beleaguered sanctuary.

I was seeking a killer, a thoughtful, cunning, plan-ahead killer.

The washcloth had told me that. The killer had grabbed it, carried it along in a pocket. The plan: to use the washcloth when gripping the statuette. There would be no incriminating fingerprints.

The washcloth told me even more:

That the attack on Burton was premeditated.

That the killer was well acquainted with Chase's study and the mantel with its twin statuettes.

That Burton sought out the killer for a clandestine meeting.

Further, I was confident I knew the reason for this clandestine meeting. Burton knew—somehow—who had shot at Chase.

That person could be anyone on the island except myself, Trevor Dunnaway, and Haskell. Trevor and I were excluded because we had been together when the shots rang out. Haskell was excluded because he was no longer on the island and could not possibly have attacked Burton. (I would not think about the size of the waves now pounding the coast.)

I looked from figure to figure in this fragile shelter against the storm and knew one was my quarry. And there was the matter of Chase's missing gun. Why hadn't I noticed, after the explosion, whether the jacket of Chase's warm-up had bulged?

The gun hadn't been in his nylon warm-up or his blazer after he died. Chase could have dropped it into a dresser drawer when he put on his swimsuit. If so, that was fine. But it could well be that someone else had retrieved the gun after Chase died —and helped Miranda swallow pills.

What mattered now was whether the killer had hidden the gun somewhere in this room.

I started with the mattresses. I had Rosalia help me pull them out from the wall, taking care not to jostle Burton or

Miranda. I poked the flashlight into the space, then made certain no gun was tucked beneath any of the mattresses at any point.

I played the light along the floor by the south wall, passing Lyle in his straight chair.

He raised a dark red eyebrow. "Looking for something special?"

I hesitated. I had no intention of underestimating the murderer, and it would occur to even the meanest intelligence that I was definitely searching for something. I decided to take a gamble.

"Chase's gun is missing. I couldn't find it anywhere this morning."

I motioned for Betty to stand up, flashed the light where she'd been sitting, then stepped past Enrique to investigate the maroon velvet drapes. I took my time over the boards, testing them to be certain one wasn't loose—with a gun behind it.

"Christ." Lyle swung off the chair, then picked it up and slammed it on the floor to get attention. "Okay, everybody, on your feet. Instead of Who's Got the Thimble, we're playing a grown-up version, Who's Got Chase's Gun. First rule, stand where you are and don't move until Henrie checks you out. Any sudden movements may result in a broken back—I play rugby and I won't tackle you for the fun of it."

Out of the corner of my eye I saw even Rosalia scramble to her feet. Everyone was standing now, including Valerie by the piano.

I wasn't sure whether to be irritated or amused. But it was effective, I'd give Lyle that. Maybe the direct way, in this instance, was best. I suppose I do have a tendency to be serpentine. And it didn't escape my notice that he was standing guard while I did the searching, the act of a man with nothing to fear or the ploy of a man who knew the gun would turn up but wanted to focus suspicion on the others.

I pulled the screen away from the fireplace, got down on one knee, and craned my head to look up into the chimney. It was thoroughly nasty, not having been designed to repel the kind of rain we were enduring. Water ran in driblets down the sides. Pools of black gooey gunk were collecting beneath the andiron. I yanked my head back and motioned for Betty to bring me one of the extra two-by-fours lying near the windows.

I stuck the plank up into the interior of the fireplace and prodded the shelving where the chimney widened.

All I got was more gunk.

When I wriggled back and stood on the hearth, holding the two-by-four, Valerie called out in a portentous voice, "And what can the Wicked Witch of the West tell us about our future?"

"Santa Claus won't be coming down this chimney. More than that I cannot say." I propped the board against the fireplace. Next I checked the table. It took only a moment to be certain that no gun was hidden beneath a fold of cloth.

In quick succession I explored the curtains of the second window, again yanking and tugging on the boards, opened the corner china cabinet, pulled up the cushions of the two couches along the north wall, including the one where Trevor had rested.

"Trevor, if you'll pull the couches out from the wall . . ."

He did, and I checked out that area.

"Now lift up one end of this one . . ."

The housekeeping on the island was certainly spectacular. Not a scrap of paper, a Kleenex, or a pen lay on the floor where the couch had sat. And ditto for the second one.

"Thanks, Trevor."

The lawyer put down the second couch, rubbed his back, then glared at me. "I guess I can sit down again, can't I?"

"Sure." I generally waved a hand around the room. "Thanks, Lyle. At ease, everybody. No gun, so we can all relax a—"

Valerie lifted the lid of the piano. "Hot, hot, hot," she cried, pointing with a crimson-tipped forefinger.

Lyle and I reached the piano together.

I made a quick decision—consequences be damned—and grabbed the weapon that rested on the strings of the piano. I looked up at Lyle. "Thanks, I'll take care of it."

"I'm sure you will. And you've effectively destroyed any fingerprints on it." His glance was cold and thoughtful.

"What are the odds there were any?" I wasn't going to worry about fingerprints; I was glad simply to have the weapon in hand. My hand.

It was either the gun Chase had had in the living room on Friday or its twin, a .32 Smith & Wesson revolver. I released the barrel latch to check the five-shot cylinder. It was full. I closed the latch and shoved the gun into the pocket of my slacks. A large patch pocket, fortunately. Probably designed for gardening tools. It served splendidly for a revolver.

Valerie gave an elaborate shrug. "Sorry I didn't detect a false note as I played, but what the hey! I'm only an actress, not Miss Marple."

"Anyone could have put the gun there," I said crisply. But it certainly underscored the reality that Valerie must have been absent from the piano at some time during the morning.

In any event, I felt the gun was almost an omen. At least the murderer wasn't armed. And, if not a sharpshooter, I am adequate with a handgun.

I should have remembered the old warning that possessing a gun is only meaningful if you are willing to shoot.

But I wasn't thinking about shooting. The gun was safely in my pocket, and now I felt free to begin my real quest.

Valerie slipped back onto the piano bench. Her fingers gently touched the keys. A hymn this time: "Nearer My God to Thee." Her eyes gazed off unseeingly. I wished I was close enough to look into their depths. But her face looked tranquil.

Roger still stood by the sideboard, filling his plate. He ate stolidly, seemingly voraciously hungry.

Lyle returned to his straight chair, straddled it again, his chin resting on his arms atop the rail. But his air of leashed strength betrayed that this man was ready to respond, whatever happened.

Enrique leaned against the wall, near the boarded-over windows, his arms folded tightly against his chest. His eyes were on me, and they were sullen.

Rosalia settled back down beside Burton.

Of them all, obviously I trusted the housekeeper the most. Or distrusted her the least. This murderer made quick decisions. I doubted if Rosalia had been capable of a decision since she married Enrique.

And there was Miranda to consider. After Chase's murder, Valerie had led the young widow off and put her to bed, leaving her to rest. But if Burton had gone down to see Miranda, could she have risen, found an excuse to accompany him to the study, and struck him down?

Oh, yes. She could have.

Then, stricken not so much by remorse as by despair—the husband she'd slain through jealousy, the secretary attacked in frantic self-protection, the storm that terrified her—Miranda might have gobbled down the pills, seeking oblivion from pain and fear.

No, I couldn't leave Miranda out of my calculations.

Or Betty.

Betty was back in her place against the wall, her arms locked around her upright knees, her head resting on her arms. Betty missed very little, yet she denied giving thought to her surroundings and the people for whom she worked. That interested me. And Betty had obviously had the opportunity to club Burton. In fact, I might have given her that opportunity when I sent her to find him.

Who else could have done it?

I prepared a tray: empty mugs, a thermos of coffee, sugar, cream, some cookies, several pieces of Bundt cake.

My first stop was the piano. If I listened hard, I could hear it despite the scream of the wind.

Valerie played the finishing chords of "Amazing Grace," then looked at me coolly. "From gun hunting to hostessing. My, you're versatile. But, sure, I'd like a cup. What's the price?"

"Some observations. Cream? Sugar?"

"Both. Lots."

I was generous.

She took the steaming mug, sipped appreciatively. "I could definitely play a heroine in a tumbril going to the guillotine. Wrenched from luxury—that's pure cream, you know, as rare today as milk in bottles—bound to the world by strings of silk and wondering what lies ahead. Everything. Nothing. Yes, I'd like that role."

I sipped my coffee. "What's the role you'll have in your next play?"

My light tone didn't fool Valerie, but the hand lifting the mug didn't waver.

In fact, she flicked me an amused glance. "You mean in the play that's going to be bankrolled by Chase's estate, pursuant to his generous promise at his final family dinner?"

"Yes. I'm sure Roger will honor his father's wishes." I ate a cucumber tea sandwich and wondered what had possessed Rosalia to fix tea sandwiches. It was delicious.

"I'm sure of it, too. Or I would be if I were sitting on dry land right now." She flexed her fingers, ran them up the scale. "And, believe me, if I were smart enough to engineer money for this play, I'd certainly be too smart to get stuck on an island like this."

It always came back to that. Why would Chase's murderer maroon all of us on the island in the path of a hurricane? If I understood that and discovered what Burton knew about the shots . . .

". . . clear to me," Valerie was saying thoughtfully, "that only two people are above suspicion—you and Trevor. Anyone else here could have shot at Chase. Anyone could have booby-trapped the tub. This morning anyone could have struck down that horrid little man." Her hand struck several dirgelike chords. She looked across the room toward the mattresses. The fine lines at the edges of her eyes deepened. "Did you find what hit Burton?"

I stood quite still. But, of course, she hadn't come to the study.

Or was that the point she was making?

Was I dealing with an honest woman or an extremely clever one?

I looked at her blandly. "The poker from the fireplace was lying beside him."

She shuddered. "God, can you imagine—think how a poker feels in your hand, heavy and smooth and cold. Think of raising it and swinging down hard, how that would feel, and the sound . . . Oh, Jesus, the sound! Poor little man."

If it was Valerie's hand that had lifted the marble statuette and swung it down onto flesh and bone, she was a consummate actress.

But the one thing I knew about her was that she *was* a consummate actress.

I swallowed another gulp of the hot, sharp French-roast coffee. "I know you were absorbed in your music, but do you have any idea if the others who were here—say between nine o'clock and ten—left for any period of time?"

Her right hand picked out harshly in single notes "Three Blind Mice." "Be nice if I could alibi someone, wouldn't it?" Her mouth twisted in a sardonic smile. "Be nice since it would give me an alibi, too. But you're out of luck. People were in and out." She shot a venomous look in Enrique's direction. "He can't give his wife a hand with carrying up the food and water, but he damn sure managed to slip out himself and come back a half hour or so later, plenty fat around the middle."

I, too, glanced toward Enrique. Yes, his shirt did blouse out around his waist.

"That's not cellulite," the actress drawled. "In fact, honey, I'll bet you that's a money belt, and it might be pretty interesting to know where he got it—and when."

"I'll find out."

She tilted her head, played a few bars from "The Pink Panther." "Damned if I don't think you will, Henrie O. Just for the record, why do you care?" Her tone was amused, with just the faintest undertone of admiration.

I finished my coffee, put it down, and picked up the tray. "Why not?" I retorted. "And also for the record, when did you leave the music room?"

"Bitch." But her tone was genial. "Sure, I left. A couple of times." Once again her eyes moved across the room. "For what it's worth, I don't like to see any living thing hurt. Not cats or dogs. Not even bugs. Certainly not humans."

"Right." As I moved away from the piano, I reminded myself that Valerie was an actress, a superb one. Had someone else forgotten that and lost his life as a consequence?

I offered Roger the sandwich tray.

"No more, thanks." He shot a hesitant look at me and cleared his throat. "You knew my dad pretty well, didn't you? A long time ago."

"Yes, Roger." Oh, yes, so well. But perhaps never well enough.

"When you were young." He looked uncomfortable. "I mean—I don't mean . . ."

I laughed. It was nice, it was wonderful, to have a reason to laugh. My self-esteem has never been keyed to age. "Roger, I'm an old lady—and glad enough to be one. I'd enjoy being one a bit longer. Look at it this way, everyone's nineteen only once. Or thirty-two. Or forty-six. Or whatever. Fair enough, right?"

Obviously, my laughter eased his mind. He even managed an uncertain grin in return.

"Please." And now his plea was open, unabashed. "Tell me, what was Dad like when he was young?"

"Exciting." I could hear the echo of youth in my voice, lighter and higher than usual.

My answer was honest. I wasn't naive enough to think that Roger had to be innocent because he asked about Chase. Roger appeared to be rather innocent and open, but that would be a useful guise to adopt, should he instead be devious and calculating. And he could have loved his father and still hated him enough to be his murderer and yet, on one level of his being, hunger to know more about the man who had both given him life and ruthlessly shaped that life.

A clatter on the roof brought every head up.

Lyle gripped the back of the straight chair. "One of the chimneys is going." Rosalia put her hands to her face. Valerie's hands came down hard on the keys. The music ended in a discordant crash.

Again I had the sense of urgency, of time running out. But if the end was coming soon, so soon, I might as well spend some of those final minutes responding to a human need. So I told Roger about Chase's vigor—"He could work all day, play poker half the night, and cover a train wreck at three the next morning. He was a good writer. That's what most people don't mention now. They concentrate on how he built an empire, the battles he fought to beat down competitors, buy up the best talent, corner markets. But he was a hell of a good writer."

Roger's face was puzzled. "I can hear in your voice that you cared for him, really cared. Why didn't it work out?"

I hadn't realized I was so transparent. But this was the

rock-bottom question, the question I would never answer for Roger. It was the judgment I'd made so many years ago: Chase was brilliant and creative and enormously gifted, handsome and entertaining and incredibly disciplined—and he was a man without principle.

But I didn't have to answer.

The deep, cavernous, enveloping roar of the wind was now a part of our being. We did not so much ignore it as unquestioningly accept it, expect it. For hours the house had quivered and shaken, moaned and rattled.

But the final onslaught still came as a shock.

An abrupt, heart-stopping, mind-numbing shock.

The roof exploded.

It was there; then it was gone. Tiles and timber and mortar and plaster crumbled down, the tearing, rending, crashing sounds mingling with our screams and shouts.

The wind rolled back that section of roof as neatly as a key curls the lid of a sardine can. Water that had collected on the rooftop sloshed down. That was the first cold, abrupt shock. Then came the needle-sharp rain. It stung every exposed piece of flesh. The wind pulled and tugged and pummeled, butting us like invisible goats.

Survival meant clinging to the furniture, a wall, any solid stationary object.

I tried to crawl across the floor toward the mattresses.

I could not move.

I don't know how long that lasted. Five minutes? Ten? It seemed an eternity. Life came down to wetness and cold and pressure, hanging on, clinging, surviving with the tenacity of an amoeba and just about as much control, knowing that there was no hope, that either the floor would give way, plunging us into the raging waters that surrounded the house, or hypothermia would cradle us in its deadly chill.

If anyone cried or shouted or called out now, no one heard.

Then, without warning, the storm ended.

One instant we were besieged. The next the rain stopped. Stopped.

The wind dropped from more than a hundred miles an hour—down, down, down—to sixty, fifty, forty, then to intermittent and unpredictable gusts, still strong, still gusty, but bearable.

We could stand, shakily, uncertainly, but we could stand.

Even more remarkable to minds and spirits overwhelmed by the seemingly never-ending force and intensity of the storm was the sunlight.

Watery, greenish, weak. But it was sunlight.

I heard the exclamations of the others—

"My God, where's the island?" Lyle stood next to the east wall that was sheared in a diagonal from top right to bottom left. "We're all that's left. We're *all* that's left!"

"It's over, it's over!" Valerie sounded dazed. The rain or the water from the roof had loosened her hair. The scrappy wind tugged at the wet tendrils.

"Look at the water! It's almost up to the second story." Roger hung perilously over the side.

Trevor pointed at the china cabinet. "God!" The winds had dumped it forward. Only the piano had kept it from crushing him.

—and I understood their fascination, but my own gaze was riveted on the far horizon and the thick black clouds that climbed skyward to the west. I turned slowly. The sky was clear to the east, but I didn't doubt what lay beyond our sight: more thick black wall clouds, clouds climbing thousands of feet, clouds encircling us in the eye of the hurricane.

14

Only a special few ever see the eye of a hurricane and live to tell it: adrenaline-fueled pilots of weather planes, sailors in seaworthy—and lucky—ships, and some thrill-seekers who chase hurricanes with video cameras.

Most do not live to tell it.

One of the pluses of a long life in the news business is a brain packed with odds and ends of information, sometimes useful, sometimes entertaining, sometimes devastating.

Covering Camille taught me a lot about hurricanes.

The eye of a hurricane can be as much as twenty miles across. The more severe the storm, the smaller the eye.

It could take as long as two hours to pass if we were, say, at the western edge of the eye even with the center of the circumference. Or it could take, depending upon our position, as little as fifteen minutes.

So where the hell was the mobile phone!

Like a commentator viewing destruction from a helicopter, Roger's voice continued. ". . . drowned animals everywhere, deer, field rats, wild turkeys, squirrels . . . oh"—his voice dropped—"a raccoon. And there's . . ."

I was turning toward the door to the central hall—that wall was still standing, despite the partial removal of the roof—when the commentary paused, then Roger said in a puzzled tone, "Something's moving under the eaves. I can't exactly tell— Oh, my God!"

He jumped back and looked wildly around. "Quick, quick. Lyle, get me a two-by-four!"

I saw the snake.

"No, Roger," I yelled. "Back away, back away slowly. Stay still the rest of you. Absolutely still."

We had one piece of good luck. The snake was oozing calmly over the broken masonry. The reptile wasn't poised to attack. It was seeking safety.

We had one piece of bad luck. This was a huge diamond-back rattlesnake, one of the most venomous and dangerous reptiles in America.

The rattler paused, lifted its head.

"Don't move, Roger! Stay absolutely still. Listen to me, the snake isn't attacking. It will only bite if it feels threatened. Do not move."

I didn't tell him that snakes can jump more than half their body length to attack. Our wisest course was to wait, leave the diamondback alone, stay still.

Above all, we must not frighten the rattler.

The light breeze fluttered the drapes near the window. The snake turned its head. It felt the vibration.

It was big, six feet in length at least, the dark diamonds distinct on the amber back. The rattlers were darkish coils at its end.

Finally the snake lowered its head and began to move, pushing itself forward, gripping with its scales, pull-push, pull-push.

We all stood like statues.

The rattler oozed down the wall, moved forward, passing within inches of Roger's shoes.

Every eye watched its progress.

The diamondback moved toward the piano and the wreckage of the china cabinet. It swarmed up onto broken pieces of the furniture, then disappeared, slithering into the wreckage.

I held up a warning hand. We had to move, we had to go, but where? I looked around. The roof to the north appeared to be in place. "We can climb up on the roof. Everyone move quietly and slowly toward the wall." I gestured behind me. "There may be more snakes. But they'll likely stop here, once they feel safe from the flood."

I pulled the piano bench to the wall, placed a chair on it, and clambered up.

I'd not given any thought to the construction of the island house. Now I realized that tile eaves projected from the sides. The roof itself was flat and covered with a gritty tar surface. A chimney had toppled and bricks were strewn in irregular clumps.

Shards of tile, tree limbs, and clumps of tennis netting littered the rooftop. The wind, sharp and gusty, rippled standing water from the deluge.

But this portion of the central roof seemed to be intact.

If it had weak spots, I couldn't see them.

And I didn't see any snakes. At the moment. But others would come, some poisonous, some not. But even the nonpoisonous, if frightened, will bite, and some, like the brown water snake, will bite and keep on biting.

I thought about it for a moment, then slowly grinned. We were saved by the eaves. The snakes obviously sought the first secure area, the dry, protected space beneath the eaves. The reason the rattler had swarmed into the music room was because the roof above it had been peeled back and it had lost its retreat.

So, atop the roof, we might not be faced with slithery wanderers seeking sanctuary.

I pointed at the roof and yelled, "No snakes."

That got me instant cooperation.

Trevor was on his way up to the roof before I finished speaking.

I caught his arm as he climbed over. "Stay right here. We'll need you to help. When we bring Burton and Miranda."

I was a little surprised, but the lawyer meekly did as he was told, though when his eyes kept sliding past us to the music room, he shuddered.

Roger and Lyle helped me. We moved both Burton and Miranda up to the roof, and Trevor lifted them over. Roger and Lyle climbed down, intending to retrieve a mattress.

The standing water was draining—thank God for excellent architecture—and I was able to find a relatively dry spot in the middle of the roof for our injured charges. I asked Rosalia and Betty to guard them. I told Trevor to patrol the perimeter of the building. "Watch for snakes," I ordered.

I went back to the edge of the roof where Valerie stood. "Go back down and see if you can find any thermoses. And didn't Rosalia and Betty bring up some big bottles of bottled water to the music room?"

Valerie pushed back a lank lock of hair. "God, you don't

mind asking, do you? You know something, you would have made a wonderful nun."

But after a wary look below, she eased back onto the chair and dropped to the music-room floor. She was back atop the chair in a flash, passing up a pair of thermoses. "The rest are smashed. The food's gone. But there are three big bottles of water. I'll have Enrique get them."

She called to Enrique, and he nodded.

I reached down, grabbed her hand, and helped her scramble onto the roof.

Enrique retrieved the bottles and handed them up.

Valerie and I hauled them over.

Valerie rolled them, one at a time, to our little storehouse of goods near the chimney. "Next time I'm resting I'll try out for a stevedore job. God, it feels good to use muscles." She followed me back to the roof edge.

I swung my leg over the broken wall.

Valerie reached out, caught my arm. "Don't go back down. You've done your part." Her fingers tightened spasmodically. "Oh, Lord, *look*!" She pointed, and it seemed odd that the polish on her fingernail was still a brilliant crimson, as perfect as if fresh from the beauty salon. "There's a cottonmouth that got by Roger. Roger, Roger, careful, behind *you*!"

Roger froze.

Lyle wheeled around, but Roger was between him and the coiled muddy-brown snake. White mouth open wide, tail shimmying, the alarmed cottonmouth was poised to strike.

I almost pulled out the gun, but a shot that took out the snake would also have struck Roger. I had only one possible chance. I reached down, grabbed a broken half of brick, and threw it fast and hard.

The brick smacked into the snake in mid-lunge.

And Lyle plunged past Roger and brought down a plank, crushing the cottonmouth's head.

Valerie turned an astonished face toward me. "How the hell did you do that?"

"Softball. A long time ago. I played catcher." I was rather proud of my percentage of outs at second. And I could already feel a twinge in my elbow.

"When you weren't riding a broomstick," she muttered.

I climbed back down into the music room, watching where I stepped.

Lyle called out, "Get anything you want to take up there. When you're finished, we'll all go up."

I stayed away from the broken-up china cabinet. That territory belonged to a particular diamondback. But I looked diligently elsewhere. The mobile phone was gone.

Lyle helped me hunt.

"I put it on the table by the fireplace." He used the two-by-four to flip over cushions.

Roger and Lyle tossed some cushions up to the roof. I found another unbroken thermos. Enrique pulled some two-by-fours free from what was left of the windows. We even managed to drag out the middle mattress and shove it up onto the roof to provide a dry, soft resting place for Burton and Miranda.

That was our last task.

Finally on the roof to stay, I took a deep breath and looked around.

The sun seemed far, far away.

That was haze.

I looked to the west. I no longer saw that ominous wall of blackness. But I knew it wasn't time to break out the champagne. It merely meant the eye was moving. Closer at hand, the sky was hazy with a greenish cast and as far as the eye could see there was nothing but muddy, foam-flecked, roiling water.

I looked to the east. It was awesome to realize that I could see all the way to the ocean. It was as if a giant hand had reached down and snatched up the pine trees. The floodwaters swirled over the dunes and the forest and only an occasional wind-peeled branch stuck up from the angry brownish-gray water.

Nothing remained of the storage building with the generator and the room-size freezer where Chase's body had been taken. The tennis courts, of course, were long gone.

This central portion of the house, which had been built on the island's highest ridge, was the only man-made structure still standing. Floodwaters lapped above the first-floor windows. The current looked swift. The water would pull and tug at this remnant, eroding the ground beneath it, pushing on weakened walls.

When the eye passed, when the storm began again in all its ferocity, how long could this battered structure last? As for us —I looked around the roof at the band of survivors—we now had no place to hide, no protection from two-hundred-mile-an-hour winds, from cold, stiletto-sharp rain that could drive all living warmth from our bodies.

But we had survived to this point. The air was balmy. I could feel my cold, wet clothes beginning to dry.

Roger, Enrique, and Lyle patrolled the roof edge. Trevor knelt by the broken chimney. He was stacking fragments of bricks into a mound. Should it come down to a struggle for the last space, we had two-by-fours and bricks; the snakes had fangs and agility.

Valerie sat with her back against the foot or so of chimney still in place, her face lifted to the sun, her eyes closed. Her shining golden hair, beginning to dry, sprung in wiry curls around her face. She might have been sixteen.

I realized suddenly how tired I was, how very tired. The explosion—God, that seemed a lifetime ago. I looked at my watch. It was like trying to decipher foreign script. I could see the numerals, of course, but they didn't make sense. Not against the enormity of what we had endured.

Could it possibly be just eleven-forty-one?

The *Miranda B.* had exploded at half-past three, eight hours ago.

Chase had died at just after seven A.M.

We had found Burton at shortly after ten.

I wanted desperately to drop down on the roof, rest against one of the cushions.

But I turned and forced my leaden legs to cross to the center of the roof and our invalids.

Perhaps our other piece of luck—at least for Burton and Miranda—was the fact that only half of the music-room roof had been peeled back by the winds, so the mattresses and their human occupants had remained at least partially sheltered. They had been damp when we lifted them to the roof but not drenched—and not suffering from hypothermia.

When the storm resumed . . . But I wasn't going to think about that now.

I dropped down on one knee, next to Rosalia. "Any change?"

"Mrs. Prescott makes a little sound every now and then and sometimes she moves a little. But Mr. Andrews, no, no, he does nothing. But I think he is still breathing." Her hand touched Burton's shoulder protectively. "There is no shelter here. Nothing to protect them." Her eyes stared somberly out at the ocean. Rosalia had grown up in Cuba. She knew about hurricanes, and she understood that our storm wasn't over.

I slowly rose. My arthritic knee ached.

We looked at each other, and we both understood.

She touched her rosary. "I will pray," she said.

I stayed for a moment more. Miranda lay on her back, a still, beautiful sleeping princess untouched by her devastated surroundings. I wished I'd talked more to her this morning before she—or someone else—had poured out the contents of that plastic vial. Was Miranda simply one more victim? Or was she a murderess escaping the consequences of her actions? Her breathing seemed a little less labored, but that might not mean much. Had she suffered liver damage? Brain damage? What were the consequences of this long delay in treatment?

As for Burton—I felt queasy when I looked at his wound. It was crusting. Hard, black dried blood protruded from the swollen mass behind his ear. Blood had seeped down to glaze the collar of his blazer, making it dark and shiny and rigid. His skin had an ugly bluish tinge. The only improvement was that at some point when he was being moved, his teeth had come free from that poor wounded tongue. His mouth was still open, blood stained its corners, but his tongue was mercifully retracted.

I bent close to that open mouth, ignored the sweet-sickish smell of blood, and finally, finally felt the tiniest flutter of breath.

I drew back, touched his skin. Clammy.

I reached out, patted Rosalia's thin shoulder. "Thank you for taking care of him. Will you stay with him?"

"Yes, Mrs. Collins. Betty and I will. As long as we can." She glanced to the east.

I looked past Rosalia at Betty. She wasn't close enough to harm Burton. I'd like to think she wouldn't. But I still didn't have any answers. Any answers at all.

As I stood, the fatigue washed over me. It would be so easy to drop down beside Valerie and close my eyes, let the warmth of the sunlight touch me with fingers of life and let my mind drift, taking memories and thoughts as they came.

But anger flickered beneath exhaustion.

I suppose I've always been angry. That's what drives most writers, the hot, steady, consuming flame of anger against injustice and dishonesty and exploitation; against sham and artifice and greed; against arrogance and brutality and deceitfulness; against betrayal and indifference and cruelty.

I would not give up.

At the least, the very least, I wanted to confront the person who had willfully and wantonly taken Chase's life, gravely injured Burton, and brought young, frail Miranda to despair.

I glanced again at her pale, unresponsive face. It could be the face of a murderess. I knew that.

Then, unwillingly, I looked to the east.

The sky was darkening, thickening. I couldn't yet see the ribbed wall of the storm, but it was coming.

The only sounds were the scrape of the men's shoes as they patrolled the sides of the building, the gurgle and shush of water eddying around us, the bewildered cry of a disoriented gull.

It was time—I hoped I had the time—to go back, to remember, to think.

It began with a dog bounding across the room to snatch a poisoned candy.

That summer weekend, every person on this roof, other than myself, had had access to Chase's study in his New York brownstone.

Lyle Stedman abruptly stopped his patrol and stared out to sea, his hawk-strong face somber. He was a man whose appearance immediately captured attention: the sleek copper hair, bold nose, firm mouth, and blunt chin. No one would look at Lyle and expect to prevail—whatever the struggle—without a hard, long, and vicious fight. He was a man sublimely convinced of his own worth, supremely certain of his success. An ambitious man, a man who intended one day to head Prescott Communications. As I watched, Lyle's face tightened in an angry frown. He reached down, scooped up a brick, and heaved it as far as he could.

It sank into the swirling water.

Lyle's hands balled into fists. He faced a force he couldn't defeat, and his thwarted fury was palpable. It would take very little to ignite him.

Roger Prescott watched the fragment of brick disappear, too, his usually genial face empty of everything but weariness — and resignation. Roger took a step toward Lyle, then stopped, as if in recognition that he was powerless to help. Good-humored, kindly, hopeful Roger, a man passionate in his beliefs. Were ideals more important to him than people? He saw the power for good that his father's empire could provide. Had he succumbed to the old siren song of the ends justifying the means?

Roger turned suddenly, looked straight at me. He had sensed my eyes upon him. He looked like a teddy bear that had been left out in the rain, his blond hair scraggly, his clothes wrinkled. He forced a smile. "Like Robinson Crusoe, aren't we?" He didn't wait for an answer but began his walk along the edge of the roof again. Perhaps he knew there wasn't a good answer.

The sounds were the same: the scuff of the men's shoes, the swish and gurgle of water, the occasional frantic call of a gull. But no one spoke.

Trevor still crouched near the shattered chimney, working on his mound of broken bricks. His eyes followed his hands as they reached out and retrieved the pieces of chimney. His entire being was focused on the task, the better to exclude the terrifying reality of his surroundings. It was hard to recall the polished, confident, handsome man I'd met on my arrival with this frightened, diminished creature.

I walked across the roof.

"How's it going, Trevor?" I heard the rattle and scrape as he reached for another brick.

He didn't look up; his eyes never left the brick in his hand. "Fine, fine."

If ever someone was vulnerable to assault, it was this man. If he knew anything at all, this was the time to find out. How much had he been in Chase's confidence? He'd known about the insurance policy, the policy that would make all the differ-ence for Lyle Stedman and for Roger. Chase had tried to keep that from me.

Had Chase kept anything else from me?

But I must feel my way carefully. "Trevor, you owe your loyalty to the living. Not to the dead."

Reluctantly his eyes slid from the brick in his hand to my face. His look twisted my heart; it was a look of despair mixed with fear and horror.

"Trevor, tell me, did Chase have any idea at all who wanted to kill him? Did he tell you anything that would help us?"

I wasn't prepared for his response.

"Chase." Trevor's voice shook. "I wish I'd never come to this goddamned island. Never. Never. Never." His breathing was jerky. "You work for somebody, and they call the shots. Right? But it was stupid, stupid from start to finish. And now look what's happened to us. We're going to die—all because of Chase."

I wouldn't have called Chase's plan stupid. Actually, it was quite in keeping with his character: daring, arrogant, secretive, determined. Foolish, yes. Obviously, it was entering the lion's den to invite a murderer to try again. That's what this carefully engineered gathering on the island came down to. Chase had refused, as he had refused all of his life, to do it the easy way, the ordinary way. Looking back it was easy to say, yes, Chase should have called the police about the poisoned candy. And there was no doubt but that he should have contacted the police after the shooting episode.

But Chase would—at all costs—have his own way.

And cost him it had.

Trevor's voice dropped. "I didn't want to come. I didn't want to. And now we're going to die, and it's all Chase's fault."

So Trevor had known all along the purpose of this gathering—and now he would have forfeited all his possessions to have made a different decision.

But I didn't suppose he'd ever been able to resist Chase.

I didn't fault him.

I, too, hadn't resisted Chase.

I looked down at the lawyer for a moment more and once again he was searching for pieces of brick, scrabbling across the graveled roof, picking them up, adding them to his mound.

I doubted if he even remembered the reason for this stockpile. But it didn't matter. It was his focus, his reality, and it protected him from what was to come.

The eastern horizon was darkening by the minute. Too soon the wall cloud would curve closer to us and we would see the bunchy layers of blackness climbing to heaven.

Trevor wouldn't look that way.

Valerie St. Vincent wasn't looking either. She still rested against the remnant of the chimney. A bleak smile touched her mouth. Her eyes were closed. I wondered what fragment of memory touched her. Did she recall a triumphant scene upon the stage that she loved, when she and an audience had the overpowering, incredible sense of fusion that can occur only in drama? She was a woman who would wither away without a creative goal. Chase had promised to consider backing her play after dinner on our second night. She hadn't had that promise when the candy was poisoned or the gun fired on the island. But she was on very good terms with Roger. Did she feel confident that Roger would fund her? Confident enough to commit murder? Resting, her face upturned to the sun for warmth, Valerie's unstudied classic beauty was as perfect as a marble sculpture of Minerva and, like the cool, milky stone, not quite human.

A muffled cry, and a sharp crack sounded.

I whirled toward the south.

Enrique lifted his arm. The blunt board whipped down,

pounding the writhing body of a water moccasin. Enrique's tan, pocked face was utterly absorbed. The bulge around his middle, beneath his shirt, was quite evident when he lifted his arm.

I had a theory. I almost crossed the roof to confront him. I put my hand inside the patch pocket of my slacks and gripped the butt of the gun. I stood that way for a long moment, then slowly the tension eased out of my shoulders. No. Not now. Later—if later came—I would see to him.

He kept on striking the pulpy head long after the snake was dead. Although not a tall man, Enrique had a powerful physique, muscular arms, broad shoulders, thin hips, and strong legs. I thought of Haskell's Christmas Eve memory. I felt sure Enrique cared no more about the two men he'd shot that night than he did about the snake he'd just killed. He dispatched victims with ferocious competence.

I looked toward Rosalia, still guarding our wounded.

She watched her husband. Her face was expressionless.

I walked closer. "Rosalia, I've been meaning to ask you, what do you and Enrique intend to do with the money Mr. Prescott left you in his will?"

"The money?" Her eyes stared up at me, then slid past me, stopped. She drew her breath in sharply. "I don't know anything about money, Mrs. Collins. All of that my husband sees to."

I knew Enrique stood close behind me. He must have moved quickly and cat-footedly, for I heard no sound.

I turned to meet his dark and hostile stare. He still held the stained board in his right hand. I said insistently, "Quite a lot of money."

Enrique shook his head. "I know nothing about money from Mr. Prescott's will." His eyes moved down to his wife. Rosalia drew in on herself, seemed to grow smaller as we watched.

"That's a lie." Betty looked up defiantly. "I've heard them talking about it. He said it would be money for the dog races."

Enrique bolted forward, the board upraised.

Betty began to scramble backward.

"No." It wasn't a shout, but it was loud enough. "If you touch her, Enrique, you're a dead man." The gun in my hand felt good. I don't like guns. If you draw a gun, you have to be prepared to use it. I was. I didn't like the way it made me feel inside, but still I was glad—glad—to have it in my hand and to face him down.

Roger and Lyle started across the roof.

I held up my left hand. "It's all right. He's going to do just as he's told."

Enrique had beaten and brutalized women for so long, he couldn't believe the equation had changed. But, finally, slowly, he lowered his arm, his eyes full of fury, his mouth twisted with rage, his skin an ugly saffron. Then his eyes flickered toward Roger. "A misunderstanding, Mr. Prescott. That is all it is." He moved lithely back toward the edge of the roof. He did give one backward glance, and I knew I had a mortal enemy.

Roger hurried up. "What's going on?"

"A disagreement," I said easily. "But not a misunderstanding. Enrique knew your father left him money in the will. He lied about it."

Roger looked down at Rosalia.

"And there's no good your asking Rosalia. He abuses her. She's afraid to tell the truth." I stuck the gun back in my pocket.

Roger's horrified gaze swung back to me.

"I'm sure."

Roger knelt down beside the mattress. "Rosalia, when we get to shore, I'll take care of you."

Tears welled in the housekeeper's eyes.

"I mean that. Don't be frightened." His clothes were rumpled and his face pale, an odd figure for a rescuer. I liked Roger. But I also watched him closely. I didn't want anyone too near Burton.

Roger awkwardly patted Rosalia's shoulder, then stood up and turned toward me. The wind stirred his blond hair, tugged at his clothes. I was suddenly aware that the wind was stronger, harder, flatter. I looked to the east.

There was the wall cloud, huge and black and curved. Roger opened his mouth.

I didn't want to talk now. "Later." I wanted to think. There wasn't much time left. I was like a marathoner. It didn't matter now so much what the end of the race would bring, I was content merely to finish.

Rosalia, too, felt the freshening wind. She was on her knees, spreading another blanket over Burton.

Burton.

Abruptly I realized that I had gone about everything the wrong way.

Because Burton was the key.

Yes, Burton had been attacked because his continued existence threatened the murderer.

But how?

The obvious conclusion would be that Burton had demanded money for his silence.

That rang false.

Not because the secretary was honest. He wasn't honest. I was positive he'd taken the envelope filled with cash from Chase's safe once he knew Chase was dead and the house was likely to be destroyed by a hurricane. As I'd thought when I found the envelope, it was a quick, clean, comfortable, safe little crime.

That was Burton's speed.

Burton wouldn't have the guts to blackmail a murderer.

So if Burton hadn't engaged in blackmail, what had he

done that had brought the marble statuette crashing down on his head?

What did I know about Burton?

He was a toady.

He didn't know what to do if someone flouted his superior's orders.

He was always on the defensive, expecting to be blamed for whatever had gone wrong.

He loathed women.

He wouldn't want to do anything that would get him in trouble. But the envelope filled with cash—oh, that was easy. He could always claim, as naive Roger had quickly assumed, that he'd taken the money to save it, intending all along to give it to Roger or to Chase's estate.

I was scarcely breathing I was so intent. I was close, I knew it. Burton . . . authority . . . afraid . . .

Oh, God, suddenly I knew who. There was only one possible answer. I still didn't know why, but I knew who.

That's when Lyle shouted—a deep, hoarse, triumphant shout. Quickly he pulled his limp, smudged T-shirt over his head, tied it around the end of a two-by-four, raised the board, and began to wave it back and forth.

We all shouted, yet above our clamor we could hear the *whop whop* of the Coast Guard rescue helicopters coming from the west, two of them, their white and orange colors vivid against the sickly green sky.

They were coming. Oh, God, they were coming!

I made a quick and fateful decision.

Would I have done it without the gun in my pocket?

I'll never know.

But it wasn't simply the gun. I don't think it was. I hope it wasn't. It was a conviction that never again would our murderer be as vulnerable, that unless I sprang a trap now, the killer would walk away forever scot-free because no material clues would be available to help the authorities. We didn't even have Chase's body anymore.

And perhaps my subconscious had already absorbed the truth. Shielding Burton's battered head with my body, I called out, "Burton's awake. My God, he's awake!"

One person stiffened, stiffened and didn't move.

Rosalia leaned closer.

I cocked my bent head as if listening hard.

The helicopters were close now, perhaps a hundred yards away.

The noise from the rotors boomed over us: *whop whop whop whop.*

When I rose and turned, I held the gun in my hand. I began to walk toward him.

He saw me coming.

"You are under arrest—a citizen's arrest until the Coast Guard arrives—for the attempted murder of Burton Andrews."

I should have remembered that cornered animals turn savage.

15

Savage and cunning.

Trevor Dunnaway slowly raised his hands.

He glanced up at the approaching helicopters, then he started to walk toward me.

I didn't worry. It was all over now. It never occurred to me to order him to remain where he was.

But Roger surprised me.

It all happened at once, Trevor walking toward me in apparent surrender and Roger abruptly lunging toward his father's murderer.

Startled, I swung toward Roger.

That instant was all Trevor needed.

In a rush and a jump, he scrambled to his left, flung Rosalia aside, and bent over Burton to snatch up Miranda. Holding her as a shield, he backed slowly across the roof to the east edge, then swung her small, limp body out over the swift-flowing floodwaters.

Roger skidded to a stop.

I aimed the gun at Trevor. But I couldn't take the chance. If Miranda went into that swirling water unconscious, we would never find her, get her out, save her.

"I'll throw her in." The lawyer's handsome face twisted with fear and an awful determination.

I took a single step toward him. The wildness in his eyes stopped me. I put the gun in my pocket. For now, it was useless and might make everything worse.

Roger made a noise deep in his throat and tensed, poised to jump.

I grabbed his arm and hung on. For Miranda's life. "No, Roger, no. He means it." And I clung.

Roger's chest heaved, his eyes glazed. "He killed Dad. He killed Dad!"

I yelled to be heard over the *whop whop whop whop* of the helicopter rotors. The white and orange crafts were directly overhead now. "Roger, he has Miranda. Wait, let me talk to him." I could feel Roger trembling.

The door in the lead copter slid back, and a blue-helmeted rescuer bellowed through a loud hailer, her firm voice clear. "Are there casualties among those to be rescued?"

Lyle took charge. He held up two fingers, then pointed toward the mattress. Then he held up eight fingers for the ambulatory evacuees. The wash of wind from the rotors whipped our sodden clothes against us, and the *whop whop whop whop* of the rotors drummed against our ears.

The flight mechanic called down, "Roger. Two injured, eight ambulatory." She advised through the loud hailer that the basket would be lowered first for the injured, then the remainder of the party, the injured and three passengers to the first copter, the remaining five to the second.

I gestured for Roger to stay put and I cautiously edged closer to Trevor. I pled with him. "This won't do you any good. Put her down, Trevor. You can't escape. Don't make things worse."

"Stay there, Henrie O." He was a big man. It was no effort for him to continue to hold Miranda's still body out over the water.

I halted. "This doesn't make sense!" I shouted. "You can't get away. Give it up. Look, they've thrown a line down to Lyle and now the basket is swinging down. Let's go put Miranda in it."

"Give me the gun." His eyes flickered from side to side.

I didn't like their feverish shine.

The flight mechanic called down: "Hustle. We have only minutes to load if we're to get back to the station before the eye moves on."

"What good will the gun do you, Trevor?" The wash from the rotors buffeted us. "You can't hope to kill us all. Even if you did, you'd be in clear view of the pilots. Give it up. You're through."

Whop whop whop whop.

"No. No way. Listen, I'll make a deal." His shout was hoarse and emphatic. "Miranda for the gun. It's easy, it's sweet. No problem. I'm not going to shoot anybody—unless they try to take me along. I'm staying here. That's final."

"You'll die if you stay!" I screamed it at him.

Whop whop whop whop.

"The hurricane's coming back." I pointed behind him, at the monstrous dark sky, purplish and black, awesome and horrifying.

Trevor didn't so much as glance at the clouds. "I'll take my chances."

Behind me I heard Lyle's shout to the flight mechanic operating the rescue hoist. "This way, this way! Great." And then the cry, "Here he comes," and I knew Burton's limp form was swinging up to the aircraft.

Roger took a step forward.

Trevor didn't miss Roger's move. "Five seconds," he yelled. "That's all you've got and she goes in. One . . . two . . ." He meant it. The muscles in his neck were distended. He was like a shot-putter, getting ready to heave. If I waited, Chase's young wife would be gone, flung to certain death.

Slowly, I drew the gun out of my pocket, placed it carefully on the roof, and kicked it toward Trevor.

It came to rest inches from him.

"Oh, Christ." Roger bunched to jump.

I swung around and grabbed him again and doggedly hung on. "No."

Gradually Roger eased back on his heels.

Watching us with those frantic, feverish eyes, Trevor edged forward, scooped up the gun, and put Miranda down on the roof.

I started to breathe again.

With the gun in his hand, Trevor gained confidence. Brusquely he gestured for Enrique to move away from the south edge, the torn section that opened down into the shattered music room.

Enrique moved. Quickly.

Trevor ran lightly to the side, swung a leg over. And then he was gone.

Roger already had his arms around Miranda.

The basket slipped down to the roof, and she was safely ensconced and on her way up to the helicopter.

Lyle gestured for me to go next.

I pointed at Rosalia and Betty.

Then they were gone, and Valerie was in the basket, swinging up into the sky.

Whop whop whop whop.

The flight mechanic leaned out, using the loud hailer. "Clarify count, please. Were told to rescue eleven. Aboard now are two injured, three ambulatory. We see four on the roof. Where are the remaining two?"

When we'd sent out our distress message over the mobile phone, we'd reported twelve stranded. At that time, Chase had been alive and Haskell had still been on the island. When Haskell left the island, Chase was alive. Now Chase was dead and Trevor gone, hiding out in the music room, desperately, crazily hoping to ride out the hurricane.

Haskell!

Haskell had made it through! That's why they were expecting eleven. They knew Haskell was safe. Haskell was alive!

I felt a swift rush of pure happiness.

But Lyle wasn't worrying about who came why or when. He didn't waste time. He held up four fingers, pointed at them emphatically. Did it once, twice.

"I read you: four remaining to be rescued." The basket swung down.

I was the second aboard the companion helicopter. I tried, shouting to be heard, to explain to our earnest young pilot that one man indeed remained on the island but that he was armed and dangerous, he'd committed murder twice and was refusing rescue, hoping to ride out the storm and escape before the authorities reached the island.

"Two murders?" the pilot yelled.

"Two."

"He won't come aboard," Lyle yelled.

Swiftly, the pilot commanded the flight mechanic to order Trevor to surrender. She shouted over the loud hailer. They gave him twenty seconds to respond.

Twenty seconds can seem like a lifetime.

But there was no movement. Nothing.

The helicopters turned and headed back to the mainland.

I craned my neck for a final backward glance at the muddy water surging around that remnant of a mansion. That small patch of roof was the only indication man had ever set foot on Dead Man's Island.

There was no trace of Trevor.

I tried to shake a strong feeling of unfinished business. In hoarse, truncated shouts, Lyle and I fleshed out the case against Trevor Dunnaway during that bumpy and tense flight to the Coast Guard station.

Lyle started it, putting me on the spot. "Burton was dead. He didn't tell you a damned thing. So how'd you know Trevor bashed him?"

The helicopter lurched, the noise made my ears ache. "Burton either knew something about those shots at Chase . . ." I paused, then lifted my voice again. ". . . or he fired them in collusion with somebody. In the first instance, his instinct would be to tell somebody. He would have trusted only two people. If it was the second case, only the same two could have been collaborators."

Lyle saw it at once, and I had a new appreciation of his perceptiveness. He leaned close, yelled in my ear. "Yeah, sure. The shooting alibied you and Trevor. So Burton would feel safe in going to either one of you. And that's true of the second proposition: the only people who gained anything from the shooting were you and Trevor. You were automatically eliminated from the list of suspects when Chase was killed."

The sky was heavy with clouds all around us now. The helicopter wobbled from the buffeting of the wind.

"So what's the truth—was Burton a good little fellow trying to report to somebody he trusted or was he involved in a plan to kill Chase?"

We didn't solve that.

But, yelling until we were hoarse, we came up with some plausible ideas, with a lot of conjecture thrown in:

That investigation would reveal Trevor to be involved in some kind of illegality within the Prescott empire.

That Trevor had used his own hair dryer in a kind of double bluff, counting on the fact that he was alibied during the shooting incident to eliminate him as a suspect in Chase's murder.

That Trevor and Burton had been in collusion, Trevor persuading Burton to plant the box of chocolates and to shoot at Chase, missing him, of course, in some kind of elaborate scheme to persuade Chase to trust Trevor and be suspicious of Lyle and Roger. Obviously, it had required collusion because Trevor hadn't been present at the brownstone that weekend.

That's as far as we'd gotten when we reached the air station.

And that's about as far as the investigating authorities, which would include the local sheriff's office, Lloyd's of London, and the private detectives hired by Roger, ever got when all was reported.

The aftermath revealed that Trevor had indeed been involved in the illegal transfer of monies within Prescott Communications to stave off financial collapse.

Some wondered how Trevor had managed to keep his chicanery from Chase. They speculated that Trevor had been forced to kill Chase before the huge interest payments came due October 1 and that Trevor had intended to replace the illegally used funds with the huge chunk of money Lloyd's owed on the policy insuring Chase against murder. And, in fact, the insurance money did indeed make it possible to save Prescott Communications from bankruptcy.

The press, including all the newspapers and television stations within Prescott Communications, played the story to the hilt. Face it, there is nothing the press enjoys more than a good murder.

This murder had every element necessary to win 48-point heads across the country:

A murdered magnate dispatched in an imaginative way. (Hot tub companies cringed.) The accompanying Hawaiian music was an added fillip.

A gorgeous young widow who had lain perilously near death for days, affording the opportunity for running updates on Miranda's condition and the joyous relief when she survived undamaged. Much was written about her passionate love for her older husband. No one called it obsession. As it was. I felt certain that it was she who'd searched my room that first afternoon. At least she'd found nothing there to break her heart. But I wondered if she would ever be at peace.

An island kingdom, cut off from the world, steeped in luxury, doomed to sudden destruction. The newspapers carried elaborate architectural renderings, interviews with the interior-design firm, even a description of the room-size refrigerator where Chase had lain until the building succumbed to the storm. This made it possible to speculate on what had happened to his body and ditto that of his murderer, Trevor Dunnaway.

A killer hurricane that ravaged the coast with two-hundred-mile-an-hour winds, prompting a massive but successful evacuation of several hundred thousand residents, including the gallant rescue of those stranded on Dead Man's Island. The press, of course, relished the old name for the island. Spin-off stories included comparisons with previous hurricanes and the all-time death toll in the great Galveston storm, long before weather services could warn of impending danger.

The courageous and strikingly handsome stepson who had risked his life on a frail homemade raft to seek rescue for those in peril.

The famous actress who had faced death with aplomb.

The enigmatic manservant who had been arrested as he tried to leave the Coast Guard air station. (A tip, investigators said later. It was easy enough for me to pass a note to the co-pilot saying Enrique was wearing a body belt packed with cocaine. But more about that later.)

The grief-stricken son who had held a press conference to announce his intent to honor his late father's memory by directing Prescott Communications to vigorously pursue investigative reporting to root out malfeasance in office, desecration of the environment, financial fraud, the inadequate response of society to the mentally ill, drug and alcohol addiction, the insurance scandal in medicine, and children who lived in poverty.

The urbane and charming murderer was the subject of lengthy articles based on interviews with his friends and professional associates.

It afforded the juiciest peek into the world of the rich since the Claus von Bülow trial.

And a spate of articles on the retired newspaperwoman turned suspense novelist, Henrietta O'Dwyer Collins. Some old friends, no doubt, were a bit surprised by my willingness to serve as a news source. But I know my fellow reporters: a fed dog doesn't scratch to dig up bones. I was quite willing to play raconteur to focus the reporters' attention on me today and not on my past.

The sensation finally subsided, of course.

The facts about the murder of Chase Prescott provided one of the premier news stories of the decade.

But it wasn't the true story.

16

One fact was evident.

Trevor Dunnaway had struck down Burton Andrews.

But, as we spun our theories during that helicopter ride, I was never fully satisfied with our reconstruction of the crimes.

It made sense, yes.

But there were still loose ends.

Who had destroyed the *Miranda B.*? Certainly there was no

rational reason for Trevor to have marooned himself on the island.

I asked Roger to hire the private detectives. I set them to work scouring the county for purchasers of dynamite, especially those who had bought only a few sticks.

It was easier than I'd expected.

Frank Hudson, who'd taken me over to Prescott Island the day I arrived, claimed he had bought the dynamite to rid his land of some tree stumps. Ultimately, a jury didn't believe him, especially when the sheriff's office did excellent work in identifying some flotsam from the explosion that the storm had deposited inland and a forensic chemist testified that the *Miranda B.*'s porthole had been damaged by a dynamite blast. Testimony underscored Hudson's intense hatred for Chase Prescott and how Hudson believed his family's island had been stolen by Chase.

So the explosion was separate from the murders. The explosion was the act of an angry, vengeful man who had spied an opportunity to repay the Prescotts for taking what Hudson saw as his own, Dead Man's Island.

That simplified the equation. I thought that would satisfy my niggling sense that something was off-key.

And I was delighted when the news broke that Enrique's arrest had smashed a powerful smuggling ring. Enrique had removed a shipment of cocaine from the *Miranda B.* when it went in for its annual overhaul. He had had the drug shipment on the island. When the hurricane was imminent, he had hurried to the servants' quarters to get the shipment.

Chase had been clever but not clever enough to realize that his longtime employee had used the *Miranda B.* to smuggle huge quantities of cocaine. Later investigation revealed that Enrique owned a mansion in Bolivia and that the garage at his by-no-means-modest home in Miami harbored a Jaguar and a Rolls-Royce.

Rosalia wasn't implicated. Roger helped her obtain counseling and a new life where Enrique or his agents would never find her.

At my direction the private detective investigated everyone, so I learned all about Betty's family: her daughter, Mary, who had lost her job at the jeans factory and had no health insurance and couldn't pay the bills when her little girl, Alice, became severely diabetic with all the treatment and expense that entails.

Betty desperately needed money to save the life of her only grandchild. And for years she'd resented Chase's treatment of Carrie Lee Prescott. So she had found it easy to meet secretly with Jeremy Hubbard and provide all those damning and quite true stories about Chase and his family for the unauthorized biography that had created such nasty headlines.

That should have answered all my questions. But still . . .

Perhaps I've covered too many stories, asked too many questions. Deep inside I knew it wasn't over. Yet. For me.

Not even when I finally came home, more than a week later. I walked into the house and realized this was how it had begun for me.

Coming home, and a telephone call.

And there on the bed were my pictures of Richard and Emily. I gave a little salute to Richard's portrait, a good one that recalled his broad, open face, reddish-brown hair, and green eyes. And that familiar crooked grin.

I dropped my suitcase and carry-on and picked up the photograph of Emily.

The phone rang.

My heart lifted as I recognized her voice. "Hello, love. Yes, I'm glad to be home."

Emily had a lot of questions about my ordeal.

I answered so carefully.

Too carefully.

"Mother, what's wrong?" My daughter has an uncanny way of sensing when I'm not being absolutely open with her. She is utterly ruthless in prizing out the truth. "Mother, are you all right?" A definite note of suspicion.

"Of course. Just a little frustrated. I'm behind. I need to get started on the new book—and I don't even have an idea yet." I carried the phone outside and settled beside the pond. Sunlight splashed on the portrait I still held.

"Oh." Her relief was evident. "You always feel that way in the beginning. The book will come."

There's nothing quite so irritating to an author as a family member's easy confidence that, of course, the book will come.

I snapped, "It's like trying to chip an idea out of concrete. Nothing's coming!"

"It will, it will. Probably you're still emotionally involved with that island. But the excitement's dying down. It won't be news much longer, then it will be easier for you to forget."

Forget?

No, I wouldn't forget.

I managed to divert Emily, to turn the conversation to her work.

I didn't ever want to talk to Emily about Chase and what had happened and why.

So I suppose it's understandable that when our conversation ended, my thoughts turned to Chase. I sat quietly on the rustic bench, Emily's picture in my lap, and surveyed the garden. Not my garden, of course. I have no green thumb, and I've never lighted long enough in one spot to invest myself in plants. But this house came with a dreamily gorgeous backyard that includes a weeping willow–shrouded pond with a rock fountain in the center.

I welcomed the September warmth, the occasional wafting past of glorious Monarchs on their way to Mexico, and the musical splash from the fountain.

And I stopped avoiding thoughts about Chase. Perhaps I'd never be free of those traumatic days until I permitted myself to grieve. Fragments of memory slipped and slid across the surface of my mind as I watched the water trickling down and around the mossy gray rocks, so artfully constructed to look like a miniature mountain range.

I thought of Chase's unexpected telephone call and that instantly familiar voice, with its unfamiliar undercurrent of desperation.

Desperation?

Yes. Looking back, I realized Chase had been fiercely determined to persuade me to come to his island, that it was of paramount importance to him. Of course, it had all been prearranged, the guest list carefully devised so that I could play detective, identify the person who'd attempted to poison him.

He'd brilliantly played every card he'd had to enlist my aid. I suppose he knew that I'd never shed the guilt of leaving, all those years ago.

He'd subtly taken advantage of that.

A wisp of wind stirred my hair. It had just the faintest undertone of fall in it, the first hint of chill.

Like the chill that edged into my heart, remembering Chase and that phone call.

Yes, he'd played his cards beautifully. But was I surprised? I'd always known what Chase was like. Determined to win—always—no matter what the cost, no matter who was hurt, no matter . . .

Chase's character.

And Burton's character.

Burton, so terrified of being blamed for doing something wrong.

I curled my fingers around the metal arm of the bench, welcoming the warmth trapped in the iron curve.

I needed warmth because I was seeing and thinking now with a cold clarity.

I should have seen it from the very first.

One piece of poisoned candy.

Shots. Swift, carefully aimed shots.

The electricity turned off on Thursday night so that the hair dryer could not only be put in place but plugged in. That was when the killer returned to the generator and turned it back on—*to make certain that the plugged-in dryer wouldn't trip the circuit breaker*. The near encounter with me must have been nerve-racking indeed. But I'd run to safety. So then all that remained was to go to the pool, go into the cabana, trip the breaker to that line, go outside, unplug the dryer, reset the breaker. The trial run was over. Now it was certain—once the hair dryer was plugged in—that anyone entering the hot tub would be immediately, efficiently, swiftly electrocuted; there would be no tripped breaker to frustrate the planned electrocution.

And that was what had happened.

But another element to the plan was crucial to its success: those shots aimed at Chase. I'd sensed that—but not quite understood why.

What did the shots accomplish?

They gave me and Trevor an alibi. This was essential. Because obviously Trevor was part of the scheme.

What did Burton tell me about the shots?

There was an unmistakable ring of truth in his voice when he said, almost tauntingly, *"I didn't see anybody shoot at Chase."*

But after Chase's death Burton worried about it. And he decided, because he *wasn't* a part of the plan, that he should tell someone.

Who?

Someone in authority, obviously. Someone who could tell Burton what he should do.

Why did he choose Trevor? Not, as I had thought, because Trevor had an alibi for the gunshots. That didn't figure at all. Burton was still close to Chase's influence. Chase didn't confide in Roger about business. Burton didn't like Lyle. But Trevor—Trevor was Chase's main adviser.

So Burton made his decision. He would tell Trevor.

That signed his death warrant.

Because Trevor couldn't afford to have anyone know that no one had shot at Chase.

I gripped the bench rail so hard my hand ached.

Why, oh, why, hadn't I seen it from the first?

I didn't need an alibi. Trevor was the one to be alibied. His alibi was his price for cooperating with Chase in Chase's dark and final plan.

Who planned the island gathering?

Who was determined—always—to triumph?

Who said he would rather die than see his empire destroyed?

Who knew better than anyone that the Lloyd's of London money would save Prescott Communications?

And who knew better than anyone how exhaustively insurance companies investigate those kinds of death claims?

So who poisoned that candy?

Chase.

Who shot the gun on the sunny point that morning?

Chase.

That's what Burton saw. That's what he knew.

That's why Burton had to die. Because everything Chase did was known to Trevor. And Trevor had to agree with Chase's desperate scheme because he was in it up to his neck in the misuse of vast sums of monies in a desperate attempt to save Prescott Communications. Trevor knew only the Lloyd's policy would be enough to save them. There was no financing waiting in the wings. If Lloyd's disallowed the policy on the basis that

Chase's death was suicide, not murder, all would be lost. Trevor had to have the proceeds from Lloyd's.

So, with a high degree of efficiency and brilliance, Chase Prescott engineered his own murder. He didn't care about the misery it would cause those left behind as suspects. He *wanted* suspects. He wanted the hunt for a murderer to continue. It had to be murder, and Chase didn't care what it cost either his family or his associates so long as Prescott Communications, the one thing he had loved on this earth, survived.

Now I knew.

What could I do?

What should I do?

If I made this claim, I had not a shred of evidence to back it up.

Knowledge of a man's character isn't enough in a court of law.

The insurance company would be delighted and would resist the claim.

But it came down to no proof.

Still, wasn't it my duty to press to see that the truth came out?

An idealist would choose truth.

A realist would gauge whether the revelation would have any practical effect.

A leaf fluttered down onto my lap. I brushed it away from Emily's photograph.

My lovely daughter. They say daughters are so often the image of their fathers. The slender, elegant, fine-boned face, the glossy ebony hair, a mirror image of Chase Prescott as a young man.

I'd decided before she was born that she would not grow up with a father who cared nothing for what was right.

And she had not. She'd adored Richard and admired him, and, like him, grown to be an honorable person.

It was the right decision then.

It was the right decision now.

Any mother would understand.

The world might disagree, deem my choice reprehensible.

But, for now and forever, I was determined.

The world had its story, and I would let it be. Trevor was guilty of murder, that was certain. And though he hadn't murdered Chase, he had been a collaborator in Chase's death. So I would let it be. Let Roger remember his father with honor; let Miranda idealize the man she'd loved too much; let Prescott Communications take on the battles against greed and pollution and social despair; let Emily remain firm in her devotion to Richard, the father she'd known.

And let me bury the ghost of a dead lover. Forever.